In the same series

The Plays of Samuel Beckett
Selected Poems of Ezra Pound
Selected Poems of T. S. Eliot
Emily Dickinson
Edward Thomas
Seamus Heaney
Fiction of the First World War
Keith Douglas

BRIAN FRIEL
A Study

Ulf Dantanus

ff

faber and faber

LONDON · BOSTON

First published in 1988
by Faber and Faber Limited
3 Queen Square London WC1N 3AU

Photoset by Wilmaset, Birkenhead, Wirral
Printed in Great Britain by
Richard Clay Ltd Bungay Suffolk
All rights reserved

British Library Cataloguing in Publication Data

Dantanus, Ulf
Brian Friel: *a study*
1. Friel, Brian—Criticism and interpretation.
I. Title
828'.91409   PR6056.R5Z/
ISBN 0–571–14948–0

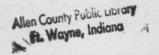

In the age when critical theory promises, or threatens, to 'cross over' into literature and to become its own object of study, there is a powerful case for re-asserting the primacy of the literary text. These studies are intended in the first instance to provide substantial critical introductions to writers of major importance. Although each contributor inevitably writes from a considered critical position, it is not the aim of the series to impose a uniformity of theoretical approach. Each book will make use of biographical material and each will conclude with a select bibliography which will in all cases take note of the latest developments usefully relevant to the subject. Beyond that, however, contributors have been chosen for their critical abilities as well as for their familiarity with the subject of their choice.

Although the primary aim of the series is to focus attention on individual writers, there will be exceptions. And although the majority of writers or periods studied will be of the twentieth century, this is not intended to preclude other writers or periods. Above all, the series aims to return readers to a sharpened awareness of those texts without which there would be no criticism.

John Lucas

Contents

Acknowledgements   ix

Introduction   1

I From Killyclogher to Ballybeg   23

II The Early Plays   50

III Development of Form and Content   84

IV New Accents   153

Conclusion   213

Notes   219

Bibliography   223

Index   227

Acknowledgements

I am greatly indebted to several people for their assistance in the course of my work; I am particularly grateful for the active help and support given by the following:

in Belfast: John Boyd for his friendly advice; the staff of BBC's Radio Drama Department and Schools Department for helping me locate unpublished material;

in Brighton: Martha for everything;

in Derry: Jude Bowles and Julie Barber of Field Day for their kind help with reviews and material about Field Day; Mrs McGinley for her Irish breakfasts that kept me going the whole day;

in Dublin: the former Press Officer Deirdre McQuillan and her assistant Mary O'Neill of the Abbey Theatre for press clippings and general information about productions of Friel's plays; Tomás MacAnna of the Abbey and Hugh Hunt for allowing me access to rehearsals; Professor Brendan Kennelly of Trinity College, Dublin, for help with accommodation and library facilities; the staffs of the Trinity College and National libraries; the Drama Department of RTE Radio and TV for tracing elusive manuscripts; Dr Christopher Murray of University College, Dublin, for his careful reading of an earlier version of this manuscript and for many helpful suggestions; Veronica and Stephen O'Mara for their hospitality and friendliness;

in Gothenburg: Professor Erik Frykman for his expert advice;

in London: the staff of BBC's Radio Drama Department for help with the manuscripts of Friel's unpublished plays;

in Muff and Greencastle: Brian Friel and his family for hospitality and kindness, for allowing me access to unpublished material, for time spent answering questions and letters.

Ulf Dantanus
Brighton, February 1987

Introduction

Irish dramatists writing today have to contend not only with contemporary criticism and current theatrical taste but frequently also with the giant spectres of past dramatic literature in Ireland, some of them distinctly unwilling to relinquish their hold on the devotions of both public and critic. If, in a wider context, an Irish dramatist is to be taken seriously as part of what we now call the Irish dramatic tradition, his achievement will have to withstand at least a fleeting comparison with the great names of the past, a Synge or an O'Casey, even if this only involves pointing out similarities and differences between these two and today's practitioners. Ireland today is rightly proud of the world-wide reputation enjoyed by these two writers, who, between them, have defined to the outside world essential aspects of Irishness and moulded two important forms of modern Irish dramatic writing.

To say that much and no more would be to articulate a commonplace. Yet the simple often hides rich and complex truths. It is interesting and highly relevant, both in terms of Irish literature in general and this study in particular, that Synge and O'Casey in their respective works seem to have divided Ireland into two distinctly different habitats, country and city, or more specifically and at its most extreme, the Aran Islands and the city of Dublin. We associate almost completely the lives of the people within their works with these two Irelands that are as dissimilar as the creative imaginations of their creators. The plays of Synge and O'Casey contain within them this basic dichotomy of place, coupled with an insistence on the place as the acting influence on the shaping of character and event. Synge's characters are always referring to places like Kerry, Mayo, Achill, Erris, Limerick, Belmullet, Connaught, Sligo, Wicklow and Castlebar, all of them from beyond the Pale (these place names are mentioned in *The Playboy of the Western World*), whereas O'Casey is all Finglas, O'Connell Street, Rathmines, Santry, Henry Street, Parnell Square, Dublin Castle, Liberty Hall, Phoenix Park, the G.P.O. and Boland's Mills (taken from *Juno and the Paycock* and *The Plough and the Stars*). There are, however, some rare references to the 'other' Ireland in both Synge and O'Casey, all of them intended to suggest a sense of contrast, and frequently containing comic or ironic elements. In *Juno* Captain Boyle gives us a dismissive hint about this 'other' world and its inhabitants: 'Don't be superstitious, man; we're Dublin men, an' not boyos that's only afther comin' up from the bog o' Allen.' In *The Playboy* Jimmy has obviously heard of 'the skulls they have in the city of Dublin,' characteristically from a man who has returned to the West via Dublin from seasonal harvesting in Britain. However, Jimmy's familiar sphere of reference immediately returns him to a more intimately known habitat: the skulls are 'ranged out like blue jugs in a cabin of Connaught'. Enumerating the spoils of Christy's success at the races the crowd speaks of 'A flat and three-thorned blackthorn would lick the scholars out of Dublin town!' The contrast, though, is more suggested and felt than directly expressed, but, when it comes, nevertheless clearly obvious. Perhaps Pegeen's words to Christy hint at what could be a characteristically 'Western' attitude to the unknown parts of the world: 'And I thinking you should have been living the like of a king of Norway or the Eastern world.'

[2]

The strict heterogeneity between the locales chosen by Synge and O'Casey for their material becomes manifest as soon as one considers even briefly the titles of their plays. *Riders to the Sea, In the Shadow of the Glen, The Tinker's Wedding, The Well of the Saints, The Playboy of the Western World* and *Deirdre of the Sorrows* suggest and indeed describe an Ireland very different from that described in *The Shadow of a Gunman, Juno and the Paycock, The Plough and the Stars, The Silver Tassie, The Star Turns Red* and *Red Roses for Me*.

It must be established, though, that the two dramatists had very different ways of approaching this dichotomy of place as a possible source for their creative energies. O'Casey was never seriously interested in the Ireland beyond the Pale. He was born and brought up in Dublin and spent most of his life there. The bulk of his plays take as their subject the social and political upheavals of early twentieth-century Ireland as seen and experienced in the city of Dublin. With Synge things were very different. Born and brought up in what is now a suburb of Dublin, cosmopolitan in outlook in his early years, he came to adopt as the home of his creative writing a part of Ireland with which he seemed at first to have very little in common. It was thus a conscious effort on Synge's part to find a locale and a people whose life he could express. Though Synge may have seemed ill equipped to take up such a challenge he proved to be singularly receptive to his new subject, and he soon found that his own inner solitude was in near-perfect unison with the soul of the place he had chosen. Furthermore, the fact that he knew Dublin and Paris added a strong sense of the great contrasts involved, and made him more sensitive to the characteristics of rural Ireland. This awareness is latent everywhere in Synge, and it shows through at its most crisp and emblematic in the Preface to *The Playboy of the Western World,* where in the final sentence the simple contrast between 'straw' and 'bricks' could be seen to symbolize the contrast not only between country and city, or the West of Ireland and Dublin, but how modern life has forgotten or even destroyed many traditional and distinctly local customs and characteristics, what Synge refers to as 'the springtime of the local life'.

'I am inclined to believe that, as critics, we have paid too little attention to the importance of place in Anglo-Irish writing,' wrote A. Norman Jeffares in an article entitled 'Place, Space and Personality and the Irish Writer'.[1] He then goes on to demonstrate the validity of his own complaint by looking at 'the way in which some Anglo-Irish writers have dealt with the physical entity of Ireland'. Jeffares' aim is very modest and does little to remedy the lack of the particular approach which he was complaining about. There is no reason why the critic's task should be any less exacting than that of the creative writer. In the field of Irish literature a much more relevant and rewarding approach would be to reverse the relationship between the writer and 'the physical entity of Ireland'.[2] How has 'the physical entity of Ireland' dealt with its writers? For a full appreciation and understanding of Synge's work we must look to rural Ireland in general, and preferably to even more localized habitats, just as for O'Casey (and to an even more intense degree for Joyce) we must try to discover the spirit of Dublin. We get to know the West of Ireland from Synge, and Synge from the West of Ireland in the same way that we get to know Dublin from Joyce and O'Casey, and Joyce and O'Casey from Dublin. Contrary to what the Covey may think, the human individual is not just 'a question of the accidental gatherin' together of mollycewels an atoms'.

Although it cannot be quantified or even defined, the 'spirit of place' must be recognized as a shaping influence on the imagination of the creative writer and should merit some attention and investigation. E.

Estyn Evans in *The Personality of Ireland: Habitat, Heritage and History* quotes Lawrence Durrell on the subject: 'the important determinant of any culture is the spirit of place'. Evans also refers to 'the intuitive understanding and interpretation of the creative writer' in relation to 'regional personality' and concludes: 'Their [the creative writers'] inspiration characteristically springs from intimate association with particular landscapes, local, regional and national.'

What I see as a basic dichotomy of place in Ireland, reflecting the great contrasts that exist, historically, culturally and socially between the West of Ireland and Dublin, finds its natural expression both in literature and indirectly in literary criticism in a great number of different forms. For me to be exhaustive in this discussion is clearly an impossibility. Let me just give a few relevant and revealing examples. If we read Frank O'Connor's short story 'In the Train' we are made strongly aware of the physical and symbolic journey from East to West, from a modern basically foreign culture to a traditional and basically native one. Or the reference may be briefer and less developed: Gabriel Conroy in James Joyce's story 'The Dead' (as is pointed out by Jeffares in the article quoted above) could be seen as the typical modern Dubliner in his attitude of incomprehension or even apprehension *vis-à-vis* the West. Even in today's Ireland there is an awareness of many lasting differences in attitudes and ways of life: 'There are still huge disparities between rural and urban attitudes. "If I go into a Dublin pub" said one man from Mayo, "people are either deep in an English paper like the *Mirror* or the *Sun*, or watching darts, racing or BBC comedy on TV. The influences on them are British, by and large, but they'd shoot you if you said that. Now rural Ireland is very different." '[3]

In criticism the link between rural Ireland and, for instance, the Abbey 'peasant play' is well known. The word 'peasant' is also often used to denote a certain

[5]

kind of writer dealing with the rural parts of Ireland. In his *Modern Irish Fiction – A Critique* Benedict Kiely discusses some of his contemporaries under headings such as 'Rebels', 'Peasants' and 'Townsmen'. In a more recent study, *The Irish Renaissance: An Introduction to Anglo-Irish Literature,* Richard Fallis in one of his chapter headings, uses a slight variation on the theme: 'Peasants, Visionaries, and Rebels'.

Though Ireland is a relatively small country which possesses, in relation to the outside world, a separate and individual racial and national identity, what Estyn Evans calls its own 'personality', there is also a strong sense of various localized 'personalities' in the regions of Ireland. The strongest of these can be seen in terms of the dichotomy of place between East and West, or more precisely, Dublin and the West. Through an examination of this dichotomy we are led back to the very origins of Irish drama. It is a well-known fact that the original Gaelic civilization had no theatrical tradition at all, and that the birth of the Irish Dramatic Movement at the very end of the nineteenth century was the first expression of a native Irish drama. The reasons for this lack of a Gaelic theatre were simple enough:

> ... it was at bottom the exclusively rural pattern of Gaelic culture which prevented the growth of an indigenous formal drama. Such drama everywhere has been the product of communal living, has been a town art supported by fixed patronage. Now the Irish never founded a town. Even villages of the English or Continental kind did not exist in the original Irish civilization. The towns and cities of Ireland are of Danish, Norman, or English descent.[4]

In *The Irish* Seán O'Faoláin expressed the same truth more pointedly: 'We have always feared towns.'

Thus, in order to emphasize the East-West division,

it could even be argued, be it contentiously, that Dublin was never really or truly an *Irish* city. There the theatre had been an important and flourishing part of the social life of the resident ruling class since the first theatre was built in Werburgh Street in 1637. This and later playhouses were, however, totally the preserve of this same class, and the theatre 'was to remain a foreign thing, a colonial creation, and the plays staged had little real connection with Irish life, and as a consequence had little influence or impact on the people as a whole'.[5] The situation in the provinces was even less encouraging. O'Faoláin tells us about how, before his first visit to the Abbey Theatre at the age of fifteen, (since O'Faoláin was born in 1900 this would have been when the National Theatre was well under way) he 'had seen nothing but plays brought to Cork "straight from the West End". (They never needed to add the words "of London": where else could it be?)' The same was true of other regional theatres in Belfast, Limerick, Galway, Waterford, Newry, Kilkenny, and Derry. They were all pale replicas of the Dublin theatres, but received, as early as from the end of the eighteenth century, occasional visits from English touring companies.

It is highly significant that when the founders of the Irish Literary Theatre were looking for a venue where their Irish plays could be staged they found that the existing theatres in Dublin were either booked or far too expensive for their modest budget. In the end, and after additional problems in obtaining a licence to perform the plays, they rented, on a very temporary basis, a large hall seating 800 people, the Antient Concert Rooms in Great Brunswick Street. Thus the beginnings of Ireland's National Theatre and the Irish Dramatic Movement had to be foisted upon a reluctant Dublin, and had many characteristics of what would today have been described as a 'fringe event'.

The first efforts to create a national theatre were

[7]

part of the Irish Literary Revival and set out, in a reaction against what the founders saw as a limited, stereotyped and frequently insulting portrayal of Ireland and the Irish in contemporary literature, to 'bring upon the stage the deeper thoughts and emotions of Ireland'.[6] The new literature of the Revival, poetry, prose and drama, had an enormous influence on emerging Ireland. It was, to quote O'Faoláin again, 'a whole people giving tongue'. Here he touches on a problem that has haunted many Irish writers in the twentieth century. The great irony is that the 'tongue' that O'Faoláin is referring to, and that he himself is using, is English and not, of course, the native Irish Gaelic. For many writers the impossibility of Gaelic as the language of modern Ireland has been accepted, albeit reluctantly; for others, Gaelic has continued to be the main symbol of nationality. On the whole, though, it is true to say that 'the language question' has continued to exercise the conscience and imagination of the Irish writer. The dilemma was succinctly, and ironically, summed up by Michael O'Beirne in a motto to his *Mister: A Dublin Childhood*: 'One day the master said we were to write a comp on "Ireland, my own country". I was glad of that, as my favourite subject was English.' There are innumerable references in modern Irish literature to this bilingual heritage and complication. Even the great European James Joyce was aware of the quandary. In his discussion with the dean, Stephen is made painfully aware of the insidious confusion operating in the linguistic consciousness of any sensitive Irishman using the English language. Stephen's thoughts are probably the best and most eloquent expression there is of the predicament.

He felt with a smart of dejection that the man to whom he was speaking was a countryman of Ben Jonson. He thought: The language in which we are speaking is his before it is mine. How different are the words *home*,

Christ, ale, master, on his lips and on mine! I cannot
speak or write these words without unrest of spirit. His
language, so familiar and so foreign, will always be for
me an acquired speech. I have not made or accepted its
words. My voice holds them at bay. My soul frets in the
shadow of his language.

Writing in 1931, Daniel Corkery stated in *Synge and
Anglo-Irish Literature* that 'the Irishman feels it in his
bones that Ireland has not yet learned how to express
its own life through the medium of the English
language.'

It is a further undeniable and ironic fact, if completely understandable, that when Ireland came to
express herself in dramatic literature the lead was
taken, not primarily and initially by members of the
native Catholic community but by representatives of
the ruling resident Anglo-Irish Protestant Ascendancy.
Yeats, Synge and Lady Gregory were all, as a simple
consequence of their religious background, cut off from
one of Corkery's 'three great forces which, working for
long in the Irish national being, have made it so
different from the English national being', namely 'The
Religious Consciousness of the People'. In respect of
another of these 'forces', 'The Land', they were still
severely handicapped, whereas in the third, 'Irish
Nationalism', they could feel more at home. It is ample
proof of Yeats's greatness that, in spite of these
overwhelming shortcomings, he could become such a
centralizing figure in modern Irish literature. His
genius quickly traced the roots of the 'Irish national
being':

> John Synge, I and Augusta Gregory, thought
> All that we did, all that we said or sang
> Must come from contact with the soil, from that
> Contact everything Antaeus-like grew strong.

His lack of 'The Religious Consciousness of the People'
was made up for by his dedication to what could be

termed 'the other-worldly' in various forms. His use of the old Irish sagas, the popular myths and superstitions of the Irish people, frequently touch their soul and frequently approach and overlap with Corkery's more conventional 'Religious Consciousness'.

Pursuing for a little while further Corkery's definition of the 'Irish national being' and projecting it on to the Ireland of today, a relevant and very revealing set of discordant notes can be heard. Leaving aside the question of 'The Land' and its corollary 'rural Ireland', which, even today, seems to be, as I have suggested earlier, an established manifestation of Irish life, and concentrating instead on 'Religion' and 'Nationalism', we come up against two formidable and basically unresolved complications. I am referring, naturally, to the existence of the statelet of Northern Ireland and the festering wounds of religious and nationalistic feuding so evident there. This political dimension would be the second of the two dichotomies of place mentioned earlier. It is frequently expressed in terms of a North–South context, even to the extent of confusing normal geographical terminology. 'People in the South' refers not to those living in Cork or Killarney as opposed to Donegal, but to the Irish Republic as a whole, just as 'people in the North' are the inhabitants of the part of Ireland that is still within the United Kingdom, not those living in Sligo or Donegal. It is not my intention here to deal directly with the immense problems facing any commentator on the history, past or present, of this part of Ireland, but to refer to some aspects of the conflict where it seems relevant for the purposes of this study. In order to do this, however, it becomes necessary to establish something about the nature of this North–South dichotomy. There are basically two important and conflicting views regarding the origins of the present problems in Ireland. Is the tragedy of Ulster a result, solely or at least principally, of the seventeenth-century plantations and to the partition of

Ireland in 1920? The Nationalist would no doubt answer 'yes' to this question; there would be no tension if the whole of Ireland were to be united. To others the issue is more complicated. 'To see the problems of modern Ulster as having their sole source in the plantations seems to be as far from the truth as to lay the entire blame on partition and on the machinations of the British Government.' Estyn Evans sees the 'personality of Ulster' as 'a strong regional variant, in habitat, heritage and history'. He strengthens the North–South dichotomy further: 'The two communities in the North, however deeply divided by religion, share an outlook on life which is different from that prevailing in the South and which bears the stamp of a common heritage. They are alike in their intransigence.' He calls on history to prove his contention:

> New cultures have entered Ireland most easily in the north, by the short sea route: those reaching the south had many possible entries and might come either from England or direct from the Continent. The north thus tended to form a distinct cultural region or group of regions, behind its frontier belt of drumlins and, if we can believe the heroic tales, its leaders – the Men of Ulster – were prepared to defend it to the end against the Men of Ireland.

These regional characteristics and differences must of course be recognized, and they provide the Unionist with strong arguments. Whether they would justify the political division of the island into two separate states is an entirely different matter. There are equally strong arguments, looking at Ireland from above, for a one-nation island. It is the complexity of the situation, fraught with historical, political, religious, social and economic indeterminacies that keeps the conflict alive.

In the life of any country, historical, racial, national, religious and linguistic concepts can be potent symbols of unity and serve to express a sense of origin and identity. The fact that within 'the personality' of the island of Ireland all of these notions are afflicted with what could with a modern term be described as schizophrenia (the word is often used to describe the divisions in Ulster), goes a long way towards explaining the political turmoil in contemporary Ireland. It becomes part of the 'personality' not only of the island itself but of its people. It touches all, but perhaps most acutely and actively the sensibilities of the writer in its midst. Its existence inevitably influences the creative writer. The pressures of these unresolved uncertainties and the resultant search for a sense of place, origin and identity are obvious in much twentieth-century Irish writing. For the individual author there are two equally difficult courses to take. He can decide to conduct his search by immersing himself in the history and heritage of Ireland, adopting, in Frank O'Connor's famous phrase, 'the backward look', in the hope of finding there his own, and by implication, every Irishman's true identity. This was the cure favoured by most writers of the Irish Renaissance. It is no exaggeration to claim that this was necessary field work for the subsequent emergence of a (partly) independent Ireland, and that it has lasted well into our days, tempered and adjusted with time, but still expressing an important aspect of the Irish identity. For many writers, remaining in Ireland was in itself a difficult course to take. Daniel Corkery enumerates 'without any searching into the matter' more than thirty names of writers who decided to leave Ireland for other parts of the world in order to achieve greater artistic freedom and greater financial rewards. In trying to ease the pains of his birth-place he frequently inflicted upon himself pangs of a different order. Exile and emigration have been, and still are, powerful themes in Irish literature. Like the protagonist in George Moore's 'Homesickness' there can be no definite and clear-cut answer for the émigré to the question whether his decision was right or wrong, but the pull of the homeland will stay with him as long as he stays away.

In his recent study, *A Guide to Anglo-Irish Literature,* Alan Warner points to the great differences in attitude between two contemporary poets, Seamus Heaney and Philip Larkin, in their relations to their place of birth. Quoting Larkin's poem 'I Remember, I Remember' Warner highlights the poet's indifference to his home town Coventry. After revealing his dislike for the city the poet makes it rather clear that the whole idea of a 'place of birth' is something rather silly and sentimental, and perhaps un-British. ' "Oh well, I suppose it's not the place's fault," I said.' In Heaney, as in most modern Irish writers, even if it may not be 'the place's fault', the formative influence of place is felt to be extremely strong. The place of birth, the native or adopted region, and frequently Ireland herself become prominent characters in Irish fiction. In Heaney's work there is temporarily even an obsession with the local background and its historical perspective. The now well-known analogy between the contemporary violence in Ulster and its counterpart in Viking times, as expressed in the collection *North,* is his most far-reaching effort in this vein. In the Englishman Larkin's poem there is not the same search for the past as a partial definition of identity. He, and, it is probably true to say, most other contemporary English writers, share a more secure sense of a unified and central historical, political and national background, in which there is little that does not carry with it a centuries-long unquestioning acceptance.

For obvious reasons, it is in the North of Ireland, and in the generation that has experienced the recurring troubles of this century, and perhaps even more importantly, who were born into or brought up in a divided Ireland, that the conflict is most pressingly felt. Seamus Heaney, of course, is not alone here. Other poets in the North, like John Hewitt, Derek Mahon, Michael Longley and Paul Muldoon, have all more or less frequently returned, in their work, to the unresolved divisions mentioned earlier. They have done so less obliquely than their Southern contemporaries. Speaking in 1970, after the present troubles started, Seamus Heaney and Derek Mahon both referred to the effects that events in the North were having on them as creative writers. 'The spirit of place' has become part of the individual and comes to express itself both consciously and subconsciously. Heaney has this to say about one of his own poems ('The Last Mummer'): 'I didn't, at the time of writing, mean this to be a poem about Northern Ireland, but in some way I think it is' (*Irish Times*, 14 August 1970). In the same article Derek Mahon stresses how the personal experience infiltrates the creative process:

> These poems on the surface are not about the North. They're intensely personal poems. Some of them are love poems, for example. But they are about the North because I'm choosing to use my own personal dilemmas as metaphors for the Northern situation.

To study contemporary Irish literature in terms of place and the writer's attitude to place is not a limiting but an illuminating experience. The two basic dichotomies of place, East–West and North–South, that I have sketched or at least, I hope, suggested, in this Introduction, are still powerful in their implications for Irish literature. And the pattern of the exiled Irish writer still remains. Today we can progress from Joyce, O'Casey and Beckett to Brian Moore, Aidan Higgins and William Trevor (or returned exiles like Francis Stuart). Three of the best-known living Irish dramatists, John B. Keane, Thomas Murphy and Hugh Leonard, were all for some time 'seasonal labourers' in England. Emigration and exile continue to be important themes in Irish literature.

The relation between the Irish writer and his locality is always of vital interest and seems singularly significant in the work of Brian Friel. The strong attachment to a recognizable physical locality in Friel's work has been noticed by several commentators. In his monograph on Friel D. E. S. Maxwell places him firmly in 'his own region, the northwestern counties of Ireland' and then goes on to give a more detailed description: 'The "real" world of Brian Friel's short stories reaches from Kincasslagh in the west of Donegal through Strabane, Derry City, and Coleraine to Omagh and County Tyrone.' John Wilson Foster in *Forces and Themes in Ulster Fiction* refers to Friel's stories as being 'usually set in MacGill country, among the hard, empty hills and obscure villages of Donegal and Derry'. Foster also introduces the subject of the 'social deprivation' of this particular area, a point taken up and given political and religious substance by Seamus Deane in *Ireland Today*: 'The territory of Brian Friel's short stories and plays is that borderland of Derry, Donegal and Tyrone in which a largely Catholic community leads a reduced existence under the pressure of political and economic oppression.' There can be little doubt that this insistence on his own chosen locality is a conscious constituent in Friel's craft. In a discussion on 'The Future of Irish Drama', in what has now turned into a significant statement, Friel points to the direction his work was to take, and in doing so also describes his career up to then: 'I would like to write a play that would capture the peculiar spiritual, and indeed material, flux that this country is in at the moment. This has got to be done, for me anyway, and I think it has got to be done *at a local, parochial level*, [my italics] and hopefully this will have meaning for other people in other countries' (*Irish Times*, 12 February 1970). He has voiced similar thoughts elsewhere: 'The canvas can be as small as you wish, but the more accurately you write and the more

[15]

truthful you are the more validity your play will have for the world.'[7] The focusing of his fictional reality on an acknowledged habitat is strengthened by his persistent demand for 'truthfulness' in the description of this habitat. (The same point is made by Friel in the article from the *Irish Times* mentioned above.) He writes about places he knows or has known intimately, but his aim is not so much to be true to the geographical and physical characteristics of a place but to capture the 'atmosphere of a place or a person' (*Acorn*, spring, 1965). In his short stories he ranges over a fairly wide area of the North-West of Ireland, whereas the early plays seem to stay within the political entity of Northern Ireland. From *Philadelphia, Here I Come!*, however, there has been what seems to me a remarkable concentration on one specific fictional locality in the bulk of his plays. The village of Ballybeg in County Donegal becomes the microcosm of contemporary Ireland.[8] The village, as created by Friel, has established a presence in his work, and has a clearly identifiable 'spirit of place'. There are interesting parallels between this creative movement in place towards a settled point and Friel's own real-life changes of residence. Omagh to Derry to Muff and then Greencastle in Co. Donegal may be part of the normal necessities of life, but one might be forgiven for seeing some sort of symbolic meaning in it. Friel himself would not agree. He moved from Derry to Donegal he says, 'simply because I had made some money on *Philadelphia, Here I Come* and wanted a house in the country. The most suitable site was Muff. If it wasn't for the border it would be a suburb of Derry' (*Belfast Telegraph*, 6 March 1981). Here two words, 'the country' and 'the border' lead us back to the two fundamental dichotomies of place that I referred to earlier.

In a number of different contexts Friel has emphasized the 'peasant' quality of Ireland. Being, as he himself has expressed it, the 'grandson of peasants who could neither read nor write', Friel places himself firmly in rural Ireland (*Aquarius*, 5, 1972). And then in another interview: 'I think I'm a sort of peasant at heart. I'm certainly not "citified" and I never will be. There are certain atmospheres which I find totally alien to me and I'm much more at ease in a rural setting' (*Acorn*). In an article written for *The Times Literary Supplement* and given the wittily relevant title 'Plays Peasant and Unpeasant' he deliberates on the state of Irish drama and the general background of Ireland: 'But to understand anything about the history or present health of Irish drama, one must first acknowledge the peasant mind.' The three 'great forces' that Corkery was stressing as part of the Irish mind again turn up here, given a more personal and perhaps more eloquent expression by Friel: 'a passion for the land'; 'loyalty to the most authoritarian church in the world'; and 'devotion to a romantic ideal we call Kathleen'. In the article Friel deplores the low state of Irish drama. In many ways he seems to be talking to himself, trying to map out a territory where Irish drama (his own and other writers') can flourish. Perhaps rather surprisingly he suggests that 'the deep schizophrenia' of Dublin 'should ignite a dramatic instinct'. Giving the reason for this suggestion he introduces again the general contrast between East and West: 'because it is there, and only there, that the urban man and the rural man meet and attempt to mingle'. This is, of course, a subject that has exercised the imagination of many modern Irish writers, who have focused their work on the radical changes that have taken place in Ireland (not only Dublin but gradually also the rest of Ireland) since the coming of the modern age. The conflict between the values of two completely different ways of life has meant a gradual loss of or at least dissolution of many local and traditionally Irish ways. Friel has been acutely aware of this. 'We are rapidly losing our identity as a people and because of this that special quality an Irish writer should have will be lost . . . We are no longer even West Britons; we are East Americans' (*A Paler Shade of Green*). These fears, though they may be verbally exaggerated here, are intensely felt by Friel and other Irish writers. It may lay them open to accusations of traditional Irish conservatism and insular introspection, but I feel that the major reason for their worries is that the process of modernization confuses their search for an Irish identity.

> And when I referred to Ireland as being inbred and claustrophobic and talked of the tortuous task of surveying the mixed holding I had inherited, I had in mind how difficult it is for an Irish writer to find his faith: he is born into a certainty that is cast-iron and absolute. The generation of writers immediately before mine never allowed this burden to weigh them down. They learned to speak Irish, took their genetic purity for granted, and soldiered on. For us today the situation is more complex. We are more concerned with defining our Irishness than with pursuing it. We want to know what the word native means, what the word foreign means. We want to know have the words any meaning at all. And persistent considerations like these erode old certainties and help clear the building site. (*Aquarius*)

When seen in an abstract and critical light this persistent inquiry into the boundaries of racial, national, cultural and linguistic identity may seem a singularly narrow and unfruitful exercise. In their creative work, though, the search is often managed with inventiveness and it rarely becomes obtrusive. Far from being an obsession, it is a necessary adjunct to organic growth. It helps, as Friel says, 'to clear the building site' where future structures will be erected.

In terms of the North–South dichotomy of place, Friel is keenly aware of the problems of a split identity, as occasioned by the political, religious and social divisions that he has experienced in Northern Ireland. (He refers to it as 'living in a schizophrenic community' (*Aquarius*).) He has 'a strong belief in racial memory' (*Acorn*), which leads him to conclude that there is a 'foreignness' in English literature that makes it different from Irish literature; 'It is the literature of a different race' (*Magill*). These conclusions are far from extreme, and the solution he offers to the 'language problem', for instance, although it may not have been consciously expressed by contemporary Irish writers, is one which, in reality, the vast majority of Irish people seem to have accepted. Despite the strong (though mainly symbolic) role as the official language, Irish plays a very small part in the life of the Irish nation – English is spoken by the vast majority. Friel, though, is most scrupulous in his claim that '[w]e must make them (English language words) distinctive and unique to us' (*Magill*). 'I query the assumption that the two languages are the same,' he has said in an interview with the present writer.

Friel's nationalist leanings are well known. 'I was a member of the Nationalist Party in Derry for a number of years, but I resigned about five years ago because I felt the party had lost initiative' (*A Paler Shade of Green*). He cannot accept the legitimacy of the border and believes that there 'will be no solution until the British leave this island' (*Magill*). Again these attitudes would seem to suggest a rather harsh and uncompromising nature. Nothing could be further from the truth. Friel has arrived at his point of view through a process of constant re-examination of the problems involved. Though there are certain questions on which he is not prepared to compromise (the border and the idea of a united Ireland) the events of post-1969 Ulster have had him moving between deep despair and complete certainty of civil war on the one hand, and a more optimistic note on the other. 'Still, I don't think the gap is too wide to be breached. People are pliable

[19]

and generous. In a family the most outrageous things may be said, yet within a week, although they have not been forgotten, they can be glossed over. The same can apply to our religious and political differences' (*A Paler Shade of Green*). In Friel's life and work, the reference to 'a family' in the quotation above becomes indicative of many of his concerns. As early as 1964, shortly after his first success with *Philadelphia, Here I Come!*, he rather unexpectedly described James Joyce as 'a saint' (*Guardian*, 8 October 1964). He was talking about one of his early plays, *The Enemy Within,* in which he wanted to 'discover how he [St Columba] acquired sanctity'. The definition of sanctity here is, however, a fairly limited one: 'Sanctity in the sense of a man having tremendous integrity and the courage to back it up'. Being asked how Joyce acquired integrity, Friel answered: 'By turning his back on Ireland and on his family.' This, of course, is exactly what Friel has consistently refused to do. He has centred his life and work on Ireland, and the concept of the family has been a cornerstone in much of his work. This basic nucleus has been strengthened and vitalized by the frequent presence in his work of its own opposite, exile and emigration, uprooting and dislocation of place.

The purpose of this study is to examine the growth of the work of Brian Friel. In this Introduction I have dwelt at some length on certain aspects of modern Irish literature, first of all because they seem to me to be essential qualities in the making of any modern Irish writer, constituting as they do a common heritage, but more importantly since they are at the heart of Brian Friel's work. The habitat, heritage and history of Ireland have made him an Irish writer. In the Introduction I have wanted to establish some of the natural consequences of this fact so as to be able to deal more directly with Friel's work in the coming chapters. Likewise, and for the same reason, I wanted to give some idea of the man before turning to his work. I have hinted at some major thematic concerns for Friel as a writer. These will be revisited and developed as his plays are discussed in greater detail. Well aware of Friel's dislike of being quoted in definite statements, I have allowed him to speak for himself on important issues rather than relying on reported evidence. This seemed to me not only preferable but necessary in order to be brief and at the same time relevant. I hope that his words will be seen in their proper context in the discussion of his work.

In the first chapter of this study I shall try to establish the relevance of a pertinent attention to the question of 'place' in Friel's work. This question frequently comes up in the short stories. Unfortunately the scope of the present study prevents much attention being given to them. It could, however, be said that Friel's handling of the short story is largely traditional and the influence of, in particular, Frank O'Connor, is strongly felt. It may in fact have been Friel's failure (as he saw it) to free himself from this influence that helped him decide to turn to drama instead. Chapter II will introduce the early dramatic works, radio and stage plays, problems of form as well as pointers to later techniques. Next I shall turn my attention to the relation between, and the development of, form and content in what could perhaps be described (in the scope of the present study) as his middle period (approximately 1964–75), a period of energetic experimentation, and I hope that finally some sort of totality will emerge, when his later plays are considered in the light of his earlier work. My aim is to show that Brian Friel is a 'successful' writer in the same sense as Friel himself defines a 'successful' play:

> What he [the dramatist] means is that this particular work is in tune with the body of his previous work; that it is a forward step in the revelation of his relationship with his own world; and that at the time of writing the idea and form are coincidental and congruent and at one,

or that, and again I am using his own words, Friel has given 'organic form to the totality of [his] work' (*Aquarius*).

My method is basically chronological. That seemed to me the best and, in dealing with the early plays, the only possible approach. From the early or mid seventies there seems to me to be a significant shift in Friel's approach to his own subject matter. In the later plays, and in particular since the foundation of Field Day Theatre Company in 1980, Friel has increasingly pursued questions about the historical, political and linguistic identity of Ireland. This stage of Friel's career is very much linked to the North and to Field Day. It reflects the turmoil of the continuing troubles in Ulster. The founders of Field Day knew, Friel has said, that 'we must have impermanence built in . . . If a great new play emerged tomorrow, specially if it was a Northern play, we'd jump at it. Or else we might put out a magazine or do something completely different' (*Irish Times,* 5 September 1981). In 1983 appeared the first three Field Day Pamphlets, whose commitment to questions about the historical, political and linguistic identity of Ireland is obvious in style and content. These pamphlets are formalizing in brief, concentrated form the same concerns that preoccupy Friel in his later plays.

His devotion to Field Day has not prevented Friel from pursuing his own career as a writer. The production of *Fathers and Sons,* his own reworking of Turgenev's novel, at the National Theatre in London represents a further remarkable extension of his powers and his reputation as a dramatist.

I

From Killyclogher to Ballybeg

Friel had his first story published by *The Bell* in July 1952. The story, almost too short to be called a short story (a mere 780 words), approaches several themes that, we can now see, are at the heart of Friel's creative sensibility, containing some of his major concerns as a writer. It strives to overcome the limitations of its own brevity by reaching for nothing less than universality. Its title, 'The Child', the only words used to describe the individual at its centre, is repeated through the story. We know he is a boy, but the relative impersonality of the word 'child', like 'father' and 'mother' or 'Ma and Da', suit the broader implications of the story better. Nor is the place given a specific or even general name. To the boy, squatting at the top of the stairs, the sounds coming from the kitchen below are 'the sounds of a home', a much more personal and yet universal concept. But despite the absence of a named locality, the story strongly establishes an atmosphere which assumes a reality by means of recognizable characteristics. There is a definite sense of place here, growing out of subtly given specific details. The place is distinctly felt to be rural Ireland, agrarian, Catholic, poor. This is the habitat working on the young protagonist of the story, this is the environment which is going to help determine his personality and his future. As a brief story, 'The Child' is little short of a feat of compressed thematic exploration. With great economy of detail, Friel introduces us to the reality of rural Ireland.

'The Child' is in fact different from the rest of Friel's stories and plays in that it lacks a name for the place he is describing. Most commonly he insists on placing the action in real or imagined, but always named, places in Ireland. But the difference here is a superficial one. In all his work it is the atmosphere of the place, assembled from the given localized detail, that is Friel's main interest. One of the characters in another story, 'Among the Ruins', is referring to this as 'the feel of the place', a phrase suggesting emotional and psychological links between people and places. In the same story this link is further developed and given a definite hint of a personal relationship. Admonished by his wife for driving too fast and making the children in the back sick, Joe briefly forgets the here and now in favour of the treasured memory of his own family home, 'the ruins' that they are on their way to visit:

> At this moment, I don't give a damn, he thought without callousness; at this moment, with Meenalaragan and Pigeon Top on my left and Glenmakennif and Altanure on my right. Because these are my hills, and I knew them before I knew wife or children.

The name of a place or area can be used to great advantage when it comes to investing a place with symbolic and connotative detail. It is not just an arbitrary label. It is a description of a locality; it has a history longer and stronger than the generations who have lived in this place. Perhaps, for reasons suggested in the Introduction, the interest in and affection for one's own place has grown especially strong in Ireland. In one of his essays, Seamus Heaney quotes Carson McCullers' remark 'that to know who you are, you have to have a place to come from'. He even suggests that 'a new found pride in our own places' was one of the moving forces behind the Irish Renaissance at the end of the nineteenth century. The same notion has been expressed by other modern Irish writers. For John

[24]

Montague 'the least Irish place name can net a world with its associations'.

The place in any work of fiction exerts an influence, consciously or subconsciously, on a reader or an audience. If a writer is placing his characters in the Garden of Eden, the Palace of Argos, the Forest of Arden, Wessex, Sussex, Dublin or Ballybeg, he is writing about these places as much as about his characters. In realistic fiction, this becomes the agreed meeting-place between author and reader/audience. If a writer places the action in, say, The World, he is by definition moving outside the confines of realism. Some of Beckett's settings clearly suggest that reality as we know it has been tampered with in order to cut the link between the work and a conventionally realistic appreciation of it. If the setting of a play is given as 'A house in west London, or 'A country public house' there is enough of an indication for the audience to give them some kind of security of place, affording them, so to speak, an anchoring place for their appreciation and understanding of the play. As long as it conforms to our picture of reality, the question whether this place is real or invented by its author is beside the point. So too is the question whether, as Joyce claimed, Dublin could be rebuilt from the pages of *Ulysses*; so too would be the effort to search the villages of Donegal for a model of Friel's fictional Ballybeg. The fictional reality of an invented place like Ballybeg need not be different from the topographical detail of Dublin or the Aran Islands. We know that the Bank of Ireland is opposite Trinity College in College Green, that Kilronan is the only harbour on Inishmore, but we cannot check that the houses of Ballybeg are lined out in the order that Friel tells us. This is important only insofar as it relates to the physical reality of a real place, and can be disregarded completely when we come to look at the more important influences of 'the spirit of place', working on the author and the characters he is writing about. In its social, economic and religious characteristics, in its implied political history, the village of Ballybeg is emblematic of Ireland and a part of Ireland rather than any one specific village in that area. In this respect Ballybeg represents an effort, on Friel's part, at the wider application of a place, towards some kind of local universality. Friel's intention here is obvious: 'So on the last day of August we crossed from Stranraer to Larne and drove through the night to County Donegal. And there we got lodgings in a pub, a lounge bar, really, outside a village called Ballybeg, not far from Donegal Town.' Significantly, this sentence is repeated almost verbatim by all three characters in *Faith Healer* in their respective narrations of the events of a particular day. The directions given here are so accurate and point so precisely to a certain area that we are not disturbed by the inclusion of a fictional village among the real place-names. It is important to realize that Ballybeg is, in fact, the only invention in *Faith Healer,* a play where real place-names abound. However, the introduction of a name like Killybegs or Ardara would have invited unwanted comparisons with the real thing and moved the attention away from more important aspects of the play, and the name Ballybeg, with its wider and more sustained connotative meanings, does in fact add something to the structure of meaning not only in this play but wherever it is used. In *Faith Healer* the wider universe of London on the one hand, and Welsh and Scottish villages on the other, is inexorably narrowed down to Ballybeg for the central episode; 'narrowed down' is not a limiting concept here. As Friel himself has suggested, (see e.g. the interview in the *Irish Times* quoted in the Introduction) the place has to achieve some kind of local reality and existence before it can become universal; or to quote, with Heaney, Patrick Kavanagh: 'Parochialism is universal; it deals with the fundamentals.'

[26]

We must note, however, that it is Friel's fictional use of Ballybeg that is an invention. The name Ballybeg, as expected, is not uncommon elsewhere in Ireland; there is a Ballybeg in County Meath, another in County Tipperary, one in County Cork, and there is a Ballybeg House in County Wicklow. But there is no Ballybeg in County Donegal. Before setting, for the first time, *Philadelphia, Here I Come!* firmly in 'the village of Ballybeg' Friel had used the name in the background of some of his short stories, 'The Skelper', 'The Flower of Kiltymore', and 'The Gold in the Sea'. Since *Philadelphia* (1964) Friel's fictional focus has been moving towards Ballybeg, and from *Living Quarters* (1977) all (with the exception of one short unpublished play, *American Welcome*, in 1980) his plays have converged on the same village.

Throughout his work Friel has mixed real and imaginary places. Often, as the quotation from *Faith Healer* shows, they are put close together, unobtrusively shifting the emphasis from the particular place to the general region. There is a finely struck balance between the fictional villages of Mullaghduff, Beannafreaghan, Corradinna, Glennafuiseog, and Knockenagh, for example, and the larger area or region, always localized in the existing and known counties, Donegal and Tyrone most frequently, Derry on a few occasions, and in the larger context, modern Ireland. The only towns with any true and genuine presence in Friel's work are Omagh in the early short stories, and Derry in some stories and plays. It is rural Ireland that is his fictional habitat, areas outside any large conglomeration of people or buildings. Increasingly, in order to describe these places, he has come to use a word that has no real existence in any English-speaking area outside of Ireland. The word 'town-land' is an English word to translate something intrinsically Irish.

Friel achieves this local focus by progressing from the

larger unit of the whole island of Ireland, through the north-western counties of the province of Ulster, and at this stage he is still true to the existing names of Irish geography, to find the pivotal action localized in a fictionalized centre. When a name is given for this place, which is almost always, this name will frequently be an invented one. The example of Ballybeg has been quoted, and is, without a doubt, the most obvious one. The invented names quoted above, Mullaghduff, Beannafreaghan, Corradinna, Glennafuiseog and Knockenagh, perform the same function.

As suggested earlier, this leap from geographic fact into the greater freedom of the invented place liberates both author and reader/audience without diminishing the topicality of the fiction, still firmly rooted in the essentially Irish experience by its established regional radix. It seems reasonable to expect that it is these larger regional influences that determine what I have called 'the spirit of place', rather than the more strictly local qualities of a particular place. The difference between Mullaghduff and Kincasslagh is of less importance than the fact that they are both within the same region of Ireland. That the climatic, cultural, social, economic, and religious conditions, past and present, will become part of any individual exposed to them also seems a reasonable expectation. What must also be accepted, I think, is that similar sensitive minds exposed to these conditions, even for a short period of time, will be similarly affected. At the beginning of *Faith Healer* the lyrical evocation of 'those dying Welsh villages'

> Aberarder, Aberayron,
> Llangranog, Llangurig,
> Abergorlech, Abergynolwyn,
> Llandefeilog, Llanerchymedd,
> Aberhosan, Aberporth . . .

is much more than a repetition of place-names. Their reality, factual or imagined, has entered Francis Hardy

himself, the itinerant faith healer, and established a
meaningful presence in his mind to become part of his
personality and of his life, more so than he himself
thinks: 'I'd recite the names to myself just for the
mesmerism, the sedation, of the incantation.' The fact
is, and this looks like much more than a remarkable
coincidence, that Grace, his wife, introduces herself
with the almost identical 'incantation', and then goes
on to echo Frank's similar conjurations through her
monologue. Frank and Grace, husband and wife, or at
least living as such, have assimilated with their
memories of each other and their life together these
Welsh (and Scottish) place-names, strongly suggestive
of meaning and a shared experience. Teddy, the
London Cockney, does not immediately share the same
community of feeling. When, however, the issues
involved touch on some fundamental aspect of the
human situation, the birth of Grace's still-born baby at
the side of an isolated road on the northernmost tip of
Scotland, even he becomes part of the community and
can join the name of Kinlochbervie to an event of
human tragedy. Significantly, though, he does not at
first get the name right. As an outsider and Englishman, he is also able to accept and face the actual
circumstances of the event, where Frank, the Irishman, prefers to superimpose his own truth.

The symbolic significance suggested by these joint
incantations of place-names is, in its applied meaning,
wistful and vaguely allusive rather than clear and
precise. The connection between a place-name and
functional meaning is expressed more directly and
plainly in *Translations*. Yolland, the English officer,
and Maire, the Irish country girl, separated from each
other by the lack of a common tongue, are brought
closer together through the attempted assimilation of
place-names in their respective backgrounds. By
repeating the names of the places that 'made' Yolland,
Maire seems to be able to get closer to him in his

absence. 'Winfarthing – Barton Bendish – Saxingham Nethergate – Little Walsingham – Norwich – Norfolk. Strange sounds, aren't they? But nice sounds; like Jimmy Jack reciting his Homer.' By drawing a map of the area where Yolland grew up she virtually becomes capable of conjuring up his presence again after he has disappeared. Maire, in her rather gauche but sensitive way, seems to realize that these names give a kind of existence to Yolland as well as establishing certain natural and basic qualities in his habitat, which are part of the description of Yolland himself as well as the larger themes of the play. The list of English place-names could, of course, though it is redundant here, be completed by adding 'England', thus stressing the central contrast of the play, the conflict between England and the English language and Ireland and the Irish language.

Earlier in the play Yolland was physically and symbolically united with Maire when he perceptively and sensitively appealed to her sense of place:

YOLLAND: Bun na hAbhann? (*He says the name softly, almost privately, very tentatively, as if he were searching for a sound she might respond to. He tries again.*)
Druim Dubh?
(*Maire stops. She is listening. Yolland is encouraged.*)
Poll na gCaorach. Lis Maol.
(*Maire turns towards him.*)
Lis na nGall.
MAIRE: Lis na nGradh.
(*They are now facing each other and begin moving – almost imperceptibly – towards one another.*)
MAIRE: Carraig an Phoill.
YOLLAND: Carraig na Ri. Loch na nEan.
MAIRE: Loch an Iubhair. Machaire Buidhe.
YOLLAND: Machaire Mor. Cnoc na Mona.
MAIRE: Cnoc na nGabhar.

[30]

YOLLAND: Mullach.

MAIRE: Port.

YOLLAND: Tor.

MAIRE: Lag. (*She holds out her hands to Yolland. He takes them. Each now speaks almost to himself/herself.*)

Here Yolland can sacrifice whatever local prejudice he had to assume not only the existence of these places but their own distinctive spirit and atmosphere. This is the vital meeting-point between the two of them, a moment of great symbolic value in Friel's play. Here the whole question of 'the meaning of place' becomes clear. In Maire's map and Yolland's Irish place-names two individuals have seen the way to overcome local and national conditioning to become united almost in spite of history. The power of these place-names has shown the way, because, to quote Seamus Heaney once again, they 'lie deep, like some script indelibly written into the nervous system'.

The name Friel (or O'Friel) carries distinct local connotations. Statistics relating to the modern distribution of the population show that it is seldom met with outside County Donegal and contiguous areas. It is the anglicized version of the Irish ÓFirghil (pronounced and often written Frighil, with the same meaning as Farrell [ÓFeargháil], 'man of valour') and can be traced back to Eoghan, brother of St Columcille. The Chief of the leading Friel family had the hereditary right of inaugurating O'Donnell as lord of Tirconnell (Donegal). The reference to St Columcille hints at a distinguished origin and may explain the choice of subject for one of Friel's early plays, *The Enemy Within,* which dealt with the private life of St Columcille on Iona. This in its turn typifies Friel's interest in his own local roots and his continued affection for Derry and the North-West of Ireland.

Brian Patrick Friel was born in Killyclogher, one and a half miles north-east of Omagh in County Tyrone, on 9 January 1929.[1] His father was principal of the local

Culmore Primary School, and the atmosphere and experience of school life, and especially the tribulations involved in having one's father as teacher, were to provide Friel with rich material for his short stories and plays. The town of Omagh was close and convenient for practical purposes and must have contributed in giving Friel, from an early age, a definite sense of the opposition and contrast between town and country. In addition, there were, like in many of the short stories, through family background, impulses not towards Omagh but in a north-westerly direction. Friel's paternal grandfather was born in Donegal but came to live and marry (a McCabe) in Derry where he worked as a jarvey. Both grandparents were Irish speakers and his grandfather illiterate. It was towards Derry and Donegal that the family kept looking and the sojourn in Omagh was also to be of a temporary nature. In 1939 his father, Patrick Friel, was appointed to the Long Tower School in Derry, and the family left the relatively close contact with the country for the more cityish character of Derry. The move was an important one also in another respect. When Friel was born the political entity of Northern Ireland was only nine years old. The precarious nature of its existence was most strongly sensed and most vividly expressed in areas where its *raison d'être* was weak or non-existent. Although the six counties had an overall Protestant majority of almost two to one at the time of Partition, its geographic distribution was far from even. County Tyrone had a Catholic majority of 55.4 per cent, and Nationalist and Republican attitudes have always been strong in the County Council, various urban councils and many rural councils. In Derry City, however, the political situation was from the beginning even more explosive. In local elections in 1920 the whole concept of Partition was violently questioned by the Catholic majority (56.2 per cent). With the help of proportional representation (used for the first time in Northern

Ireland) the Nationalists won control of Derry City and immediately pledged allegiance to the Dáil in Dublin. To the Protestants Derry was of central, almost symbolic, importance in the new state. For them it was thus vital that the Nationalists' control of office should be brief. With PR swiftly abolished and election boundaries cunningly adjusted, sweeping changes took place, and there was from 1924 a continuous process of gerrymandering in key parts of the province. The clearest example of this can be seen in Derry. In 1966 an adult population of 30,376, made up of 20,102 Catholics and 10,274 Protestants, still returned Unionist-controlled corporations. The whole process had been stage-managed in two steps: first, through restrictions in the franchise, limited to rate-payers and their wives, and thus automatically discriminating against the poorer Catholic population, and reducing the Catholic majority substantially with a voting population of 14,429 Catholics to 8,781 Protestants, and, secondly, through almost constant revisions of the constituency boundaries. The city was, in 1966, divided into three wards:

South Ward	North Ward	Waterside Ward
11,185 voters	6,476 voters	5,549 voters
10,047 Catholics	2,530 Catholics	1,852 Catholics
1,138 Protestants	3,946 Protestants	3,697 Protestants
returning	returning	returning
8 (Nationalist)	8 (Unionist)	8 (Unionist)
councillors	councillors	councillors

From the institution of the political entity of Northern Ireland in 1920 up to the introduction of direct Westminster rule in 1972 – and in this Northern Ireland is unique among Western states in the twentieth century – it has been governed by a system guided almost completely by the principle of religious discrimination. To shy away from this recognition is to make the understanding of its history almost totally impossible.

One of the eight Nationalist councillors representing the South Ward (including Bogside, Creggan, and Brandywell) on the Derry Corporation was Paddy Friel of 5 St Joseph's Avenue, Brian's father. He served three terms before the corporation was suspended in 1969 as a result of the troubles. It was in Derry, when the first civil rights march was stopped and batoned by the police on 5 October 1968, that the conflagration had started. It started in Derry, Friel has said, 'because it was there the suppression was greatest', and 'one was always conscious of discrimination in Derry' (*A Paler Shade of Green*). In many ways Derry had always been a city under siege. The historic city walls themselves suggest the mentality of a Protestant enclave in a Catholic country. Today the terrible reality behind the graffiti demonstrates the deep confusion in the religious and political consciousness: 'God made the Catholics and the Armalite made us equal', and 'Blessed are those who hunger for justice'. It is easy to see how the close proximity of a politically unstable and inflamed situation with frequent outbreaks of ugly violence could lead to confusion in the impressionable young. 'I was reared in a very traditional, Catholic, nationalist home. I came to Derry in 1939 when war was beginning. We believed then that Germany was right and that England was wrong, that sort of thing' (*Irish Times,* 12 August 1970). Unless childhood ignorance is freed from its narrow range by an adult widening of the horizon it could easily be perverted into adult prejudice and sectarianism. Friel's nationalist sympathies are not doctrinaire and dogmatic, but nonetheless firm and unwavering. In his Irish context there is no place for the Border, and it does not seem to exist in his writing, where his characters, especially in the short stories and early plays, move from West to East and from North to South without the Border being mentioned. In an early reference to Friel's work in *Threshold* Sean MacMahon remarked that Partition 'seems not yet to have affected his writing'. This statement still holds true. Friel frequently deals, both directly and indirectly, with the tragic consequences of Partition, but his subject matter is the whole island of Ireland.

After primary and secondary education in Omagh and Derry followed St Patrick's College, Maynooth, where Friel passed the First Arts Examination in 1947 in Latin, English, Logic, Greek, and Mathematics. In the summer of 1949 he was awarded the BA degree in Latin, English, Ethics, Logic and General Metaphysics, Psychology and Special Metaphysics. Friel has described his years at this well-known ecclesiastical college as 'a very disturbing experience' (*Acorn*). On the whole, however, he has preferred to keep this experience a private matter and, with the exception of one early play, not to deal with it directly in his writing. Faced with the problem of choosing a career for himself he found that teaching 'was an obvious thing to do . . . My father had been a teacher, two sisters were teachers. It was the obvious and easy thing to slip into' (*Acorn*). This entailed a year in Belfast, at St Joseph's College of Education (then named St Mary's Training College, being the men's department of St Mary's Training College for women). After successfully completing this course in June 1950 Friel again gravitated towards Derry, where he taught in various Primary and Intermediate schools until 1960, when he started to work full time as a writer. The early fifties saw the beginnings of Friel as a creative writer. Settled in Derry, married in 1954, he began to spend more and more time writing. These were important and decisive years that cemented his already close association with Derry, and he was to remain there until 1967. In some ways the move from Derry into the village of Muff and the Republic of Ireland could be seen as a liberating

[35]

influence. Friel has spoken of 'the frustration' he felt 'under the tight and immovable Unionist régime' (*A Paler Shade of Green*). The suppression experienced by Derry's Catholic population was capable of suffocating and stifling the best intentions. So, for example, during the years of gerrymandering in Northern Ireland, many seats remained uncontested in the elections. The results were a foregone conclusion. In a similar way, literature and the arts generally laboured under very unfavourable conditions. When Friel started writing as an after-hours activity he believed that he was 'the only writer in Derry'. There was little there that would naturally express itself in artistic form: 'from a spiritual point of view, it wasn't a good town.' One is reminded of Yeats's famous 'great hatred, little room', and other, more contemporary feelings: Stewart Parker, in an interview in the *Irish Times*, referring to Ireland in general, complained that 'the artistic air that you breathe here is too thin to support you for a lifetime' (13 August 1977).

Nevertheless, and perhaps rather surprisingly, given Friel's close connection with the city, and excluding one or two of the early stories, *A Doubtful Paradise* and *The Freedom of the City*, Derry does not figure at all prominently in his work. Even the subject and setting of *Freedom* seem to have come upon Friel in a somewhat unplanned and perhaps even instinctive manner. When asked, after the outbreak of violence at the end of the sixties, to express in dramatic form the dramatic events of the everyday political situation in Northern Ireland, Friel's immediate reaction was to question its suitability as fictional material, both generally, because '[t]o have a conflict in drama you must have a conflict of equals or at least near equals. There is no drama in Rhodesia or South Africa, and similarly there is no drama in the North of Ireland' (*A Paler Shade of Green*), but more importantly for his own position, because, 'first of all, I am emotionally much too involved about it; secondly, because the thing is in transition at the moment. A play about the civil rights situation in the North won't be written, I hope, for another ten or fifteen years' (*Irish Times,* 12 February 1970). Friel, of course, was to be shown to be completely mistaken in his hopes here. The North very quickly became a new addition to the well-known traditional subjects of Irish literature, and he himself was to write *The Freedom of the City* before three years had passed after the quoted interview in the *Irish Times*. Perhaps it would not be too facile or far-fetched to refer again to Yeats, whose dictum in 1915 'that in times like these A poet's mouth be silent', suggesting that there are topics too base and inhuman to merit artistic expression, would be exploded by the 'terrible beauty' of Easter 1916. For both Yeats and Friel it was the nearness of, and, one could almost say, the personal experience of, tragic events of mythic proportions that prodded their creative sensibilities into expression. Yeats knew several of the leaders behind the Easter Rising, soon to be shot by the English, and the Bloody Sunday of 30 January 1972 in Derry made the play Friel was working on take definitive shape.

For an aspiring writer in Derry (or anywhere in Ireland for that matter) in the fifties there were important considerations of a practical nature to be dealt with. Once a story had been completed, where could one turn for publication? After all, this is one important criterion of success as a writer. If publication was the aim, to become a professional writer actually being paid for one's work looked like a very distant prospect. Complaining about the number of expatriates in Irish literature and listing over thirty examples, Daniel Corkery puts his finger on the major obstacle: 'Why our writers have to go abroad is obvious: a home market hardly exists for their wares.' Even in the fifties there had been very little change for the better and Corkery's judgement was still largely true.

Literary journals like *Irish Writing* (1946–57), *Envoy* (1949–51), and the vital and influential *The Bell* (1940–54) achieved a great deal by opening their pages to budding writers, but other opportunities within Ireland were scarce, and in the July 1952 issue of *The Bell* John Hewitt reiterated Corkery's complaint. (Significantly, but coincidentally, however, in the same issue was included Friel's first published story, 'The Child'.) Then, in the midst of these publication problems, as Friel himself explains it, a new and 'golden opportunity' presented itself. 'And that opportunity was the American market!' In a pointedly ironic little article in *Commonweal*, 'For Export Only', Friel dwells on the moral and aesthetic questions involved for an Irish writer facing this situation. The irony is aimed at all quarters: at Ireland, for failing to provide adequate opportunities for creative writing; at America, for wanting only its own traditional and leprechaunish version of Ireland; at the writer himself for yielding to the temptation of this crass commercialism; and finally, to complete the circle, at those who begrudged others this good turn. Artistically, the predicament was of the same kind as that faced by Corkery's 'expatriates', only in a lesser degree. 'Can expatriates, writing for an alien market, produce national literature?' he asks. By 'national literature' Corkery meant 'a normal literature, for normal and national are synonymous in literary criticism' – and since 'a normal literature is written within the confines of the country which names it', the expatriates are normally excluded. The major danger, though, since it works insidiously, is that the writer adjusts to the requirements of his audience. 'The typical Irish expatriate writer continues to find his matter in Irish life; his choice of it, however, and his treatment of it when chosen, are to a greater or less extent imposed on him by alien considerations.' Friel was very much aware that for an Irish writer to write for an American audience meant that 'there are certain aspects of Irish life that you ignore lest you upset the traditional concept of Irish life which Americans have'. He would have to forget, for instance, that 'Cork boys and girls can jitterbug as expertly as boys and girls from Chicago', and that 'our fishermen now work on radar-equipped government-supplied ships and that the hazardous canvas-bottomed curraghs are relatively few' (*Commonweal*). Irony apart, however, it is true to say that American journals, in particular the *New Yorker,* with which Friel had a favourable contract in the early sixties, played a vital part in launching Friel's writing career. Apart from providing him with a certain amount of financial security it also served to help him learn his craft while practising it full time after years of burning his candle at both ends, giving him the necessary confidence to grow and to try his hand at new things. Since then the North American market has continued to show great interest in Friel's work. Most of his plays have been produced, some with great success, and a few of them even received their première over there. In his work the Irish-American connection, often in the shape of themes like emigration and exile, has remained an important influence.

If the primary aspiration of a writer of short stories is publication, the main concern for a playwright must be the production of his play. Again, in the mid fifties Derry had very little to offer for the hopeful playwright. On the horizon there were two different directions in which he might at first look for recognition, Belfast and Dublin. In the fifties generally, the state of Irish drama was far from notable. After the disastrous fire at the Abbey in 1951 the National Theatre, it seemed, had lost more than its home. The old Abbey, of course, was hopelessly short of space, and in that sense the fire was a blessing, but the years at the Queen's seemed like an exile. A more serious problem, though, was the shortage of promising material. Few events could rise above the ordinary everyday fare in the Dublin theatres, and few writers could lay claim to international recognition or fame. The exception, of course, was Brendan Behan, whose irreverent genius, however, was first honed into an organized and structured whole by Joan Littlewood's Theatre Workshop at Stratford East. The reputation of the Abbey and of Dublin as a theatrical centre suffered greatly, and it was only in 1958, and with the aid of another famous theatrical controversy over the inclusion of an adapted version of *Ulysses* in the Dublin An Tóstal, that notoriety and misfortune returned to the Irish capital.

As far as Irish theatre went, Belfast had always had to accept the role of second string to Dublin. Bitten by the Dublin bug, some Belfast enthusiasts had started the Ulster Branch of the Irish Literary Theatre in 1902. For a brief period Ireland had two theatrical centres and a fruitful exchange between North and South seemed possible. But in Belfast Cathleen Ni Houlihan cut much less of a figure than in Dublin, and there was neither the genius of Yeats nor Miss Horniman's cash to pull or provide the strings. The work had to be done by gifted amateurs. Moreover, a rift between North and South soon opened, and the Belfast company had their knuckles severely rapped by the secretary of the Dublin Irish National Literary Theatre for presuming to call themselves a branch of that company. So Belfast went its own way, and the Ulster Literary Theatre was formed in 1904. It had its own distinctive direction, aiming to encourage their own Northern talent. Some Ulster playwrights made a name for themselves in Dublin, and visits by Belfast and Dublin companies were exchanged, but, essentially, the rift remained. In the fifties, however, there was a fair amount of theatrical activity in Belfast, and thanks to, among other things, his year at St Joseph's, Friel had some knowledge of the theatrical climate of the city. The Group Theatre was still a force to be reckoned with, and the Belfast Arts Theatre occasionally scaled some heights. With the opening of the new Lyric Players Theatre in 1951 there was some hope for the future. For the aspiring playwright there was also the BBC, which regularly provided encouragement and hope for writers presenting new material. This is where Friel's first opening came. In 1958 he was given a professional production by the Northern Ireland Home Service for two of his plays. His career as a dramatist had begun, and in August 1960 the Group Theatre presented *A Doubtful Paradise*. Almost exactly two years later Friel was given the great accolade of having a play put on by the Abbey at the Queen's. *The Enemy Within* was well received in Dublin and then for a number of years the Irish capital took over Friel as the most promising new Irish dramatist. Except in two cases, both of which were premièred in the US, all Friel's stage plays between 1962 and 1979 received their first production in a Dublin theatre. Then, in 1980, Friel was at the helm of a new and unique theatrical enterprise in Ireland. Together with the Belfast-born actor Stephen Rea, he founded a new company, Field Day Theatre Company, with grants from the Arts Councils of both North and South, and with the intention of touring every production over the whole island. In spite of the importance given to touring, and the symbolic significance of this, the company has a distinct Northern anchorage, and represents for Friel a kind of homecoming. For five weeks in August–September 1980–82, Derry turned into a city dedicated to Friel and Field Day. Its 'psychic energy', to quote Friel himself, has been a vital force in launching Field Day.

On the maternal side, Friel had strong links with Donegal. His mother was born near Glenties, and from an early age there were frequent visits to her old home. Summer holidays were spent there and the area soon became a significant part of Friel's childhood memories and exercised a strong influence on his writing career.

In Friel's work there has been a gradual and increasingly realized concentration on the north-western corner of Ireland. Many of his short stories, and even more so the plays, took the County of Donegal as their fictional home. Even apart from family connections Donegal seems to have held strong attractions for Friel. Its soul and spirit, or to use one of his own words, its 'atmosphere', expressed in both nature and people, was a potent influence on man and writer. 'We spend a lot of our time in the west of Donegal. It is the wildest, most beautiful, and most barren part of Ireland, and the people are almost completely untouched by present-day hysteria and hypocrisy.' It is an area with a clearly recognizable and strongly felt 'personality'. Up till recent times, like most of the West, people were settled mostly in coastal areas. The sea, both as the giver and taker of life, has been part of the folk imagination. Farming was chronically difficult and yielded little but hard work. The area was classified as a 'congested district' in 1891. The Commissioners divided the population into two classes – 'the poor and the destitute'. It is part of the Gaeltacht, the Irish-speaking areas of Eire. Its geographical position has made progress and innovation, which has tended to spread from the East and South, very slow, and Donegal has kept many local customs and traditions, preserving elements and features of an earlier age. Migrations, both seasonal, temporary, and permanent have formed a natural part of life well into our days. Sometimes nature and economic necessity have combined to highlight the precariousness of life in the area. In November 1935 a small boat carrying migratory workers returning from seasonal work in the Scottish harvest fields capsized after hitting a rock in the strait between Burtonport and Arranmore. Nineteen lives were lost. The only survivor spent fifteen hours in the water holding on to his dead brother. The emotional appeal made by Peadar O'Donnell after the tragedy cannot fail to move:

Morning. And the world hears. And the world says it was a rock. And the world says: Put up a beacon. And the world says it was a fog . . . But it was not a rock. It was Society. The world has spelled out one of its crimes in corpses. The order of life that impounds the Gael, that drags him to sleep on the steps of Glasgow Central, to slave in the tatie fields in Scotland may decree beacons along Arranmore coast.

But, O'Donnell pleads, 'the impounding of the Gael' must be ended, and migratory work in Scotland stopped.

In spite of the general difficulty and laboriousness of existence, or perhaps because of it, there seem to exist compensatory attractions for the population. The stark natural beauty seems to exercise a strong influence on the individual, and the bond between people and place is strong. It is frequently expressed in rather sentimental terms, where the harsh reality has been forgotten or pushed aside in favour of a romantically nostalgic emotion.

> I'm going back to Glenties when the harvest fields are
> brown,
> And the Autumn sunset lingers on my little Irish town.
> When the gossamer is shining, where the moorland
> blossoms blow,
> I'll take the road across the hills I tramped so long ago –
> 'Tis far I am beyond the seas, but yearning voices call,
> Will you not come back to Glenties, and your wave-
> washed Donegal.

When asked in an interview if he would like to live in America, Friel himself answered: 'I'd be very lonely, I think, in the way a child is lonely. I get very nostalgic and very homesick' (*Acorn*).

In a society where members have to rely to a great extent on each other and interdependence is a necessity, there is bound to develop a strong sense of community. The community, while allowing for a fair amount of personal freedom and individuality, is inevitably cemented by common considerations and values. Inherent in this type of situation is the potential conflict between individual and community. The difference, essentially, is that between town and country, or in larger Irish terms, between East and West. Friel has made use of the conflict in his short stories, emphasizing the wariness with which newcomers are treated.

Generally speaking, the West of Ireland has always been associated with the original Gaelic civilization, and after the Irish Renaissance life in the West represented for many writers the lost Irish identity, a sort of national psyche, which was being rediscovered as part of a conscious effort for Ireland to define herself and to justify her claim to national selfhood and independence. And what was originally the perceptions of individual writers soon became, in the Irish Free State, official policy. This whole process was, as Seán O'Faoláin has testified, a discovery of monumental importance.

> It was like taking off one's clothes for a swim naked in some mountain-pool. Nobody who has not had this sensation of suddenly 'belonging' somewhere – of finding the lap of the lost mother – can understand what a release the discovery of Gaelic Ireland meant to modern Ireland. I know that not for years and years did I get free of this heavenly bond of an ancient, lyrical, permanent, continuous immemorial self, symbolized by the lonely mountains, the virginal lakes, the traditional language, the simple, certain, uncomplex modes of life, that world of the lost childhood of my race where I, too, became for a while eternally young. (*An Irish Journey*)

The first and best known of these 'discoveries' of the West is Synge's classic *The Aran Islands* (1907). As Corkery has pointed out, Synge went further than any other Protestant Ascendancy writer in his efforts to portray accurately the native Gaelic Catholic population of Ireland. Despite the handicaps of class and religion Synge succeeded extraordinarily well and Corkery's reluctant praise of his achievement is very great praise indeed. In the final analysis, though, Synge was found wanting in one important respect:

> If he failed to give us a true reading of the people he would deal with, except in *Riders to the Sea,* it was not from any want of sympathy with them. His sympathy with them was true and deep; but his range of mind was limited, and was not quite free from inherited prejudices. He saw in them what he had brought with him: he noted their delight in the miraculous, the unrestrained outbursts of emotion they indulged in; he noted what their living so close to mother earth had made of them. He drenched himself in all the features of the physical world they moved in, but he made choice among the features of their mental environment. Of their spiritual environment he did not even do that same.

The conventional picture of Synge on the Aran Islands is that of an onlooker: 'he remained as an observer among the peasants, a sympathetic outsider but an outsider nevertheless, unable to understand completely the people he observed and, at the deepest level, unable to commmunicate with them.'[2] Although it would have been extremely difficult for anyone to find his way into the heart of this community, certain characteristics in Synge's own personality, his feelings of alienation and isolation, did little to help.

> In some ways these men and women seem strangely far away from me. They have the same emotions that I have, and the animals have, yet I cannot talk to them when there is much to say, more than to the dog that whines beside me in a mountain fog. There is hardly an hour I am with them that I do not feel the shock of some inconceivable idea, and then again the shock of some vague emotion that is familiar to them and to me. On

some days I feel this island as a perfect home and resting place; on other days I feel that I am a waif among the people. I can feel more with them than they can feel with me, and while I wander among them, they like me sometimes, and laugh at me sometimes, yet never know what I am doing. (J. M. Synge, *Collected Works,* vol. 2)

While there are some obvious and important differences between Synge and Friel in their conscious adoption of a locale, there are also, on a number of occasions, points where the experiences of the two writers meet. A careful reading of Friel's stories strengthened by some occasional comments he has made elsewhere clearly shows that Friel, in spite of having some claim, on the strength of family background, to a much more direct and immediate knowledge of Donegal than Synge had of the Aran Islands, approaches his subject with the same sensitivity and caution as Synge did. Friel was no stranger to the 'mental' or 'spiritual environment' of his fictional habitat. Both lead a natural underground existence in Friel's work, surfacing sometimes to stress some point or other, but always constituting the basic fabric of his description of life in that part of Ireland. Friel's urban conditioning, however, set him apart from the 'native' Donegal community. In 1962, while he was, of course, still living in Derry, Friel was a frequent contributor to the *Irish Press.* Apart from the occasional review he also wrote for a time a regular Saturday column. It was light, personal, and frequently ironic. On Saturday 14 July he tells us how he had recently bought a cottage in Kincasslagh in the west of Donegal, and how, as a result of worries about bills to pay and other complications, he had come to ask himself whether he really needed such a place. They are the little complaints of everyday life. The important thing here, however, is that the reader soon gets the impression that they were written by an outsider who was slowly feeling his way into the spirit of the area. Going fishing with the locals he gets seasick, and he needs time to get used to the greeting, saying 'yes' and turning your head slightly, so common in the West. Certain habits and customs of the country people seem quaint to him. On one occasion he emphasizes his sense of exclusion by calling himself 'a stupid townie'. To some extent this may be a consciously adopted literary stance, but what matters more is the genuine insight into the distinctive qualities of country life that is presented. Friel had gone to the local shop to inquire about poison for some rats he had seen in the house. To his surprise it turns out that all the people in the shop are having the same problem. After worrying briefly about the truth of their talk he decides that they were not 'taking a hand at me. They wanted to make me feel at ease and socially acceptable. Perhaps they did tell – well, call it lies for want of a better word. But their purpose was not to deceive but to convince a stupid townie that a rat between friends is nothing.' And then, with typical reciprocal irony, he concludes: 'But now and again an odd visitor makes an eejit of himself and sure it's only kindness to give him his head, isn't it?' (*Irish Press,* 11 August 1962).

In these light columns Friel frequently ventures into the world of fiction, and sometimes a story presented here returns later in slightly reworked form in a collection of short stories. His attitude to his material can be exemplified by another journalistic or semi-fictional piece, 'A Fine Day at Glenties', where he records the events of the day of a fair, from the awakening of the village at five o'clock in the morning, through the modulations of tempo during the day, till the evening. There are reminders of common Irish themes, the hardship of an agrarian existence, the attractions of emigration, and the contrast between town and country. In a note at the end, Friel suggests the mixture of real life and fictional treatment that is so typical of his stories and plays. 'The events in this piece have happened at one time or another; the people are fictitious and bear no resemblance to anybody, living or dead.' Many of these early pieces, in the *Irish Press* and elsewhere, are built around Friel's own personal experience, and the direct use of his gradual initiation into the 'mysteries' of the Donegal community can be seen working more obliquely in many of the short stories. In the two collections, *The Saucer of Larks* (1962) and *The Gold in the Sea* (1966), the settings and backgrounds are fairly evenly distributed between County Tyrone and County Donegal, with the early stories perhaps tending more towards Tyrone. These stories, moreover, seem to contain more purely autobiographical material with the teacher/father turning up in the life of a young boy. The background here is a well-established and fairly safe location with few of the frictions between a visitor or newcomer and the indigenous population that occur in the Donegal stories. 'My Father and the Sergeant', 'The Fawn Pup', 'Everything Neat and Tidy', 'Foundry House' and the other Tyrone stories are inhabited by people whose political, social, and economic (but not religious) reality is of a different complexion from that of the natives of Donegal in 'The Skelper', 'Mr Sing My Heart's Delight', 'The Gold in the Sea' and 'The Diviner', to take but a few examples.

In the *Irish Press* some of Friel's contributions were cast in the mould of journeys: 'The Wild Life. Brian Friel goes to the Country' (14 July 1962) or 'A Journey with Brian Friel To the Wee Lake Beyond' (4 August 1962). In 'Among the Ruins' the protagonist sets out with his family to revisit his now abandoned and derelict home in Donegal. The fictional direction of this story is typical, even though the underlying reason is not. The movement in general is not 'back to Donegal' but rather, as I have suggested earlier, in the shape of a visitor or newcomer 'into Donegal'.

A similar shift of focus has taken place in the plays. The early radio and stage plays, *A Sort of Freedom, To*

This Hard House, A Doubtful Paradise, and *The Blind Mice* are all firmly set in the North rather than in the North-West, and look, in their thematic concerns, east rather than west. From *Philadelphia, Here I Come!* the Donegal dimension dominates Friel's work. The major consequence of this change of place has been an added and deepened interest in the two dichotomies of place in Irish life and literature, East–West, and North–South.

II

The Early Plays

Philadelphia, Here I Come!: Before and After

There are several reasons why *Philadelphia, Here I Come!* should be seen as a watershed in Friel's career as a dramatist. It represents a significant development for Friel, both as a public and private man. His venture into full-time writing was shown to be well founded and the early promise was fulfilled with remarkable speed. The play immediately established him as one of the most important contemporary Irish dramatists, and gave him creative confidence for the future. It opened on 28 September 1964 at the Gaiety as part of the Dublin Theatre Festival, and was acclaimed as 'the best new Irish play this year' by the drama critic of the *Irish Independent*. Working backwards from the success of *Philadelphia, Here I Come!* one becomes aware of certain shaping influences that created the play. The most immediate, and Friel would gladly concur, is that of Tyrone Guthrie. The time that Friel spent at the Tyrone Guthrie Theatre in Minneapolis in April–May 1963 has been elevated to the status of myth. For eleven weeks he watched Guthrie directing the opening productions of the new theatre, an experience that may have determined Friel's future in a way similar to that whereby Yeats directed Synge to the Aran Islands. Guthrie was more than a mentor; he was a friend, who admired Friel's stories immensely, and who now wanted to share his experience and knowledge of practical theatre with the budding dramatist. Friel was a quick learner. The first play he wrote after this American adventure was *Philadelphia, Here I Come!* Friel himself has paid ample tribute to the value of this experience. 'That period is a story in itself . . . But it was an important period in a practical way. I learned about the physical elements of plays, how they are designed, built, landscaped. I learned how actors thought, how they approached a text, their various ways of trying to realise it' (*Aquarius*). The combination of Guthrie and America pointed the road forwards.

> I learned a great deal about the iron discipline of theatre, and I discovered a dedication and a nobility and a selflessness that one associates with a theoretical priesthood. But much more important than all these, those months in America gave me a sense of liberation – remember this was my first parole from inbred claustrophobic Ireland – and that sense of liberation conferred on me a valuable self-confidence and a necessary perspective so that the first play I wrote immediately after I came home, *Philadelphia, Here I Come!* was a lot more assured than anything I had attempted before. (*Aquarius*)

In concluding his treatment of the early plays, Maxwell, in *Brian Friel,* suggests that their shortcoming is 'linguistic'. He develops a vocabulary Friel himself had used to distinguish between the very different techniques used by the short-story writer or novelist on the one hand and the dramatist on the other. The first two 'function privately, man to man, a personal conversation. Everything they write has the implicit preface, "Come here till I whisper in your ear"' (*Everyman*). The intimate contact between writer and reader is lost in the theatre, and in reaching the individual the dramatist has to approach him through 'the collective mind'. 'But the dramatist functions through the group; not a personal conversation but a public address.' It is this element of 'public address' that Maxwell finds lacking in these plays (he makes an exception for *The Enemy Within,* which he considers a 'significant development'). This is a useful insight into the early plays, but Maxwell has a tendency to see these plays too much through the eyes of Friel himself. *The Blind Mice* is 'bad' and *The Enemy Within* is 'solid' because Friel himself says so. There are in fact essential differences between the early plays, and one becomes gradually aware of a more conscious and secure point of approach both in technique and thematic treatment. *Philadelphia, Here I Come!* certainly owed a great deal to Guthrie and America, but there was in Friel's work an organic growth through the radio plays and the first few stage plays that paved the way for his first great success. To see it as purely a result of Friel's four months in America is clearly unsatisfactory. There had been, however, in the period before *Philadelphia, Here I Come!* a vacillation in terms of Friel's approach to his chosen medium. It was largely a question of who the audience to whom he directed himself really was. The private reader of the short stories became the anonymous radio listener who in turn changed into the collective mind of the live theatre. Each of these clearly required to be treated with its own separate technique. The success behind *Philadelphia, Here I Come!* is Friel's newly won intimate knowledge of the people he is addressing, the people in the theatre. But it is not simply a question of form. Friel has always maintained that content and form must go together, that they are inseparable in the creative process, that what has to be said presents itself in a certain form. 'If a play can find its voice in straight narrative form, well and good. If it requires a chorus, a narrator, an alter ego (as in *Philadelphia, Here I Come!*) then I'll use one.'[1] It is true that the most valuable insight gained from Guthrie and America advanced Friel's success as a dramatist considerably. Guthrie provided the inspiration. 'His frivolous intent is to have audiences enjoy themselves, to move them emotionally, to make them laugh and cry and gasp and hold their breath and sit on the edge of their seats and – how Philistine! – "to participate in lavish and luxurious goings-on" ' (*Holiday*). It was precisely this dimension that had been lacking in his previous plays.

Tracing the Friel–Guthrie connection one is forced to move backwards as far as September 1924, five years before Friel was born. That was when Guthrie started his job with the BBC in Belfast and, it could be argued, the history of radio drama in Northern Ireland and for that matter, Britain, began. He quickly realized the potential for dramatic representation in the new medium, and his pioneer work gave to radio drama an accepted, though inferior, place in the arts. In the fifties there was still a lively tradition of radio drama in Belfast, with Ronald Mason actively encouraging new work and producing it regularly. As a short-story writer Friel may have been attracted by this new medium for a number of different reasons. Its most important and unique qualities are, paradoxically, range and intimacy. While speaking to large numbers of anonymous listeners you can still remain intimately confidential with one individual, making the traffic seem to function from one source, the writer, to one recipient, the listener. The role performed by the listener is much closer to that of the reader, and there is a sense in which 'writing for radio is much closer to writing for the printed page than it is to writing for television or the theatre'.[2] In contemplating some form of dramatic writing, radio drama may have seemed to Friel a first and perhaps even natural extension of the short story. The dramatic possibilities of the spoken voice are obvious in Friel's stories, where descriptive passages mix comfortably with dialogue. Telling a story on the radio could indeed be seen as a return to the Irish tradition of oral story-telling, giving total predominance to the voice and the spoken word, in the same way that the modern short story, in its original conception, could be seen as a printed version of the live story.

As well as possessing these rather attractive qualities, however, radio also presented Friel with a range of challenges to which he was not accustomed. In the first two radio plays that he wrote, the new medium defeated Friel on nearly all fronts. *A Sort of Freedom*, transmitted on the Northern Ireland Home Service on 16 January 1958, and *To This Hard House*, transmitted on 24 April of the same year, openly reveal his technical innocence. In thematic content, as we shall see, they, and the other early plays, are essentially Friel, but the techniques used confuse his ability to express his themes even to the point of wrecking such sure-footed modes as irony and suggestive understatement. Both are short plays, fifty-five and sixty minutes, respectively, and introduce a host of themes at what seems to be break-neck speed, leaving them all hovering in the air at the end. It is the chronic problem of a short play that it has to arrive at the central theme or conflict without wasting too much time. In his handling of the radio medium Friel, in these two plays, uses only the most conventional of the freedoms at his disposal. The telephone plays an important part in forwarding the action of *A Sort of Freedom,* and in *To This Hard House* newcomers and visitors perform the same function. There are some swift changes of scene between an inner and an outer office, some brief visits indoors and to the main character's home, to a bar in the golf club in the first play, whereas in the second the action is firmly located in the protagonist's house with only two lightning visits outside.

A Sort of Freedom

Jack Frazer, a haulage contractor and employer of thirty-three men in his reasonably successful business, is at the centre of the action in *A Sort of Freedom*. His principal motives are greed and blunt self-interest, a self-made man who will only accept his own standards. His trusty employee, Joe Reddin, has worked for Frazer for over twenty years. We are left in no doubt as to the honourable qualities of Reddin. But Reddin is not equally popular with Bill Hamilton, the trade union secretary. The reason is that he is refusing to join the union, advocating the right of the individual not to do so. This is the major issue in the theme of freedom referred to in the title of the play. In retrospect it becomes a relevant piece of social and political prediction, presenting what is today a highly controversial bone of contention. It is also, in introducing the subject of individual right versus communal and societal pressures, pointing forward to what has become one of the most insistently returning subject matters in Friel's later plays. In the meantime Frazer himself adds another dimension to the issue of freedom, in his case a far less convincing predicament. An enormous gap in his domestic situation is being bridged by the adoption of a baby into his previously childless marriage. But there is a risk that the Frazers may not be able to keep the baby since he refuses to let it be inoculated against TB. Normally, we are told by Dr Murray, 'Inoculation against TB is not compulsory – it's a matter for the individual parent.' But since Frazer's wife Rita has been ill with TB it now becomes a necessary and urgent matter. Frazer, however, persists in his refusal and tries to bribe the doctor into falsely signing the papers. The reasons for Frazer's refusal are absurd and ridiculous. 'It's against my conscience to have this done, and it's wrong to force me to act contrary to the way I think.' The two cases, Reddin's refusal to join the union and Frazer's rejection of the idea of having the baby inoculated, are far too dissimilar to stand as an expression of the rights of the individual. Concepts like 'freedom', 'honesty', 'conscience' and 'principles' are too 'easy' words, and they enter the play too quickly and abruptly and are never comfortably accommodated by the thesis of the play. Friel is too insistent on making a point, and his characters repeat and overstate their stubborn arguments. Even the drunken doctor, upstanding and honest man that he is, can see this:

> FRAZER: There's no freedom in a thing like that. They
>   should let every parent do as they want.
> DOCTOR: Bravo! Well spoken! Let's drink to the individual.
>   I propose a toast to 'The individual versus the
>   State'.

A nice touch, though, is Frazer's subsequent betrayal of Reddin as hinted at in his conversation with the doctor. 'I'm in a wee spot of trouble with a pigheaded driver who won't join his union, but that's all.' We knew it had to happen, and here Frazer confirms the outcome. But before the end the plot thickens in a web of ironic contrasts and cross references. The infertility of Frazer's marriage is more starkly exposed by the eight Reddin children, who, Reddin wrongly remembers, were not inoculated, thus providing more fuel for Frazer's folly. Edward, Reddin's first-born son, is an active trade union member who will have nothing to do with his father's absurd feudal loyalty to his employer. 'Didn't he send us a chicken the Christmas before last?' is Reddin's pathetic response to his wife's sound and sensible question: 'Do you really think he's worried about you, just one man in his big concern?' The play finally runs out of control in an excess of dramatic irony. During his act of betrayal of Reddin, Frazer refuses to talk to his wife on the phone. The communication was that their adopted son had suffocated in his cot. In the play the enormity of this event inhibits any sense of tragedy. Frazer is indeed struck by tragedy, but his own grief becomes self-indulgent when we know his personality, and any pity he may evoke is soon lost in a burst of unrestrained egotism: 'He was called Jack Frazer after me. He would have been me.' To confuse the issue even further the baby *had* been inoculated the previous day. This suggests a possible link between the inoculation and the baby's death, thus, in a sense, proving Frazer right in his initial refusal. This link, of course, can never be established, and instead the doctor's words provide the only explanation, that Fate was to blame. 'It was one of those tragic accidents that occasionally occur.' (This sentence, incidentally, is an example of Friel's linguistic innocence in these early plays. In my photocopy of the manuscript the heavy 'occasionally occur' has been changed to 'happen now and again'.)

If the climax of the play is emotionally overcharged and overstated the final two scenes go some way toward redressing the balance. There is an intimation here of a more private and intimate expression of the individuals and their relationships with each other. In the first of these scenes a subdued Frazer listens to his wife describing the precarious nature of their relationship. Her bitterness at their failure to be happy together is accepted, and she can instead use it to generate some understanding for the plight of Joe Reddin and his family. 'He has children too, live children'. Her analysis of their marriage rings true and, in its implicit criticism of her husband, carries the play into a different mood, enlarging and extending its meanings. Frazer's obsessive grief over his own loss is countered by his wife's wider and deeper sense of loss. Reluctantly, Frazer is forced to accept some financial responsibility for Reddin's situation. But the manner in which this is done only reinforces Reddin's feudal and serf-like dependence on the local 'squire' and strengthens the contrast between an old and distinctly

unmodern social fabric and the advent of organized
trade unionism. Something of the old order is lost, and,
at the same time, its inadequacy in a modern economic
framework is openly revealed. The bartering between
Frazer and his wife about the price of his absolution
leads to the play's final scene in Reddin's home. The
£400 suggested at first by Mrs Frazer is ultimately
reduced (without Frazer telling his wife) to £150 when
the cheque reaches the Reddins. In that house wife and
husband are also quietly arguing, but here it is the
hardships of their economic reality that dominate the
controversy. Friel, in a small way, was before his time
in his use of the idea of unemployment and its effects on
people. He had touched it briefly in a short story, 'A
Man's World', and would return to it later in other
plays. The social and economic reality underlying and
influencing the lives of his characters is always present
as a necessary condition, but only rarely does it impose
itself on our attention. One possible casualty with
unemployed people could be their dignity. Reddin,
however, has not (yet?) lost his in the final scene of the
play. His spirit is not broken.

The cheque arrives and relieves their predicament.
But it changes nothing. It only confirms Reddin's
attachment to the old social order. And yet, his stand
on the question of the freedom of the individual is an
important one, and one to which Friel was to return in
later plays. Mary is grateful for the cheque, but she
remains cautious. Her task is to keep the family
together, to stand with both feet on the ground, looking
after the basics of life with a sensible, down-to-earth
humanity. She is suspicious of words with abstract
meanings: 'Talk's cheap,' she says. And she goes
further:

MARY: Rights, rights! That's all I hear these days. You
talking about your rights, and your conscience, and
now him talking about his rights. I'm through-

[58]

other listening to rights and liberties so that
I don't know any more what's right and what's
wrong. But one thing I do know, Joe, rights are all
very fine when you have money to support them,
like Jack Frazer there. He won't be fighting with
his bare fists.

REDDIN: There you go again. Always money. Money has
nothing to do with a thing of that nature – with a
principle.

The next few lines might well have been: 'Yis; an' when
I go into oul' Murphy's tomorrow, an' he gets to know
that, instead o' payin' all, I'm goin' to borry more,
what'll he say when I tell him a principle's a principle?
What'll we do if he refuses to give us any more on tick?'
But they are not. They are taken from *Juno and the
Paycock*, and it is, of course, Mrs Boyle who is speaking.
Friel's play remembers O'Casey and his women. Friel's
early women are all tea-making and cake-baking
towers of strength, propping up their out-of-work, old,
half-blind and extravagant husbands.

To This Hard House

Daniel Stone in *To This Hard House* is described by his
wife Lily: 'proud perhaps and cock-of-the-walk in a
transparent sort of way,' a peacock in fact, 'but for all
that, a simple man ... a good man,' something Mrs
Boyle would never say of her husband. In Friel's early
plays the male–female contrast always emphasizes
similar opposites. The women face, because they have
to, the reality of life where the men self-obsessively
hang on to their own 'higher' version of life. Perhaps it
is left to St Columba in the all-male monastic community to try to sum up this argument:

OSWALD: And their endless joking and camaraderie and
coarse humour so that if you make a serious
comment, they pounce on it and turn it to ridicule.

COLUMBA: That is something you will discover always

[59]

> where men are cut off from the refining influence of
> women, Oswald. The same with soldiers, the same
> with sailors. (*The Enemy Within*)

It is a beautiful thought, but it does not win the day. Women, in Friel's early plays, do suffer at the hands of men. They patiently perform their conventional roles and produce the expected meals, but the men do not appreciate or even realize their contribution. Lily in *To This Hard House* stands solidly behind her husband, protecting and humouring him in his difficult times. Daniel Stone, principal of a two-teacher school in a rural area, is about to suffer the degradation of becoming redundant, and, older than Joe Reddin, his sense of failure is much more acute. Behind the seemingly simple question of the number of children attending his small Meenbanid school lies one of the most fundamental developments of modern Irish history, the depopulation of the countryside. In urbanization, and emigration, its causes and its effects, Friel has found one of his most potent and powerful themes. If the exodus starts in Meenbanid, it does not end in Clareford, the fast-growing, industry-based town that attracts Meenbanid's families, including Daniel Stone's children. In the background lies Belfast, and further still, and yet very close, the ever-present threat of England. One of Stone's two daughters, Rita, has already been swallowed up by England and may even, it is said at the end of the play, end up in Canada. The other daughter, Fiona, goes to London in the course of the play, but is forced, almost against her own will, to return home. It is the younger generation that leaves the farm and the village for the town, that emigrates to Liverpool or New York. In the generation gap, the wistful and difficult relationship between young and old, and more particularly between parents and their children, Friel finds another aspect of individual relationships attractive as subject matter. In *To This Hard*

House the gap between two different generations has become much wider with the advent of modern society. The sort of life that Daniel and Lily Stone had worked hard to get, and that they were humbly grateful to accept, holds few attractions for their children. They expect much more from life, their appetites having been whetted by the close proximity or media portrayal of the modern and fashionable but materialistic city. Again, what is mirrored in the play is the breaking up of a traditional way of life. In *To This Hard House*, as in the rest of his work, Friel never dwells on economic factors, but the power of these regrettably unstoppable forces is strongly felt. Their attractions are physically obvious. The migrated Meenbanid families, happily installed in Clareford, love their 'bathroom and hot and cold water and two post deliveries a day', and, Fiona says, 'they have TV too.' For a teacher, the new school there seems like heaven: 'twenty-five in each class and every possible facility you could think of; cinema, swimming pool, milk-bar and do you know what? . . . a rest-room for the teachers!' And for Judy, the assistant teacher at Meenbanid, the move to Clareford may hold a promise even more urgent and alluring: 'Not many single girls would take a job in a place like this nowadays. Indeed I doubt if Judy will be content to spend her life here. No chance of meeting anyone suitable or anything.' Meenbanid, in that sense, is losing its life-blood. But to the older generation, Clareford is a threat, which clashes with the values of a more traditional society. The mother's hopeless innocence singles her out as a victim.

Meenbanid is dying, and the young generation refuses to accept the old values. Lily's definition of 'home' is very different from that of her daughter's. The people were born in Meenbanid; that is where they belong; 'home' is the hard house of the play's title, not the 'comfortable homes' in Clareford; they are asked to remain peacefully in the place that made them, asking modernity to by-pass them and progress to spare their lives. But some well-known dangers of urbanization are already clearly visible in Clareford. The new school is indeed described as having all the problems of the modern city. It will be 'overcrowded before the year is out', and, as a result of its showpiece importance, 'inspectors never seem to leave the place'. Overcrowding, and surveillance coupled with anonymity and lack of human contact and personality are becoming the most striking characteristics of the new school. As is so frequent in Friel, it is immediately balanced, in the whole and in pieces, by its own opposites. Judy Flanagan, Daniel Stone's assistant teacher in the small village school of Meenbanid, 'goes mad, doesn't she, when Father looks through the wee pane of glass between their rooms'; a totally different perspective, whichever way you are looking. But Friel is just describing the process, not apportioning blame, or judging for or against. Nevertheless, one cannot mistake the sadness experienced in the loss of a way of life that was, and the passing-over of the older generation. It is neatly condensed in the argument between the teacher-son and the teacher-father about the declining numbers in the village school. The son, Walter, is able to quote from more recent regulations than his father and unavoidably wins the case. He is also competently supported by (the suitably named) Mr Blackley, a senior Ministry of Education inspector, blind to the needs of the individual, devious in his treatment of Daniel Stone's personal tragedy, and as impersonal as a Ministry of Education paragraph. In his defence it must be said that, as the representative of official policy, he only responds to the reality of the situation.

In a technical sense, *To This Hard House* is even more flawed than *A Sort of Freedom*. Both plays are structured round broken promises and disappointments. But whereas in the latter play Frazer's promise to stand by Reddin in his refusal to join the union is a comparatively minor though necessary issue, Blackley's calculated betrayal of Daniel Stone raises larger questions, and increases the play's dependence on it as a structural component. In *A Sort of Freedom* there is little more than Frazer's self-interest to blame for it, but in *To This Hard House* Blackley, in the name of political authority, changes the fabric of a traditional society. All the basic issues of *To This Hard House* are revealed in the opening exchange between mother and daughter: the worsening state of the father's eyes (no more than an awkward symbol of his refusal to 'see' the coming changes); the falling number of children attending the Meenbanid school as a result of the exodus to Clareford; the threat of two more families about to move (which everyone except Daniel Stone seems to be aware of); the unlikelihood of Judy Flanagan staying on in Meenbanid as assistant teacher; the gulf between the generations; Mrs Stone's loyalty to her husband and her intention to spare him uncomfortable truths. Each issue is then repeatedly returned to, and further hints are given. After the initial conversation the play can only go in one direction, and what follows does indeed realize everybody's worst fears. The eyes do get worse; the Sweeneys and the Richardsons do ask for a transfer for their (altogether eleven) children; Judy Flanagan does leave to take up a position at the new school in Clareford. The irony is heavy and overwritten. Blackley's consideration is deeply false: 'Don't worry yourself, Mrs Stone. This will all pass over and you'll find Mr Stone in full command until the day he retires . . . if his health holds out, and Miss Flanagan doesn't leave.' Miss Flanagan's letter, which she insisted must be given to Mr Stone immediately, is conveniently left for a significant moment. And there are further complications, some rather loosely attached to the main plot. The attractive position as principal in the new Clareford school (much talked about before the appointment) is landed by Walter, the son, who becomes a personification of the evil influences. Daniel Stone, forced to retire, is left to indulge himself in the sad memory of his first-emigrated daughter Rita. Here, as in much of the second half of the play, melodrama completely unbalances the action. Stone, or, more correctly, Friel, tells us too much, going over the same ground three or four times, repeating extremely familiar feelings.

At the centre of all the early plays stands the family. This becomes overwhelmingly clear as we approach *Philadelphia, Here I Come!*. Friel's interest in the family as the first and most important societal community, the internal and external tensions and pressures affecting it, as seen against the background of the inevitable passing of time and the resultant succession of generations, is the most obvious constant of these plays. There are in fact very few plays where this issue is not directly or indirectly dealt with. It raises a multitude of complications inseparable from their thematic source. In *To This Hard House* it is particularly the subtle but significant disparity of the relationships between father and son on the one hand, and father and daughter on the other, that exercises Friel's creative efforts. His sons are uncomfortably removed from their fathers, sharing only deep embarrassment and sometimes distrust of each other; his daughters are, like their mothers, causing a higher degree of personal involvement and feeling, be it loyalty or betrayal. Fiona's dilemma is doubly difficult. She is torn between the loyalty demanded of her as the only child still left at home, and her love for freedom and Ned Daly, the second an even worse form of betrayal than the first. Ned Daly, on account of a court action he once brought against Daniel Stone, has become the arch-enemy of the family. Fiona's father, therefore, is particularly aggrieved that his daughter has struck up a relationship with this man. In the context of the play this episode introduces two subsidiary themes. It suggests the existence of fierce family feuding, an Irish subject at once historical and contemporary, and it tries to add to the King Lear connotation brought up later. Fiona leaves for London to meet Ned Daly, who never turns up. This, Fiona insists, is the reason why she returns home. She is forgiven by her father, who, protected by his wife from the truth that Rita has emigrated to Canada, is left hopelessly hoping for her return, too. Ned Daly, we are told by Walter, later returns to Meenbanid to win the lucrative trade of transporting the remaining children in his minibus to the Clareford school. With Walter, he thus becomes another embodiment of the evil force of change. This whole dimension of the play, however, can be seen to be typical of the overloading of intentional meanings with which the play is lumbered. We are certainly made well aware of the cruelties that the young are prepared to inflict on the old, but the expression of this theme is overstated and tenuous.

A Doubtful Paradise

Like the two previous plays, *A Doubtful Paradise* progresses toward the disappointment of expectations. Willie Logue (a transmutation of Arthur Miller's Willie Loman?) is not going to be confirmed as overseer in the Derry GPO. He is a man desperately trying to invest the ordinariness of his own life with pretentious and extravagant distractions. His latest craze is for French (he is 'the Francophile'), an innocuous enough spare-time occupation in normal circumstances but one which is going to precipitate him and his family into a recriminatory show-down. One daughter, Una, has emigrated to London, another, Chris, is, in the course of the play, willingly abducted by a Frenchman, a traveller for a wine merchant, but elevated by 'the Francophile' into a French count. Willie's son, Kevin, returns unexpectedly from Belfast with news of his disbarment. The generation gap in general, and the lack of understanding between father and son in particular, is vividly expressed. His wife, Maggie, although criticizing him for his follies in private, is a realistic, unpretentious and loving mother, loyally defending him against Kevin's strictures: 'It takes courage to keep on going and your father has that courage.' Yet she knows that Willie is to blame for the break in family unity that grows as events are precipitated (as they were in the two previous plays) into a crisis. As a character, Maggie Logue again reminds us of Mrs Boyle. She knows where the blame lies. Accepting her own responsibility for not stopping Willie's ridiculous posturings, she is convinced that it was all instigated by his pretentious attempts at social aggrandizement. 'Chris is out there and we're all responsible. You Willie, for bringing this madness into the house, this madness about culture and learning and all that stuff that was away above and beyond us. You had the wee girl crazed with dreams and images.' Social hubris, then, was Willie's crime against the gods, and consequently the family must be punished. The key words here are 'away above and beyond us', and the contrast is with the Graham family (Mr Graham is the new overseer) whose children 'aren't barristers and things but they're a happy family and a contented family, and that's more than we can lay claim to'. In the ruins of his own family, Willie's earlier assertion that 'this is a home. We're all one here. This is a home,' becomes another piece of empty rhetoric. His high-flying plans for the children, one 'destined for a business career', another to 'grace the legal profession' and a third to 'care for the sick', all backfire, and they turn instead into serious failures, 'hard and unhappy'. The lesson is clear. The play speaks for the right of children to be left alone, to spare them the dangers of vicarious parental pride, another variation on a frequent theme in Friel's work. But Willie's efforts to rise socially through the success of his children hide a more serious and monumental flaw in his character, his inability to accept reality for what it is. At the end of the play he is clearly prepared to accept the lure of the life-lie.[3] He will want to escape the ruins of his own life, and create his own illusion of reality, making up a past that he can tolerate and even cherish. Willie Logue, too, is a 'peacock', worse and more dangerous than Daniel Stone in *To This Hard House* in his dishonesty to himself and the members of his own family.

In several respects *A Doubtful Paradise* repeats familiar elements in the two previous plays. The basic background is similar, and we recognize several of Friel's major thematic concerns. In structure too, these three plays resemble each other in the quick build-up to a point of crisis, and a following irresolute ending that suggests no development or action, but expresses 'continuance, life repeating itself and surviving'. *A Doubtful Paradise* has the same shortcomings as Friel's first two plays, tempered slightly by his growing experience of play-writing. But in the character of Willie Logue we can see suggestions of other Friel characters to come. He may be exaggerated and overdrawn but he introduces elements of a genuinely tragic character. His rather pathetic piece of doggerel (published in the local newspaper!) reveals him as sensitive to the fragility of individual life and the precariousness of existence. And yet he himself is responsible for his disappointments by creating the circumstances in which they are likely to occur. It is in this region we sense Friel's basically tragic creative imagination: certain preconditions for life exist, and man is limited (or free) to operate within what has been ordained, always risking confrontation with the forces of Fate.

The Blind Mice

With three radio plays to his credit one would expect a surer handling of the medium. This came in *The Blind Mice*. The play, however, was first performed as a stage

[67]

play at the Eblana Theatre in Dublin in February 1963. Its production there was no doubt the result of the encouraging success of *The Enemy Within* at the Queen's the previous year, a play which had introduced Friel to Dublin audiences and created curiosity around his name. *The Blind Mice*, written before *The Enemy Within*, has been both denounced and withdrawn by Friel. The reasons for this, I suspect, are more emotional and personal than critical. The play is suffused with Catholicism, and perhaps, as Maxwell has suggested, 'at some distant level it is a transmutation of Friel's own decision of conscience as a novice at Maynooth.' As such it is a rare occurrence in Friel's work. The first three plays are based in the same mental environment but this is only a condition of these plays. *The Blind Mice* has religion and priesthood as its sole moving force, and there is the zest of personal involvement in it. It introduces Friel's first 'dramatic' priest, a character which was to return in later plays, but never again given the same extended analysis. Perhaps the play was an attempt by Friel to de-church himself, to face honestly his own attitudes to religion and the priesthood. And it may have worked. Two years later he could remove himself from the experience. 'I was in Maynooth even, for two years when I was sixteen. An awful experience, it nearly drove me cracked. It is one thing I want to forget. I never talk about it – the priesthood. You know the kind of Catholicism we have in this country, it's unique' (*Guardian*, 8 October 1964). He considers it a 'very poor' play, and probably, almost by implication, too personal a statement. 'It's a play I'm sorry about'; 'It was too solemn, too intense – I wanted to hit at too many things,' he says in the same interview. As subject matter *The Blind Mice* comes into the same category as the political situation in Northern Ireland after the renewed outbreak of violence in 1968. This, we will remember, was something Friel did not want to write about in 1970, because he was

[68]

'emotionally much too involved about it'. In contemporary political terms *The Blind Mice* has an unmistakable Northern flavour; in pre-1968 terms, it is ominous in its portrayal of the easy inflammability of sectarian feelings. This then, would be another reason for Friel's bad feelings about the play. His unwillingness to pronounce unequivocally on the situation wins through. The threat of sectarian violence, 'There'll be a riot, that's what there'll be! The other side won't stand for it!' is given a remarkable twist, and the sectarian issue evaporates into extremes of one-sided (Catholic) religious fervour.

In spite of Friel's own view of *The Blind Mice* the play represents, in some respects, an important step forward. There is considerably more control of theme and technique than in any of the previous plays. Friel approaches resolutely the difficult and delicate subject he has chosen. There is far less overwriting, and for the first time he is able to invest events and lines with extended figurative meanings, thus adding a further dimension to the action. For the first time also, there is a more varied approach to dialogue, expressing character better, and better equipped to carry the play into its different moods. The fine scenes between mother and son contain genuinely moving language, and the lighthearted mimicking of the younger characters is well on its way towards the happy humour of *Philadelphia, Here I Come!*.

As a radio play, *The Blind Mice* represents an enormous advance on its predecessors. It makes wider and more variegated use of the possibilities of the medium. The three radio announcements that initiate the action, starting in China and arriving in Northern Ireland via the United States, give both local and thematic focus a good and concise introduction. Some brief outdoor scenes are deftly handled, and the brisk activities of the Carroll household are well suggested in telephone calls and visits. Exposition, such a problem for Friel in previous plays, is much easier and controlled in this (slightly longer) play. Background noises are used imaginatively and suggestively to add further dimensions to action and dialogue.

A strong sense of local history past and present is felt in the play. *The Blind Mice* is the first play to permit elements of the Northern Irish conflict to develop. About ten years later, in *The Freedom of the City,* Friel would attempt a much more wide-ranging and far-reaching appraisal of what was then a more open and inflamed situation.

In its dealings with 'authority' in various guises *The Blind Mice* harks back to the question of the individual versus the community, as it had been dealt with by Friel in the short stories and in a play like *A Sort of Freedom*, and also points forward again to later plays. It is in particular the psychology of this clash between the individual and various authority structures that Friel finds so fascinating.

Before turning to *The Enemy Within* it is time to conclude the discussion of one important aspect of Friel's early dramatic works and attempt some sort of overall view of this period by looking at three different plays, two written for radio and one for TV. One of the radio plays, *The Loves of Cass McGuire,* subsequently had considerable success as a stage play and will be treated mainly as such in my discussion of it. In technical terms it represents a further extension of Friel's radio plays and will therefore be briefly referred to as a radio play in this section.

The Founder Members

Two of the three plays are closely connected by time and theme. *Three Fathers, Three Sons,* a play for television, was transmitted on 7 January 1964 by Radio Telefis Eireann in Dublin and contributed in broadening and extending Friel's reputation. So did a short piece on BBC's Light Programme on 9 March of the same year, *The Founder Members*. In its brief fourteen minutes *The Founder Members* tries to epitomize some well-known Frielian themes. Harry and Joe are the only adult members who have turned up for the choir's annual excursion to the seaside. Among the young boys they are sadly out of place and only barely tolerated by the organizer of the outing, a Father Harte (another insensitive priest). The young show no respect for the founder members who have futilely dedicated their lives to the choir and now find themselves passed over by time. Harry and Joe indulge rather unashamedly in nostalgia in their efforts to age with dignity. At the end of the day, when the coach returns home, they are left behind, physically and symbolically, in despair dulled with drink. Harry and Joe are both bachelors. The choir, it seems, had turned into a substitute for marriage. But the odds against having a happy life if you are a single man keep piling up in Friel's work. The tendency was there in the short stories and it is confirmed in the plays. This is not to say that marriage automatically guarantees happiness. We have Rita Frazer and Maggie Logue as proof of that. But they are women, and many of Friel's women suffer when they are married. Friel's men, on the other hand, seem to suffer if they are not married. As a play *The Founder Members* remains a bagatelle. It covers familiar ground and does not extend Friel's thematic landscape. Its mood has been influenced by an awareness of the transience of individual life, the gap between generations, and it involves the question of how to age with dignity and where to find that dignity.

Three Fathers, Three Sons

As I have already suggested, Friel frequently aims for effects through the use of contrasts both internally within individual plays, and externally between different plays. This allows for a more extended and balanced look at the subjects he is dealing with. I believe it could even be argued that the major flaw of some of the early plays was his effort to include too much material in too short a space, to cover one subject from too many angles. A cleaner and more direct treatment of one issue or theme can often arrive at a wider statement. This can be exemplified if we put *The Founder Members* beside the TV play *Three Fathers, Three Sons*. The middle-aged bachelors in the first play have as their male counterparts three generations of fathers, so that instead of childlessness we have male fertility. The suggestions of memories in *The Founder Members* become almost ritualized in the second play, where the father's memories of the son are counterpointed by the son's memories of the father twice over. The relationship between fathers and sons is the pure theme of *Three Fathers, Three Sons,* untrammelled by side-issues even to the extent of almost excluding the mothers. The action of the play is simple and straightforward. A young man is alone at home, waiting for a telephone call from the maternity unit of the local hospital where his wife is about to give birth to his first son. On the wall of the room there are portraits of the young man's father and grandfather. Suddenly the portraits start talking to each other and then enter the room to engage in conversation with the young man. Grandfather, Father and Son become locked in a war of words with recriminatory accusations and counter-accusations revealing again the difficult nature of the father–son relationship. Within this triangle Friel once more stresses the contrasts. Grandfather was a successful businessman who had no time for his son, and who is disgusted to find that the heir to his business empire is weak and emotional. In response to his own childhood Father decides to treat his Son with an interest and love that turns out to be excessive and so alienates in a different way the Son from the Father. 'I did it for you' becomes the pervasive excuse for any kind of action as Grandfather first and Father after him find that their brand of fatherhood has failed miserably. For the Son, however, there is still hope or so, at least, he believes. He will take the accumulated wisdom of two generations of fatherhood and apply it to his own. He will not make the mistake that Father and Grandfather had been guilty of.

The play repeats strands of an argument already heard in *To This Hard House* and *A Doubtful Paradise* and moves us closer to one of the most important ingredients in *Philadelphia, Here I Come!* The real question for any father is how to avoid this seemingly inevitable estrangement. The Son in *Three Fathers, Three Sons* has found the solution: 'Patience – that's the trick. Understanding – that's the trick. Sympathy, kindness, tolerance – that's the trick!' But as the play continues, his youthful enthusiasm is gradually worn down by the pervading pessimism of Father and Grandfather. There is a remarkable progression in this process towards a paring down of human life into its barest and most basic qualities that is perfectly Beckettian. It can be clearly followed in the text of the play. It starts with the Grandfather bluntly dismissing the Son's happiness at having just had a son: '(*to Father*). Come on. Come on. Pay no heed to him. He'll learn like the rest of us – when it's too late.' It is enlarged and given metaphysical connotations in the Father's outcry against the failure of human communication, repeated twice in quick succession: 'Nobody ever understands anything.' The Son's resolution to succeed in his future relationships with his own son becomes desperate, and he is clearly unnerved by the common and formal attack from previous generations.

Despite its shortness, or perhaps because of it, *Three Fathers, Three Sons* is able to encompass a wide variety of aspects within its chosen theme. Through the processes of concentration and elimination – and again we are reminded of Beckett – Friel explores two different levels of existence. What happens on the level of the individual is a reflection of the rather dreary and pessimistic outlook on the metaphysical level. On the first, the play focuses on discussions heard in *To This Hard House* and *A Doubtful Paradise* about the difficult nature of parenthood and how to bring up children. It warns us about the dangers of parental expectations and vicarious pride, which inevitably stifle and destroy, and it advocates privacy and freedom for the child. Friendship should be the essential quality in any parent–child relationship, and, as the Son in *Three Fathers, Three Sons* has told us, it must always come in the first instance from the grown-up. Friel's young men somewhere lose their childlike simplicity, and if there is no friendship to sustain the relationship, it goes to waste. There are several cases of a similar kind in Friel's stories and plays.

On the metaphysical level – and *Three Fathers, Three Sons* is unusual in allowing such interpretations – its insistence on impermanence and death, that 'Life – any life – is always preferable' (to death), the play approaches a tragic conception of life to a degree that is rare in Friel. It is, as we have seen, a common enough condition of life in the stories and plays, but its expression is customarily a much more muted one.

In its structure *Three Fathers, Three Sons* contains in a stylized form the fundamental idea that past events always penetrate present reality. With Grandfather, Father and Son able to ignore temporarily the existence of death (in itself an instance of the 'Irish macabre' but without the humour), past and present intermingle. The three characters compare events in the past and, as could be expected, disagree on most points. The Son will be allowed to present his view of the Grandfather 'provided it's the truth', whereupon the Father exclaims: 'He [Son] doesn't know what the word means.' The right version of the past depends for its truth on the individual telling or re-telling it. In this brief reference to the idea of an individual rather than general truth in dealing with the past, the play, like others before it, looks forward to *The Loves of Cass McGuire*. The radio version of the latter play, broadcast by the BBC Third Programme in August 1966, preceded by only two months the opening of the stage play on Broadway. It was in fact the last play of Friel's to be first produced on radio.

The Loves of Cass McGuire

There is a sense in which the techniques employed by Friel in structuring *The Loves of Cass McGuire* are, in conventional terms, more suited to the radio medium than to the stage. The play demands a high degree of flexibility in terms of space and movement. Scenes change quickly, and the protagonist, Cass McGuire herself, moves easily between them. She guides herself and the listeners through the play, making them her confidants. She speaks to them directly, and this contact with the listening audience becomes her only link with reality as she slowly and gradually subsides into the atmosphere of make-believe that rules Eden House, a rest home for elderly people. And yet it is in the vital relationship between Cass and the audience that the radio version finds it most difficult to function properly, and where one of the most striking differences between radio and stage version appears. In its basic content the play differs little between the two versions. Certain obvious variations occur: on the radio Cass refers to the listeners, on stage to the members of the audience. There is slightly more expository and additional material in the stage version, used to extend character and event, but nothing that influences the thematic foundation of the play. The introduction of new scenes from the past via echo/memory microphone sometimes becomes a confusing factor. The absence of a physical dimension to the other characters disturbs the flow of the play. In the stage version the gradual loss of Cass's contact with the audience and so with reality becomes the thread of the play. Here again the limitations on one-dimensional radio prevent a fuller and more varied understanding of some of the most important features of *The Loves of Cass McGuire*. Radio, with its seemingly limitless freedom, can do nothing to counter this shortcoming. Subtle variations between private and public voices cannot easily be achieved. The ability to create the atmosphere and mood of a place are similarly curtailed.

> Guthrie grasped that radio does not move in space but almost wholly in time, even though it can, by sounds and descriptions, give the illusion of place, and even though voices can be heard from near and far, depending on their relationship to the microphone, to give the impression of depth. It cannot give us a precise picture of characters grouped in a room – one reason why Chekhov's plays, which often convey complex emotional undercurrents through spatial relationships between characters, rarely succeed on radio.[4]

For Friel's plays, it would never be enough to create an 'illusion' or 'impression' of place. The idea of a securely rooted locale is one of the corner-stones of Friel's work. It cannot rise to that status on radio. The reference to Chekhov is highly relevant. He is probably the writer for whom Friel has expressed the greatest admiration. There are many similarities between the plays of these two writers, particularly as regards mood and atmosphere, the intricate emotional relationships between characters, and an overall ironic and even tragic attitude to life. If we relate these comparisons to the medium of radio, there are again further correspondences. 'Of non-Shakespearean plays, those of Chekhov were considered unsuitable [for radio production] largely because of the way in which dialogue and action are often made to work at cross-purposes in them.'[5] These 'cross-purposes' are one aspect of the irony so frequent in Friel's work. Finally, there is an obvious visual dimension that can only work on stage: 'the unspoken but so to say "faced" thoughts of Chekhov's sad ladies by their absence in this medium affect the balance of the play and diminish their creator's fame.'[6] These observations, when put together, add up to a gradual dissatisfaction with the possibilities of radio drama for the kind of plays that Friel wanted to write. In the first few plays Friel had been guilty of overstating inner thoughts and feelings. With the help of other more physical dimensions they could be expressed with greater economy, accuracy and subtlety. The radio version of *The Loves of Cass McGuire* cannot carry all the meanings of the script to the listener. It suggests instead that Friel had grown out of the medium of radio.

Since *The Enemy Within* Friel has written mainly original plays for the stage. It would be wrong, however, to disregard the experiences of writing for and working in radio in a general overview of Friel's work. It taught him, perhaps more than anything else, that dialogue written for dramatic presentation is widely different from that of a short story. The problems of narration had to be solved without the help of direct authorial intervention. Occasionally, in later plays, some commentators have detected a certain distrust of the audience and its ability to 'understand' everything, which may account for the use of a chorus or a commentator. The progression from short stories to stage plays via radio could be seen as having left some traces in Friel's later plays. It would hardly be surprising if the more experimental techniques that Friel was to use owed at least part of their origin to a cross-fertilization between different media.

The Enemy Within

In *The Blind Mice* Friel had touched on the question of
what the role of the priest should be. Father Rooney
sums up the difficult place held by the priest in the
community. 'Everyone has his own idea of what a priest
should be. That's what makes life so difficult for us.'
The position of St Columba in *The Enemy Within* is
equally if not even more problematic. The concept of
sanctity may lead some people to expect a play dealing
with a saint's life to move in an atmosphere of pure and
elevated piety, far removed from everyday life. The
truth of the matter is, of course, that Columba was first
and foremost a simple priest who at the time of the
play's action had not been canonized. Friel wanted, in
his own words, 'to discover how he acquired sanctity.
Sanctity in the sense of a man having tremendous
integrity and the courage to back it up,' not, perhaps, a
wholly conventional definition of the word (*Guardian*).
This definition, and Friel's avowed intention as
described in greater detail in a Preface to the play,
sheds light on some of the religious implications of his
chosen subject. 'I have avoided the two spectacular and
better-known aspects of the saint – the builder of
monasteries in Ireland and in Scotland, and the
Prophet and Miracle-worker, both of which are
described generously in St Adamnan's *Life* – and have
concentrated instead on the private man.' The fact is
that for most of the feats that Columba accomplishes in
the play he would hardly have been canonized at all.
But his involvement in bloody warfare and clannish
feuding must be seen against the background of his
own times, as Friel points out in the Preface.

When considering these days, one should remember that
they were violent and bloody, that Columba was reared
'among a people whose Constitution and National Construction rendered civil faction almost inseparable from

[78]

their existence' (Reeves), and that it was not until 804, over two hundred years after Columba's death, that monastic communities were formally exempted from military service.

Even though the question of Columba's conventionally religious merits is overshadowed by his personal struggle against the twin influences of homeland and family, the underlying condition of the play is his relationship with God. 'He that loveth father or mother more than me is not worthy of me' ring as words of warning in Columba's ears and illustrate the central conflict. But, true to the time it is portraying, the play allows little distinction between the role of priest and political leader. When the appeal is made to Columba to return to Ireland to fight for his family, it is made just because he is a priest.

The first act is ample proof of Friel's increasing control over the handling and expression of plot. It is structured round the first demand of family and home, coming in the shape of a messenger from Columba's cousin Hugh. But it is subtly and unobtrusively introduced and prepared for by Columba's own memories of Donegal. First Friel establishes the everyday, almost leisurely and good-natured atmosphere of the monastic community. There is no suggestion of family feuding or violence. But Columba's accidental reading of the scriptures and 'He that loveth father or mother more than me is not worthy of me' evokes a lyrical description of home and family.

Columba's exile is conscious and self-imposed. It is part of his calling as a missionary for God. In Ireland his religious work was frequently affected by the worldly demands of community and family. On Iona he was hoping, in what was at least a partial withdrawal from the world, to escape its claims and purify himself of its irreligiosity. And yet, in doing this, he also removes himself from his place and family, an uprooting which is bound to interfere with his equanimity. What may have forced him to leave is an integral part of what is now attracting him back. This seems to be the permanent condition of the Irish exile, love and hatred existing together but pulling in opposite directions. It can hardly be given a more powerful expression than in Columba's final rejection of Ireland, reduced to extreme purity and strength.

Get out of my monastery! Get out of my island! Get out of my life! Go back to those damned mountains and seductive hills that have robbed me of my Christ! You soaked my sweat! You sucked my blood! You stole my manhood, my best years! What more do you demand of me, damned Ireland? My soul? My immortal soul? Damned, damned, damned Ireland! – (*His voice breaks.*) Soft, green Ireland – beautiful, green Ireland – my lovely green Ireland. O my Ireland –

The Enemy Within is balanced on the two scenes of temptation from home and family, one in act I and the second in act III. In the first Columba is assisted by his prior Grillaan in his effort to ignore the call. In his detachment Grillaan can see dangerous connection between Columba's two roles as priest and military leader.

GRILLAAN: And [Hugh] wants you to bless his men and pray over them and dignify his brawl with a crucifix?
COLUMBA: Our churches in Tyrone and Tirconnail are in danger.
GRILLAAN: They always are.
COLUMBA: I mean it, Grillaan.
GRILLAAN: And his enemies – whoever they are this time – no doubt they have a churchman to bless their standards too, with the result that God is fighting for both causes. Isn't that the usual pattern?
COLUMBA: A mad monk leading a gang of murderers!
GRILLAAN: You are a priest – not a rallying cry!

[80]

There is an ominous note of contemporaneity in Grillaan's words. What may have been unavoidable in the less civilized days of the crusades certainly seems out of place in modern times. In these passages Friel's play has a relevance for any wholly or partly religious conflict today. The scene climaxes in a ritualized duel for Columba's soul.

GRILLAAN: The last tie, Columba. Cut it now. Cut it. Cut it.
BRIAN: They are your people. It is your land.
GRILLAAN: A priest or a politician – which?
BRIAN: They rallied round you at Sligo and at Coleraine.
    All they ask is your blessing.
GRILLAAN: He that loveth father or mother more than me
    is not worthy of me.
BRIAN: Are they to die in their sins at the hands of
    murderers?
GRILLAAN: You are a priest in voluntary exile for God – not
    a private chaplain to your family.
BRIAN: Son of Fedhlimidh and Eithne.
GRILLAAN: Abbot!

Columba yields. He cannot resist his own blood. 'We come of kings, Prior. To lead is in our blood. We are not savages.'

The brief calm of act II is only a preliminary to the second call of home. It is made all the stronger by being represented by Columba's own brother Eoghan and his son. In a long scene the arguments of act I are repeated. But events have steeled Columba's determination to withstand the challenge. The demands of 'the inner man – the soul – chained irrevocably to the earth, to the green wooded earth of Ireland!' have not been fully satisfied. He pleads with his brother to be given the last years of his life 'to do battle with the flesh' and to prepare for his Maker. There is a strong and obvious contrast between the inner and the outer man in Columba's personality.

The conflict between the inner and outer man can

only be resolved through the subjection of one to the other. That, in a sense, is Columba's tragedy. The victory of the one is the defeat of the other. In his refusal to leave Iona and return to Ireland and family he is denied and cursed by his brother. To Eoghan, Columba has failed in his duty, not only to Ireland and family, but as a priest. Ireland with Eoghan and his family may have lost a priest and a brother. Christianity, however, has gained a saint. At the very end of the play, for the first time, Columba uses the word 'home' to refer to Iona and his monastic community. His exile has been completed, but at a high cost.

The thematic content of *The Enemy Within* represents a further extension of Friel's familiar territory. The concepts of home and family are seen from a new and different point of view. It is a pessimistic play in the sense that Columba's aspirations can only be achieved through the sacrifice of the corrupting influence of these values. But it was also, we must remember, in the same way that, according to Friel, Joyce was a saint, by 'turning his back on Ireland and on his family' (*Guardian*). The struggle to keep one's own individuality and aspirations alive may leave no other alternative. But the play also suggests the rewards available to the exile. The all-male monastic community leaves Columba to give his undivided attention to his calling, just like, you might say, exile left Joyce to his artistic undertaking. As always, Friel makes the passing of time an unavoidable reality by opposing to the old age of the senior members of the community the idealistic zeal of the novice Oswald. The serious mood of the greater part of the play is balanced by the pointed but friendly jokes the monks enjoy at each other's expense. The neat structure of the three acts, the increasing tension of act I resolved in the release of energy at the end, the quiet of act II counteracted by a further conflict in act III, while revealing Friel's surer control of plot, may seem, as Maxwell has suggested 'a little contrived'. The two scenes of Columba's temptations from home and family may be too synchronized, punctuating and stressing Columba's dilemma and the two contrasting sides of his personality. The timing of the arrival, disappearance and return of Oswald threatens to fall into the same category. The character plays a part in the overall design of the play, but his role in accentuating the different stages of Columba's crises becomes a little too obvious. These weaknesses, however, never destroy the impression of the play as an important stage in Friel's growth as a dramatist. Its strengths derive from his determined approach to his subject, and his decision to stick to it. It contains both the sediments of his previous work in terms of thematic content and the seeds of the future. In its largely psychological interest and its insistence on the workings of the individual mind, in the division between the inner and outer man, between the private and public Columba, *The Enemy Within* was to find a natural successor in *Philadelphia, Here I Come!*

III

Development of Form and Content

Not Just a Question of Form

In progressing chronologically towards 1964 and *Philadelphia, Here I Come!* we have become increasingly aware of the various strands that make up the thematic fabric of Brian Friel's stories and plays. These are all conditioned by and given expression in the strongly localized habitat the author has chosen for his literary landscape. At its most general, his work realizes, to use a phrase suggested by Friel himself, 'concepts of Irishness'. In the making of the play *Aristocrats* in 1976–7, these 'concepts' included 'religion, politics, money, position, marriages, revolts, affairs, love, loyalty, disaffection', set against the background of 'a family saga of three generations'.[1] If we incorporate into this list of nouns their own opposites, we would have a reasonably comprehensive vantage point from which we could also survey the rest of Friel's work and its outer boundaries. The focus of each play is then brought down to the level of the individual where these 'concepts' are finally tested and defined, both within the self and in its relations with other people and with society. This, in turn, is where the notion of communication enters, and where language as a medium of communication becomes of paramount importance in Friel's work.

If the 'concepts' above refer to the content of Friel's plays, and if most critics and commentators on his work would agree about its basic characteristics, there is no such consensus when we turn to the question of form. In discussing Friel's plays words like 'experiment' and 'device' are frequently used to describe some of the techniques employed by the dramatist. Yet it must be remembered, when considering the totality of Friel's dramatic output up to now, that only comparatively few of his plays are 'experimental' in any genuine sense. There are two reasons why Friel's plays are often discussed in these terms. The first is the predominantly 'realistic' nature of all modern Irish drama. The second is the striking and even innovative quality of Friel's 'experimentation'.

Friel's interest in non-realistic presentation is evidence of a dramatist who is willing to test the formal possibilities of his chosen medium. Any contemporary dramatist has a rich variety of sources to draw on. He faces the problem of mirroring the fragmented complexity of modern life, of presenting a subject that has a common interest in a form that will seem both adequate and familiar to a contemporary audience. Despite the seemingly limitless freedom of the dramatist in choosing a form that will suit his particular purpose, it can still be argued that, whereas a basically realistic play will elicit few comments about its technical characteristics, any non-realistic presentation will be noticed and commented upon. Although 'experimentation' is accepted and sometimes even appreciated, realism still seems to be the norm. Samuel Beckett is a case in point. He treads on common grounds, but achieves, by the processes of elimination and concentration, a presentation of the human experience through an admittedly complicated yet clear picture of a shared situation. His methods have been termed 'absurd', but Beckett has found this to be an adequate means of expressing the predicament of the modern human being. The relation between method and subject matter, between form and content, is of vital importance for an understanding of modern drama. The two concepts cannot work independently of each other. As a dramatist Friel is very much aware of this problem. His aim is 'this happy fusion that occurs so seldom between content and form', so necessary that 'there's no point in discussing them separately' (*Irish Times*, 12 February, 1970). Yet, he admits, his first consideration, when beginning a new play, becomes its form rather than its content:

> The crux with the new play arises – as usual with me – with its form. Whether to reveal slowly and painstakingly and with almost realised tedium the workings of the family; or with some kind of supra-realism, epiphanies, in some way to make real the essences of these men and women by side-stepping or leaping across the boredom of their small talk, their trivial chatterings, etc. etc. But I suppose the answer to this will reveal itself when I know/possess the play. Now I am only laying siege to it.[2]

In his preparations for *Aristocrats,* Friel's search for form also included 'considerations of masks, verse, expressionism', none of which appeared in the final product. The making of any play necessarily concerns problems of different forms of presentation. The final test of the suitability of the chosen form comes in performance, with form working together with content and not separated from it. Why, then, is there frequently an inclination on the part of critics and commentators to single out particular items in the plays, and deal separately with, for instance, the *alter ego* in *Philadelphia, Here I Come!,* the Commentators in *Lovers,* the American lecturer in *The Freedom of the City* and the character of 'Sir' in *Living Quarters*? Against the background of what I have suggested earlier and the two reasons given above, this interest is unavoidable and even relevant. But within each separate play the stress on 'devices' should be toned down in favour of a more total attention to the organic entity of form and content in the dramatic presentation. *Philadelphia, Here I Come!* did not succeed because of the *alter ego*; *Lovers* would not be the same play without the Commentators; the lecture given by the American sociologist in *The Freedom of the City* has a direct bearing on the thematic texture of the play. The fact that the statement is delivered in the form of a lecture, and not in any other way, is in itself extending the relevance of the play's thesis.[3]

There is another sense in which Friel's work is not usefully to be described as 'experimental'. To discuss the methods used in these plays in terms of 'neo-Expressionistic crutches and neo-Brechtian gimmicks', as Robert Hogan does in his essay 'Since O'Casey', is not only unhelpful but also uninformed. It postulates that any Irish or other drama can be understood solely from the point of view of this century. It is true, of course, that the concepts and trends that Hogan mentions may be relevant and important in a discussion of contemporary Irish drama. But there are other influential forces to be considered. For Friel one such force is 'ritual': 'Ritual is part of all drama. Drama without ritual is poetry without rhythm – hence not poetry, not drama. This is not to say that ritual is an 'attribute' of drama: it is the essence of drama. Drama is a RITE, and always religious in the purest sense.'[4] In this sense Friel's drama is more 'original' than 'experimental'. A great deal can be learnt by approaching some of his plays via the classical theatre of Greece. Concepts and conventions familiar to the student of Greek drama need not be repeated here. But certain vital correspondences should be established. In the context of ritual the name of Tyrone Guthrie must again be mentioned. A chapter entitled 'Theatre as Ritual' in his book *In Various Directions* begins: 'This is going to be about religion. I am not a theological scholar, nor equipped in any way to speak with

[87]

authority. To serve the theatre is my profession; it is my belief that, in trying to serve the theatre faithfully, I am offering some sort of service to God.' The link formed here leads us back to the very origins of Greek drama. At the end of the same chapter, Guthrie sums it up: 'The theatre relates itself to God by means of ritual. It does so more consciously than any other activity, except prayer, because, like organized prayer, it is the direct descendant of primitive religious ceremonies.'

Now, perhaps, the years at Maynooth take on an added significance. The Catholic mass and the priest's role in it, Friel's consideration of various dramatic techniques like, for instance, the use of masks, the appearance of a modern form of the classical chorus in his plays, all these are part of the same theorem. 'We know that the first actors of tragedy in Athens were priests. They ritually re-enacted the death and resurrection of Dionysus,' says Guthrie. But they were also the instigators of these ceremonies and therefore in a sense the playwrights. Friel's interest in classical theatre has been expressed in several ways. At times he has contemplated attempting a modern version of Sophocles' *Antigone*. It is easy to see why Friel is attracted to this play. In his own creative imagination the themes of *Antigone* would feel familiar. There is first of all the intense presence of the character of Fate ruling the lives of human beings: 'As flies to wanton boys are we to the gods; they kill us for their sport,' Mag complains ominously in 'Winners'. Fox Melarkey's rickety wheel in *Crystal and Fox* becomes another symbol of the workings of Providence, and 'Sir' in *Living Quarters* only executes the will of that erratic character. The main conflict in *Antigone,* that between the state and the individual, would fit nicely into Friel's work; the family as one of society's communities, and internal pressures within that unit, between father and son, parents and children and male and female, set against the background of a struggle between life and death, are all, as we have already noticed, important and recurring themes in Friel's work. In terms of form, the original techniques of Greek drama as used in *Antigone* would worry no commentator. They would have to be accepted as an established and integral part of that drama. We can hardly ask Sophocles to rewrite *Antigone* or to dispose of the chorus because the conventions and taste of today find it unfamiliar. When examining Friel's modern variations on the classical chorus, as, for instance, the commentators in 'Winners' and 'Sir' in *Living Quarters*, we must not forget their origin and, at the same time, try to relate their use to its contemporary function. Brecht or no Brecht, Pirandello or no Pirandello, many of the techniques used by Friel in his plays cannot be understood solely in terms of the modern theatre.

Philadelphia, Here I Come! (1964)[5]

In connection with *Philadelphia, Here I Come!*, the name of another modern dramatist has been referred to. Friel's division of the play's main character into two actors both present on stage has been likened to the technique used by Eugene O'Neill in one of his lesser-known plays, *Days Without End*. O'Neill was also greatly interested in Greek drama and his reworking of the Oresteia trilogy by Aeschylus, *Mourning Becomes Electra*, also included elements of the plays of Sophocles and Euripides. Here, then, the artistic concerns of Friel and O'Neill seem to converge. In the case of the divided protagonist of *Philadelphia, Here I Come!*, however, a careful comparison with O'Neill's main character in *Days Without End* will reveal more differences than similarities.

In Friel's play the focus is on the workings of the individual mind. It is not a picture of rational thoughts and calm deliberations but, more importantly, a description of the emotional fabric of the mind.

With the growth of modern society and its general tendencies towards increased fragmentation, the twentieth century has gradually focused more and more attention on the individual. The development of psychology as a branch of knowledge, and more especially the work of Freud and his disciples, have resulted in great interest being taken in the mind of the individual human being. Theories about the subconscious have opened up a field where everything has not been (or can be) proven and where speculation is still possible. But quite apart from the fact that the world has seen split personalities before Freud, the use of a divided protagonist should not be seen only against this modern background. There is also the underlying idea of the 'divided self' and the primitive use of masks, which is almost as old as the world itself. This belief in and use of masks is an idea that is inherent in drama. It can express, in many different ways, the disparity between seeming and being, between appearance and reality, a conflict of immense dramatic potential.

In *Philadelphia, Here I Come!* Friel's intention is to show the psychology of the implementation of a decision. How do people react in an emotionally decisive situation? Often the human brain tends to 'speed' and there is an intense increase in activity, thoughts and ideas multiply, associations suggest themselves rapidly and seemingly irrationally. To transfer this state of flux and fluidity into literature writers have, in novels and short stories, had recourse to the interior monologue, letting the characters give out their thoughts directly to the reader. But how can the same process be credibly realized in the theatre? Friel's Public and Private Gareth O'Donnell together try to achieve this difficult goal.

In comparing Friel's Public and Private Gar with O'Neill's John Loving it should first be stressed that Friel claims to have had no previous knowledge of O'Neill's play. The similarities were pointed out to him after the first production of his own play. That this is so is easy to understand if we compare the handling of the two protagonists. Friel is very explicit in emphasizing that the relationship between Public and Private Gar is that between a man and his conscience, his 'other self'. In his stage directions at the very beginning of the play Friel makes this clear: *'The two Gars, Public Gar and Private Gar, are two views of the same man. Public Gar is the Gar that people see, talk to, talk about. Private Gar is the unseen man, the man within, the conscience, the alter ego, the secret thoughts, the id.'*

In O'Neill's *Days Without End* the two characters on stage together share the name of John Loving. One of them, John, is described in realistic matter-of-fact terms at the beginning of the first act. After stressing that Loving, played by another actor, is of the same age, height and figure, and dressed in the same way, O'Neill goes on to break the realism:

> *In contrast to this similarity between the two, there is an equally strange dissimilarity. For Loving's face is a mask whose features reproduce exactly the features of John's face – the death mask of a John who has died with a sneer of scornful mockery on his lips. And this mocking scorn is repeated in the expression of the eyes which stare bleakly from behind the mask.*

The most obvious difference is, of course, O'Neill's use of the mask, which introduces a feeling of formal ritual, of a strong insistence on the two sides of the same man, and of a war (or at least enmity) between them. O'Neill's characters (as always) generate forceful undercurrents of violent emotions and inner obsessions, and the play ends in the actual death of one of the characters, Loving, when John, the other one, has finally come back to a belief in God, thus able to cast off the doubting and hateful Loving. But the most important difference, and one which, in my view, turns out to be a shortcoming that wrecks the play and fails to lift it above the class of serious melodrama, is that all through the play the other characters, John's wife and his uncle, for instance, can hear the *alter ego,* i.e. Loving, speak. This results in many strange situations where Loving blurts out uncomfortable truths to the great surprise and discomfort of the others:

> JOHN: (*begins jerkily*). Well – But before I start, there's one thing I want to impress on you both again. My plot, up to the last part, which is wholly imaginary, is taken from life. It's the story of a man I once knew.
> LOVING: (*mockingly*). Or thought I knew.
> ELSA: May I be inquisitive? Did I ever know the man?
> LOVING: (*a hostile, repellent note in his voice*). No. I can swear that. You have never known him.
> ELSA: (*taken aback, gives John a wondering look – then apologetically*). I'm sorry I butted in with a silly question. Go on, dear.

Once again, Friel is very explicit and his *alter ego,* i.e. Private Gar, functions in a different way. *'Private Gar, the spirit, is invisible to everybody, always.* Nobody except Public Gar hears him talk [my emphasis]. *But even Public Gar, although he talks to Private Gar occasionally, never sees him and never looks at him. One cannot look at one's* alter ego.' Whatever his intention may be, O'Neill's technique blurs the vital issue of the frontier between seeming and being, between individualism and conformity. He does not take advantage of the inherent possibilities in this opposition. Friel's approach differs very much, and he has found in this disparity between the inner and outer selves an effective vehicle for both pathos and humour. In order to penetrate the minds of all the characters in the play Friel would have had to provide each one of them with a 'private' voice. As we shall see, Gar's father, S. B. O'Donnell, would most certainly have needed one. But apart from the fact that this would have made it into a very strange play, it would also have precluded all opportunities for other kinds of dramatic (often ironic) expression. The conflict between Public and Private Gar is nicely pointed in the 'normal' relationship between Gar and Madge the housekeeper, where human actions and affections are truthfully shown, and where Public and Private Gar are both present, fused into one complete person, Gareth O'Donnell. Their relationship also reflects on the exchanges between Madge and S.B. Together, these two relationships, a triangle S.B.–Madge–Gar, with Madge as an emotional go-between and confessor, comment on the dearth of emotions and the lack of communication between father and son, one of the most important themes in the play.

As it turns out, the reference to O'Neill and his *Days Without End* is not at all necessary. Although Friel's divided protagonist may not have been, strictly speaking, an innovation, it was a much more successful transposition of the classical idea of the mask into a modern framework. It becomes the perfect vehicle for the thematic exploration attempted by Friel in this play. At no time is there any undue emphasis on the 'device'. Nor is there a feeling of a contrived mechanism at work. One of the most striking characteristics of *Philadelphia, Here I Come!* is how naturally and comfortably the divided protagonist sits with the other characters and with the rest of the play. This quality is in itself proof enough of how quickly Friel had acquired a well-developed sense of theatre. 'Brian Friel is a born playwright,' Tyrone Guthrie stated in a BBC Northern Ireland broadcast, reviewing the published version of the play. What Guthrie meant was that 'meaning is implicit "between the lines" of the text; in silences; in what people are thinking and doing far more than in what they are saying; in the music as much as in the meaning of a phrase.' Guthrie's appreciation of the play, while still acknowledging the contribution made by the divided protagonist, stresses features without which no play can really succeed, whatever the nature of the technique (or 'device') used in the presentation. It is the language in communication that must carry the play's meaning and assume responsibility for the development of themes. In *Philadelphia, Here I Come!* everything is subjected to this intention. Flashbacks or memory sequences have similar functions. Friel breaks up linear time to bring both past, present and future events (the latter, of course, dreamed or imagined) to bear on the emotionally charged central situation. The few hours during which the external action of the play takes place cannot in themselves contain all significant experiences. The overall structure of the play becomes an intriguing mixture of the lived-in present, including four visits by various people all of which help to shed vital light on Gar's dilemma, two flashbacks to decisive events in the past, and various romps into an imagined future in the USA. But the strength of the play is such that the central situation, the conflict in Gar's mind, is never lost sight of. There is a gradual intensification all through the play, most clearly sensed at the end of the first two episodes, culminating in Gar's final question to himself at the very end of the play: 'God, Boy, why do you have to leave? Why? Why?' His own baffled answer, 'I don't know. I–I–I don't know', sums up the frustration felt by the intending exile. Gar knows that there may be reasons enough for leaving his poor and future-less existence in the village of Ballybeg for the wealthy promise of the city of Philadelphia. But he knows too, that the same conditions that may motivate his departure inevitably bind him to home and his native soil. Michael and Mary Feeney in Liam O'Flaherty's story 'Going into Exile' who are, like Gar, leaving for America, experience this curious transformation: 'the poverty and sordidness of their home life appeared to them under the aspect of comfort and plenty.' Friel has spoken of *Philadelphia, Here I*

Come! as 'an angry play' (*Guardian*). Certainly, we may detect a sensibility offended by some west-of-Ireland conditions that provoke young people to leave, and the lack of remedying policies from official sources. We may even, in this context, usefully see Gar's father, who is unable to help his son, as a symbol of the failure of official Ireland to provide the young generation with hope and future. But Friel's play has nothing like the desperate frustration of the mother near the end of O'Flaherty's story:

> Then the mother rose and came into the kitchen. She looked at the two women, at her little son and at the hearth, as if she were looking for something she had lost. Then she threw her hands into the air and ran out into the yard.
>
> 'Come back,' she screamed; 'come back to me.'
>
> She looked wildly down the road with dilated nostrils, her bosom heaving. But there was nobody in sight. Nobody replied.

Friel's approach is always more controlled. Many situations, in both short stories and plays, contain considerable emotional charge, but Friel finds various ways of stemming the flow of emotions. Sentimentality is restrained through a consistent check on its outlets. In *Philadelphia, Here I Come!* Private Gar is the perfect antidote to any such indulgence. 'Get a grip on yourself! Don't be a damned sentimental fool! (*Sings.*) "Philadelphia, Here I Come –" ' It could also be argued that Friel's arrangement of his dramatic material militates against a possible overloading of feelings. The more formal aspects of the structure of two later plays, 'Winners' and *The Freedom of the City* perform this function.

The successful blend of the comic and the sad is, I believe, largely responsible for the triumph of *Philadelphia, Here I Come!* The two moods never exist in isolation, they undercut each other in both directions

and their constant interplay is in perfect concord with
Gar's fragile position. He alternates between sudden
euphoria at the prospect of going to America and deep
despair at having to leave Ballybeg. It is an even
greater strength of the play's comedy that it does not
just provide laughter and relief. It is always highly
relevant for the thematic structure of the play. This
passage, for instance, is not only funny, it reveals
perfectly the drab routine of the O'Donnell household:

PRIVATE: . . . (*In polite tone.*) Have a seat Screwballs. (*S.B.
sits down at the table.*) Thank you. Remove the hat.
(*S.B. takes off the hat to say grace. He blesses
himself*). On again. (*Hat on.*) Perfectly trained; the
most obedient father I ever had. And now for our
nightly lesson in the English language. Repeat
slowly after me: Another day over.

S.B.: Another day over.

PRIVATE: Good. Next phrase. I suppose we can't complain.

S.B.: I suppose we can't complain.

PRIVATE: Not bad. Now for a little free conversation. But
no obscenities, Father dear; the child is only
twenty-five. (*S.B. eats in silence. Pause.*) Well,
come on, come on! Where's that old rapier wit of
yours, the toast of the Ballybeg coffee-houses?

S.B.: Did you set the rat-trap in the store?

PUBLIC: Aye.

PRIVATE: (*hysterically*). Isn't he a riot? Oh, my God, that
father of yours just kills me! But wait – wait –
shhh–shhh–

S.B.: I didn't find as many about the year.

PRIVATE: Oooooh God! Priceless! Beautiful! Delightful! 'I
didn't find as many about the year!' Did you ever
hear the beat of that? Wonderful! But isn't he in
form tonight? But isn't he? You know, it's not every
night that jewels like that, pearls of wisdom on
rodent reproduction, drop from those lips!

And the comedy here is only a prelude to Gar's first
confession of the gap that exists between him and his

father. When we remember that this is Gar's final night at home, we begin to realize the dimensions of the problem. He is leaving, he says, not just because he is treated as if he were five years old, or because he is paid less than Madge the housekeeper, 'but worse, far worse than that, Screwballs, because – *we embarrass one another*. If one of us were to say, "You're looking tired" or "That's a bad cough you have," the other would fall over backways with embarrassment.' This distance between them cannot be traversed. Their everyday conversation is limited to the necessary and the matter-of-fact. Madge futilely tries to mediate to bring them closer together. But she is herself wrapped up in her own painful experiences. She is even refused the simple hope of having her latest grand-niece named after her, a fact she prefers not to tell Gar. Her own damning conclusion, coming at the end of the play, may be seen to sum up much of what has (and has not) been said:

> When the boss was his [Gar's] age, he was the very same as him: leppin' and eejitin' about and actin' the clown; as like as two peas. And when he's [Gar] the age the boss is now, he'll turn out just the same. And although I won't be here to see it, you'll find that he's learned nothin' in-between times. That's people for you – they'd put you astray in the head if you thought long enough about them.

Any hope that Gar and his father might have been able to approach each other without emotional inhibitions is destroyed in an eloquent and ironic double image. S.B.'s awkward suggestion that Gar should sit at the back (of the aeroplane!), 'if there was an accident or anything – it's the front gets it hardest – ', prompts Gar to ask his father about a treasured memory from the past, fishing together on Lough na Cloc Cor. But S.B. remembers only a brown boat instead of Gar's blue one, and he is certain he never knew the song ('All

[97]

Round My Hat I'll Wear a Green Coloured Ribbono')
that Gar remembers him having sung as they walked
home happily together. 'So now you know: it never
happened! Ha-ha-ha-ha-ha,' mocks Private. And immediately, S.B.'s own memory of Gar as a little boy is
questioned by Madge:

> S.B.: D'you mind the trouble we had keeping him at school
> just after he turned ten. D'you mind nothing would
> do him but he'd get behind the counter. And he had
> this wee sailor suit on him this morning –
> MADGE: A sailor suit? He never had a sailor suit.

The father–son relationship is, as we have seen in
earlier plays, familiar thematic territory for Friel. So is
the subject of emigration, the hope of a freer and more
affluent existence in England or America; so is the
attraction of an imaginary existence for those who stay:
the coarse, empty bluster of the young men and their
imaginary sexual conquests, Master Boyle's more or
less total acceptance of a life of illusion (at the end of
the play Madge also has some definite intentions in
that direction). Canon Mick O'Byrne, the parish priest,
adds another ineffectual representative of the Church
to an already long list. What is new, thematically, in
Philadelphia, Here I Come! is the unblinking attention
Friel gives to the central problem of the play. In order
to make sense, Gar's situation and the conflict in his
mind must be exhaustively developed and laid out for
examination. This necessitates a sometimes painful
exhibition of the less attractive aspects of west-of-
Ireland village life. Economically poor, socially stigma-
tic, culturally starved, religiously puritanical and sex-
ually frustrated, those are some of the most obvious
characteristics of that society. They can all be exemplified on the level of the individual; Gar's ridiculous
egg-money, his obsequious respect for Senator Doogan
and the doctor from Dublin, the lack of any kind of
cultural activities in the town, and the consciously

liberated dreams of Gar and the young men in reaction
to the teachings of the Church. But the possibility of a
resultant urge to escape such an unpromising environment is countered openly with the acknowledgment of
the existence of more subconscious forces. Gar's plucky
but exaggerated rejection of Ballybeg is never convincing: 'All this bloody yap about father and son and all
this sentimental rubbish about "homeland" and "birth-
place" – yap! Bloody yap! Impermanence – anonymity
– that's what I'm looking for; a vast restless place that
doesn't give a damn about the past. To hell with
Ballybeg, that's what I say!' He knows that the past
holds strong attractions, that any memory of Ballybeg
will be 'distilled of all its coarseness; and what's left is
going to be precious, precious gold . . .' When uncomfortable memories impinge on his consciousness, Gar
frequently tries to evade them by the repetition of the
seemingly inconsequential phrase 'It is now sixteen or
seventeen years since I saw the Queen of France, then
the Dauphiness, at Versailles.'[6] In this or a longer
version the phrase returns several times throughout
the play, and functions both as a kind of threat of the
dangers of sentimental memories and as a charm
against them.

In *Philadelphia, Here I Come!* the characters are all
isolated from each other, all imprisoned within their
own shells. The loneliness and the incommunicability of
the soul is almost total. The few attempts there are at a
genuinely personal communication fail, and the characters withdraw into themselves. Here, the divided
protagonist makes this acutely felt. On the level of
language a pattern emerges. 'Screwballs, say something! Say something, father!' Gar implores S.B. But
the kind of contact Gar is demanding is no longer
possible. Gar cannot give it himself. S.B. remembers
when things were different: 'you couldn't get a word in
edgeways with all the chatting he used to go through.'
The natural simplicity of the child can sense nothing

that would stop open-hearted communication. Then, as in *Three Fathers, Three Sons*, 'something happens' to stop it. But Madge knows that 'just because he [S.B.] doesn't say much doesn't mean that he hasn't feelings like the rest of us'. In this sort of converse, as Guthrie pointed out, silences become pregnant, for the reader or the audience, that is. For Gar, 'it's the silence that's the enemy.' Any kind of communication is preferable to that. The visiting 'boys' would willingly agree. Friel makes this clear in the stage directions: '*Another brief silence. These silences occur like regular cadences. To defeat them someone always introduces a fresh theme.*'

Another facet of the theme of language and communication comes up in another visit. The treatment of Gar's dilemma would not be complete without at least a brief view of what awaits him on the other side of the Atlantic. Aunt Lizzy is in many ways a prototypical stage Irish-American. Her sentimental love of the old country is coupled with brash ignorance of modern Ireland. Her pride in and almost obsession with material standards underline the poverty of Ballybeg. Her effusive emotions, shown both verbally and physically, Gar finds unsettling. As an alternative to staying in Ballybeg, Aunt Lizzy's Philadelphia may not be very attractive. But it could be argued that her and Con's emigration to America testifies to an active and deliberate effort to influence their future, something S.B. is not prepared to do. Those who stay do not look kindly upon the returned Yankee. Lizzy, however, was, like Gar's mother, a Gallagher, very different from the quiet and cold O'Donnells. There is a strong hint here that Gar's mother, who died just after Gar was born, would not have stood claustrophobic Ballybeg, and that Gar, in leaving, shows that he is more a Gallagher than an O'Donnell. And yet, the decision to go to America was made 'impetuously', and 'niggling reservations' still disturb Gar on the eve of his departure: 'And that's how you were got', Private tells Public. Gar himself does not know whether he has made the right decision. He is caught between two alternatives each of which has its own sanctions. In that sense his situation must be typical of the prospective émigré. But taking the whole play into account, it would seem that Friel deplores not so much the fact that Gar is leaving but the conditions that made him leave. The true tragedy of Gar's dilemma is that either alternative would leave him open to regrets.

The Loves of Cass McGuire (1966)

In my previous chapter I suggested that Friel, in order to exhibit a contrast and thus reach a wider and more varied expression of themes, frequently examines the same subject matter from different angles. This process can be well illustrated by comparing *Philadelphia, Here I Come!* with his next play, *The Loves of Cass McGuire,* the latter in many ways a sister play to the first. It was only appropriate that the two plays, for a few weeks in October 1966, should be running at the same time in New York. Together they make up an extensive statement on the themes of emigration, love and attachment to home and family. Cass McGuire, at seventy, returns home to Ireland after fifty years in America spent fixing sandwiches for washouts near Skid Row in New York. As an exile she has been dispossessed of her own country. Her only contact with home and family has been the few hard-earned dollars she regularly sent to her brother Harry and his family back in Ireland. When she returns she finds that this money has bought her nothing. Harry, a successful businessman-accountant, never wanted for anything, and the money is still untouched and intact, providing Cass, Harry's wife Alice suggests, with 'a nice little nest-egg'. And so it does. The irony becomes complete when Harry and Alice decide to move Cass from their home to Eden House, a rest-home for old people, complete with an illuminated statue of Cupid 'frozen in an absurd and impossible contortion' in the garden. This was, from Harry's point of view, the only possible solution. The Americanized Cass is loud, coarse and vulgar, she drinks too much and quickly becomes a social embarrassment to the respectable and middle-class McGuires. At this point *The Loves of Cass McGuire* starts – or does it? Early in the play Cass and Harry compete for control over the unravelling of the plot. 'It must be shown slowly and in sequence why you went to Eden house.' Cass disagrees violently with Harry's rational and organized approach. 'The story begins where I say it begins, and I say it begins with me stuck in the gawdamn workhouse! So you can all get the hell outa here!' Cass exclaims, trying to chase the others off the stage. This, she feels, is her right, and she cites the author as her authority. 'What's this goddam play called? *The Loves of Cass McGuire*. Who's Cass McGuire? Me! Me! And they'll see what happens in the order I want them to see it.' It quickly becomes obvious that this is a play not just presenting a conventionally realistic exploration of themes; it also seeks some definition of its own technique and stresses the eternal question of how to transfer life into art. In this sense it is an intensely modern play, where references to, for instance, Pirandello and Brecht's *Verfremdungseffekt* are unavoidable. It is Friel's most complete use of theatre as an expressive medium, incorporating visual effects (like the statue of Cupid), extensive use of music from Wagner's *Tristan and Isolde* for the ritual of the 'rhapsodies', three formal memory sequences in which each rhapsodist 'takes the shabby and unpromising threads of his past life and weaves it into a hymn of joy, a gay and rapturous and exaggerated celebration of a beauty that might have been'. The make-believe quality of these 'rhapsodies' is further accentuated by the regular repetition of a few lines from Yeats's poem 'He Wishes for the Cloths of Heaven': 'But I, being poor, have only my dreams . . . I have spread my dreams under your feet./Tread softly because you tread on my dreams.' From the beginning of the play Cass establishes an informal link with the audience; she speaks directly to them, and they become her only contact with reality. Gradually, as the insistent demand from two other inmates of Eden House, Ingram and Trilbe, for the acceptance of her own truth of illusion becomes stronger, Cass's awareness of the audience diminishes. 'And I could ov swore there were folks out there. (*Shrugs.*) What the hell,' signals her abandonment of the 'real' world in favour of the comfortable and safe world of illusion. The whole process is about to start again at the end of the play when Mrs Butcher, the new inmate, enters Eden House. But it would be wrong to single out Eden House as the home of unhappiness and illusion. Everything in *The Loves of Cass McGuire* is suffused with the same sense of disappointment and lack of hope. Tessa, the young maid of Eden House, exposes herself to the same danger by pitching her hopes for the future perhaps a little bit too high. Here she is talking about her fiancé:

TESSA: He's a building contractor by trade.
TRILBE: A very practical profession, too.
TESSA: Well, he's not a real contractor, yet.
TRILBE: But he's a fully fledged tradesman?
TESSA: He will be when he finishes his apprenticeship . . .

Thus it is not the veteran dreamers in Eden House who make the real statement of the play. This is made all the more poignant by coming from, above all, the respectable Alice. We know from Harry that their eagerly awaited Christmas with the children will not happen. Alice, however, cannot cope with this thwarted expectation.

ALICE: (*warmly, leaning over*). It's me, Cass . . . I know Harry has told you: none of the children . . . (*She

[103]

*checks herself in time: straightens up: continues
with a control that is touching in its rigidity. She is
on the point of tears.*) The children are all coming –
all of them – Betty and Tom and Aiden – arriving
tonight – late – a real family gathering.

The final confession comes from Harry himself: 'You
are really better off here, Cass.' The middle-class
respectability of the McGuires is only a façade of
happiness. There is no escaping life's disappointments.
The play, then, condones illusion. It becomes the only
possible escape from the painful experience of living.

Cass McGuire returning home to Ireland from
America gives us a possible projection of Gar O'Donnell's future. Cass's home-coming is mirrored in Gar's
various scenes of leave-taking. She had, at eighteen,
the same hopeless future as Gar: 'Well, what the hell
was there to do around here, I mean.' Here, too is the
same implicit criticism of the society that causes
emigration. The fates of Cass (lived) and that of Gar
(suggested) both express problems inherent in emigrating, problems of uprooting and loss of home and family.
And yet, when Cass returns to reclaim her broken
heritage, she finds that it has failed her ignominiously.
Perhaps, if she had to go, she should never have come
back. That would be the advice she would give to Gar,
the same, in fact, that Gar's old schoolmaster gives
him: 'But I would suggest that you strike out on your
own as soon as you find your feet out there. Don't keep
looking back over your shoulder. Be 100 per cent
American . . . Forget Ballybeg and Ireland.' The issue
of emigration apart, *Philadelphia, Here I Come!* and
The Loves of Cass McGuire share the same fundamental outlook on life. In these and in two other
plays from the same period, *Lovers* (1967) and *Crystal
and Fox* (1968), Friel attempted, he has said, to analyse
'different kinds of love' (*A Paler Shade of Green*). In all
four plays there is a sad awareness of the precarious-

[104]

ness of individual life and love, the inevitable passing of time and the arbitrary workings of Fate. Circumstances, at times expressing themselves in human forms, decide the fortunes of the characters. Young or old, sharing life's fragility, they search desperately for an evasive happiness and find only a wistful sadness. Looking for the same mood in other dramatists we would find, first of all, Chekhov. Friel has always expressed great admiration for Chekhov's work, whose ironic and ambiguous description of, for instance, *The Seagull* and *The Cherry Orchard,* as 'comedies' would suit many of Friel's plays as well. Chekhov's mixture of youth and old age, the frailty of human beings and the transience of life, can be seen to be summed up in Gayev's panegyric to the hundred-year-old bookcase in *The Cherry Orchard.*

> My dear venerable bookcase! I salute you! For more than a hundred years you have devoted yourself to the highest ideals of goodness and justice. For a hundred years you have never failed to fill us with an urge to useful work; several generations of our family have had their courage sustained and their faith in a better future fortified by your silent call; you have fostered in us the ideal of public good and social consciousness.

This inanimate object has survived several generations and will, no doubt, survive several more. Its longevity cannot be matched by human beings, nor can 'the ideal of public good and social consciousness' that it inspires withstand the implacable forces of change. And is there, in the whole history of modern theatre, a more remarkable stage effect than the metaphysical string snapping twice in the same play? It becomes the final symbol of nostalgic loss and change. The same note is frequently heard in Friel's plays.

Compared to *Philadelphia, Here I Come!,* with its *alter ego* and its memory sequences as the only non-realistic features, *The Loves of Cass McGuire* employs a technique of almost total fluidity. On to this is grafted a structure which allows for an extensive and varied approach to the play's subject matter. The contrast between reality and illusion, as centred in Cass, the different ways in which it affects Cass and the other characters, move the play forward. Friel himself, in his description of the set, suggests a musical analogy: 'I consider the play to be a concerto in which Cass McGuire is the soloist.' In this role Cass, to start with, plays her own tune. Linguistically, her voice disturbs both the McGuire household and the quiet rest-home. In this sense, too, she is out of place. Her raucous vulgarity contrasts sharply with guarded respectability and lyrical illusion. But it is also a sign of her energetic vitality, and when, at the very end, she is converted to a life of dreams, she loses some of her edge.

The Loves of Cass McGuire, however, does not possess the same steady and fluent integrity that characterizes *Philadelphia, Here I Come!*. On the one hand, it has never had the popular success of the previous play, and on the other, it never figures predominantly in any discussion of Friel's work. Several reasons may be adduced for this relative failure. Although a comparison with the earlier play is largely unnecessary and maybe even irrelevant, it must be established that the success of the first play had an adverse effect on the later one. The prominence of the character of Cass becomes in itself a problem, and may, in fact, have been one of the major reasons for the play's failure on Broadway (it closed after only twenty performances). One reviewer seemed insulted by the Americanized idiom used by the main character. 'The weakest scene in Friel's estimable first play, *Philadelphia, Here I Come!,* gave us an American woman returning to Ireland. Here he has expanded this scene into three acts. And his American imitation just isn't good enough for a whole evening's work . . . and since she [Cass] is linguistically improbable, she is also an improbable observer' (*Commonweal*, 28 October 1966). Another critic complained that her coarse language may have made audiences 'uncomfortable because the author was trying something that didn't appear to stem naturally from his writing style' (*New York Post*, 29 October 1966). This particular quality in Cass could be said to be unnecessarily extended in the stage version (one of the bawdy stories was not included in the radio version); it certainly is not needed to illustrate or exemplify her character. Thus Cass seems to repeat herself a little bit too much, and in her slow progress towards the acceptance of her own truth, the basic thematic contrast between reality and illusion seems at times laboured and over-clear. There is, it seems to me, a certain basic incompatibility between theme and technique in the play. The tragic fragility of the theme is not given enough time to settle into an appropriate mode before it is again disturbed by the play's forward movement. The varied approach threatens to obscure the play's obvious merits. Walter Kerr's remarks in the *New York Times* seem relevant: 'The work wasn't written to be assimilated as an orderly sequence of events. It was meant to come at us from all quarters, simultaneously, undifferentiated ... Achieving this is a long patient process; time and tenderness are wanted.' The difficult dramatic structure makes great demands on both the performers and the audience. If the play fails the fault may also be in the production. In this context Friel recognizes that for the play to open on Broadway may have been a mistake. 'The best theatre was always done, in history, with a writer working with a director and a resident company. This is, of course, what you don't have on Broadway and indeed what you don't have in Ireland except in the Abbey Theatre' (*Current Biography*, 1974). And to be fair to Friel and the play it should be mentioned that later productions in Dublin and elsewhere have met with much more understanding and appreciation.

If the above quotation seems to imply criticism of the man who directed *The Loves of Cass McGuire* in its American première it must surely be unintentional. Friel has expressed great admiration for the legendary Hilton Edwards. Together with Micheál MacLiammóir, Hilton Edwards founded, in 1928, the Gate Theatre in Dublin, with the specific intention of introducing European plays to counter the Abbey's basically 'Irish' offerings. In the sixties Hilton Edwards directed four consecutive plays of Friel's in Dublin and America, *Philadelphia, Here I Come!, The Loves of Cass McGuire, Lovers* and *Crystal and Fox.*

> I know that they [Edwards and MacLiammóir] came into my life at a point when their practical skill and their vast experience and their scholarship were of most value to me. I am not aware that I have any theatrical pedigree; but if I had to produce documentation I would be pleased to claim – to paraphrase Turgenev's comment on Gogol – that I came out from under the Edwards–MacLiammóir overcoat.[7]

In the early seventies, however, it began to look inevitable that Friel's plays would end up at the Abbey. As his reputation grew, and as his plays took on added meaning and significance, the Abbey was able to claim him as Ireland's leading dramatist. In the period between 1973 and 1979 four of Friel's plays received their première at Ireland's National Theatre. Then, in 1980, his particular Northern background inclined him in a different direction.

Lovers (1967)

The noisy and broad humour, in *The Loves of Cass McGuire* directly and openly blended with the deep compassion and brittle love in human relationships, was, in Friel's next play, given its own vehicle. *Lovers* consists of two short plays, 'Winners' and 'Losers', whose pointed titles invite interesting comparisons. Together, they complement each other thematically, observing and commenting on two different kinds of love. The prevalent mode of writing is ironic. 'Winners' is tragic in conception, fragile and poetic in style, whereas 'Losers' is a bold farce with tragic undercurrents. Friel's method of approaching the same subject from different directions is, as we have seen in previous plays, typical of his craft. Even if the first play in itself contains a wide variety of statements on the central theme, the addition of the second explains and highlights aspects of the first, and vice versa. The two plays can be made to work independently of each other, as one-act plays, but, at the same time, they belong naturally together.

Technically, the two plays are very different. In both, there is a central story being told about the hopes and frustrated love of the two couples involved. In 'Winners' this story is told in straightforward dramatic form, presenting the two young lovers sitting on top of a hill overlooking their home town Ballymore in Northern Ireland. The time perspective is brief (a few hours), and what we are witnessing is an everyday, seemingly insignificant scene in which they chat, joke and bicker with each other, argue and then make up. On to this trivial situation is superimposed a formal arrangement whereby two Commentators, sitting at either edge of the stage, enter the play, but not the central action itself. Their first function is to provide the audience with dry information relating to the background of the central dramatized scene. They direct themselves to the audience giving facts impersonally, without any emotion whatever. 'Margaret Enright was a pupil of Saint Mary's Grammar School, run by the Sisters of Mercy. And Joseph Brennan was a pupil of Saint Kevin's College, a grammar school for boys run by the clergy of the diocese. She was seventeen; he seventeen and a half.' From the Commentators we soon find out that Mag and Joe are to be married in three weeks' time; Mag is pregnant, and as a result they have had to leave school, though they will be allowed back to sit their final examinations. They have, in fact, come out together to study. It is obvious that the Commentators help the author in imparting this basic information. This and other techniques have given rise to complaints from critics about Friel's continuing dependence on the short story as his main narrative form. Fergus Linehan's reaction in *Hibernia* to the first production of *Lovers* defines the problem.

> But *Lovers* confirms one's impression that Friel has yet to come to grips with his medium and that after some half a dozen plays he still remains a short-story writer who has strayed into a medium he finds too limiting. What is more, in an effort to overcome the problems posed by swift changes in time and place (easy in literature, but inhibited by the sheer mechanics of the stage) he seems to be trying to marry two incompatible types of theatre.

These views all stem from a basic unwillingness to accept a non-realistic theatrical convention: a narrator or a flashback is regarded as undramatic and something that needs to be 'compensated for'. Referring to *The Loves of Cass McGuire,* Roger McHugh and Maurice Harmon said in *A Short History of Anglo-Irish Literature*: 'Here, as in *Lovers* (1967), Friel's strong talent for character drawing compensates for his tendency to use the explanatory devices of the flashback or the narrator.' This wholesale rejection of 'experimental' techniques may be dangerous. There is no doubt that Friel has used these techniques, not as an automatic narrative help, but to activate and extend the exploration and treatment of themes. Although, in *The Loves of Cass McGuire,* he may have tried for too much, and thus overemphasized the technical side, there is no reason why we should be disturbed by the simple structure of 'Winners'. The Commentators act as an impersonal chorus, giving information, forwarding the action, and, in a key moment in the play, transferring the central action into the past by revealing that the young couple will drown in a local lake that same afternoon. As this happens, the time scheme is prolonged into near-eternity, and the trivial central action takes on a more general meaning. Friel's intention at once becomes more of a philosophical statement which involves not only the characters on stage but also the audience. The Commentators exist for the benefit of the audience, they are between us and the action, and gradually they become us. Their impersonality is a metaphor for the failure to communicate the human and emotional aspects of the tragedy they have told us about. The few hours acted out by Mag and Joe give us the real people behind, for instance, a factual newspaper article. The absurd attention to irrelevant detail in some of their reports, about the wind, the temperature on that day, the water level in the lake etc., make the irrelevance of the deaths in cosmic terms even greater. At the end of the play, references to 'varicose veins turned septic' and a rise in the population of Ballymore 'from 13,527 to 13,569' in the past eight months, again stress this contrast. The final two lines are, strictly speaking, unnecessary: 'Life there goes on as usual,' and 'As if nothing had ever happened'. It could even be argued that in these lines the Commenators go against Friel's stage directions: '*At no time must they reveal an attitude to their material.*' There is in the last five words an implicit accusation, not so much against people as against life's recklessness and Fate. In this sense the Commentators, in revealing and controlling not just past but also future events, become manifestations of Fate.

In order to give this wider and more philosophical direction to the central action, the role of the Commentators is essential. I do not agree with the complaint made by some critics that their remarks are 'interruptive'. Their presence on stage, though, is disturbing, in a metaphysical sense. They consistently enhance the notion of tragedy.

The greatest element of non-realism in 'Winners' is, of course, the experience of watching on stage characters who are supposed to be dead. Friel was to use the same technique in later plays. In the context of this play, the main benefit for the playwright, once it has been established that they are dead, is that one of the most important questions in a conventional plot, 'What happens next?', becomes irrelevant. We may instead start looking for reasons why things turned out the way they did, and, finding none, we can only marvel at the complicated rules of existence before turning our attention to other significant details. The thematic structure of the play is built on a rich fabric of contrasting ironies. The first of these, suggested in the title, is that in death they escape an unpromising adulthood, where love seems to be impossible. Mag and Joe, prematurely it would have seemed to them, talk about being 'buried together', when we already know from the Commentators that 'the bodies were buried in separate graves in the local cemetery each in the family plot.' Running down from the hill to meet their Maker, Mag is impatient with the past: 'Let's begin the future now!' At the same time she cannot free herself from fears of the future. She has seen what adult life can contain: 'And when I look around me – at Papa and Mother and the O'Haras – I think: by God we'll never become like that, because – don't laugh at me, Joe – because I think we're unique!' There is a strong feeling of the limitations of the self in understanding or communicating with others. From a distance, Mag and Joe like and admire each others' parents, but not their own, another reminder of the destructive and limiting forces at work within the family. And, yet, in a conflict they have to stand up for their own when under attack.

Joe and his father, like Gar and S.B., only exchange the simplest, most necessary and trivial information, and Mag has been deeply hurt by her parents when they found out she was pregnant. Even between Mag and Joe there are suggestions of insurmountable private inhibitions, each of them cocooned in their own reality.

The tragedy of the middle-aged lovers, Hanna and Andy, in 'Losers' is deeper. They have resigned themselves to a life of frustrated love, where the attractions of compensatory illusion can only grow. Andy's binoculars, through which he keeps staring at a high wall in the back yard, become a 'supra-real' symbol of escape and isolation. He had inherited them from Hanna's father, who obviously also was in need of escape. Mrs Wilson, Hanna's mother, would have been the person he was escaping from. A bedridden invalid, she turned her bedroom into a shrine to St Philomena, and from there she rules the house. Downstairs, Andy tries desperately to woo his Hanna. Any silence from downstairs causes Mrs Wilson upstairs to ring her handbell. She wants attention, and she wants, of course, to interrupt the scene of love-making between Hanna and Andy. The broad farce starts when, in order to fill the silences with words, Hanna suggests that Andy recite a bit of poetry. Since the only poem he knows is Gray's 'Elegy Written in a Country Churchyard' they have to do their courting, kissing and caressing as well as they can while 'The curfew tolls the knell of parting day . . .' The hilarious situation has serious undertones, all coming out at the end of the play. Hanna and Andy are the victims of a narrowly pietistic religious observance and a society which promotes it. In spite of the humour, it is a gloomy and pessimistic play. As a man, Andy is outnumbered and outwitted by the women. He was able to dispose of St Philomena (the Vatican officially announced that all devotion to the saint must be discontinued) but he did it in a way that finally turned Hanna away from him. 'All men is animals – brute animals,' Cissy Cassidy, a next-door neighbour, pontificates. The three solemn ladies secretly choose another saint and go on with their observance unperturbed. Andy quietly accepts the routine ('anything for a quiet life') but then retreats into the back yard and his binoculars. In 'Losers' the male–female relationship, as shown in Friel's previous plays, received a sudden and unusual twist. Most of his women, in short stories and plays, had been perfectly able to deal with questions of religion, even to the extent of manipulating such problems to their own advantage in a somewhat hypocritical but down-to-earth manner. Here their abandonment to puritanism is total, and their enmity to men uncompromising. But perhaps it is wrong to apply too far-reaching considerations to this play. It cannot reach any genuine generality on which to base a more serious interpretation. Nevertheless with the juxtaposition of 'Losers' and 'Winners' Friel was obviously trying to suggest a comparison between the two plays.

The subject matter of 'Losers' is largely taken from a short story, 'The Highwayman and the Saint', published in the 1966 collection *The Gold in the Sea*. In a first-person narrative Andy tells more or less exactly the same story. Certain small changes have been made in the transposition, the poem, for instance, in the story was 'The Highwayman' by Alfred Noyes. The main additions were made in the dramatized sequences which interrupt Andy's telling of the story. Described only briefly in the short story, they were fleshed out and extended, mainly for comic effect.

As a whole, *Lovers* presents a rather depressing view of life. In spite of the energy and the will to live and love that these characters so obviously possess, circumstances combine to frustrate them. These circumstances are all expressions of various kinds of societal pressures, and, as always in Friel, the individual suffers. In 'Losers' it is clearly and overwhelmingly (and perhaps too monotonously) the authority of the Catholic church that Andy is up against. But Mrs Wilson's bell rings also to give warning of the dangerous limitations of Father Peyton's dictum: 'The family that prays together stays together.' 'Winners' includes a much broader base of society. The influences on Mag and Joe all come from their particular background. Social and economic as well as religious factors determine their existence. But superimposed on this is the force of Fate, the final authority, against which there is no appeal. It is all set down in the books that the Commentators in 'Winners' read from. Sir, in *Living Quarters,* has another (or perhaps the same) copy.

Crystal and Fox (1968)

The rickety wheel carried round by Fox Melarkey in *Crystal and Fox* is another manifestation of Fate. It is part of the building up of an elaborate symbolic design, the knitting together of different meanings and allusions in the play. In some ways, *Crystal and Fox* initiates a new development in Friel's work. As such its nearest successor was to be *Volunteers* (1975). *Crystal and Fox* completes Friel's four-part catechism of love, but in contrast to *Philadelphia, Here I Come!, The Loves of Cass McGuire* and *Lovers*, it is dominated by an unusual and dangerously unpredictable character. Fox Melarkey, in an obsessive attempt to regain an innocent and fleeting moment of love in his past, destroys everyone around him. One by one he disposes of the members of his cheap travelling show until, at the end of the play, he is left with his beloved Crystal. This is what he wanted: just 'you and me and the old accordion and the old rickety wheel – all we had thirty years ago, remember? You and me. And we'll laugh again at silly things and I'll plait seaweed into your hair again.' But you cannot go back into the past. You cannot regain lost innocence or lost love. Fox's disappointment with life and his failure to accept it, 'there must be something better than this', proves to be his downfall. Perhaps he realizes his mistake and, therefore, in deliberately lying to Crystal and forcing her to abandon him, he makes a final sacrifice of himself. Alone, at a literal and symbolic crossroads, Fox is left to ponder the absured futility of his dream: 'but we were young then, and even though our clothes were wet and even though the sun was only rising, there were hopes – there were warm hopes; and love alone isn't enough now, my Crystal, it's not, my love, not enough at all, not nearly enough.' The play deals with qualities in life that are half-real, wistful and illusive, perceptions that elude definitions because they contain no certainty. It is a kind of emotional realism that mirrors the turmoil of the mind. There can be no answers in this kind of drama because there are no questions. Perhaps *Crystal and Fox* invites the kind of reaction the play received after its opening in Dublin: 'a very strange play indeed' (*Evening Herald*); 'crudely unreal' (*Evening Press*); 'obscure actions and even more obscure motives' (*Irish Independent*); 'I am at a loss to understand its symbolic overtones' (*Irish Times*). If it does, it also contains a powerful antidote. The pathetically simple melodrama that is part of the Fox Melarkey Show, and that opens Friel's play, 'The Doctor's Story', includes all the conventional and romantic ingredients of entertainment. 'Belt it out. And plenty of tears. All the hoors want is a happy ending,' is Fox's encouraging advice as the actors enter the stage. There can be no such simplified emotions in Friel's play, and the concept of love is a much more complex one, much more genuine and true to real life, Friel seems to say.

There is, nevertheless, a problem with Fox as a character. Friel expects us to accept Fox's motives for his obsessive search for a moment of past happiness. This we can easily do. They are eloquently expressed by Fox himself:

> Once, maybe twice in your life, the fog lifts, and you get
> a glimpse, an intuition; and suddenly you know that
> this can't be all there is to it – there has to be some-
> thing better than this. . . . And afterwards all you're left
> with is a vague memory of what you thought you saw;
> and that's what you hold on to – the good thing you
> think you saw.

The problem is that Friel turns Fox into a character
who threatens to step out of the realistic convention in
an otherwise realistic play. There is a concentration in
Fox of a vagueness, an intense complexity that
changes him from a human being into an idea, a symbol of wistful human yearnings for pure love, a protest
against a trivial and degrading reality that makes
love impossible. In that sense we must be prepared to
accept him as a different kind of experiment, enlarging the confines of the convention Friel is working in.
This, too, we ought to be able to do. If, however, we
expect a more obediently realistic character, we may
fail to do so. What is essential is that Fox's enigmatic
character must not be seen to be contrived or exaggerated by the author. Only on one occasion does Friel
run the risk of doing this. Fox's impulsive lie to Crystal, that he had informed the police about their son
Gabriel (who was wanted for attempted manslaugh-
ter), is tantalizingly close to being explained by Fox
immediately after Crystal has left.

> It's a lie, Crystal, all a lie, my love, I made it all up,
> never entered my head until a few minutes ago and
> then I tried to stop myself but I couldn't, it was poor
> Papa that told the police and he didn't know what he
> was saying. I don't know why I said it, I said it just to –
> to – to –

Here, it seems to me, Friel unnecessarily teases us
into expecting or looking for a possible answer.
Although it stresses Fox's bewilderment at his own

behaviour, the passage may be going a little too far in that intention.

Any consideration of the intricate pattern of motives that moves Fox as a character has to be subordinated to stronger forces. Just as in 'Winners', the sense of an inevitable necessity in human affairs dominates the mood of the play. Turning his rickety wheel, Fox's final speech amounts to an unqualified surrender to Fate. His fairground is the world itself.

> (*Fairground voice*) Red–yellow–black or blue, whatever it is that tickles your fancy, the Fox knows all the answers – what it's all about, that's why he's dressed in velvets and drives about in a swank car, you're looking straight at the man that sleeps content at night because he's learned the secrets of the universe, strike me dead if I'm telling a lie and you wipe that grin off your jaw, lady, when you're at a wake, red–yellow–black or blue, you pays your money and you takes your choice, not that it makes a damn bit of difference because the whole thing's fixed, my love, fixed–fixed–fixed; (*almost gently*) but who am I to cloud your bright eyes or kill your belief that love is all. A penny a time and you think you'll be happy for life.

But it is also possible to see Fox as having engineered his own destruction. In his reckless obsession he is taking the ultimate risk, challenging somebody or something to oppose him. The Fates, at least, allow you to do that much. Fox and Frank Hardy in *Faith Healer* use that liberty to push themselves beyond the possible. For others, as suggested in the last few lines of the above quotation, illusion may offer some comfort.

Other familiar Frielian themes turn up in *Crystal and Fox*. The son Gabriel is an extreme case of father–son alienation. There is an undercurrent of violence in their relationship, Gabriel's physical violence inflicted on the old lady in Salford is matched by Fox's mental violence on the members of his travelling show. And there is open and covert violence too, in the appearance of the English

[118]

detectives who come and arrest Gabriel. The theme of human isolation, the inability to transcend the self, to communicate with others, even members of the same family, is here expressed by Crystal, first quietly in talking about Gabriel, 'maybe you never know anybody,' and then, in her final rejection of Fox, much more strongly, 'I don't know who you are.'

Perhaps the more conventional structure of *Crystal and Fox* had led the puzzled critics to expect a more straightforward play. There is no outward experimentation, no supra-real devices that can absorb and attract the comments. For Friel it was, nevertheless, a question of a new dramatic kind. After the initial intimations of a theme that focuses on Fox, the play advances towards the end through a gradual and consistent process of elimination, shedding all except its main character. At the curtain, leaning on the old rickety wheel, Fox has become a symbol of the inscrutability of life. *Crystal and Fox* tries to find its own form, and in doing so, helps to define itself, not in relation to conventions or agreed taste, but according to the themes and the characters that inhabit Friel's play. The melodramatic playlet with which the play opens, the memories of some of the greatest successes of the Fox Melarkey Show and the circumstances in which they happened, are all part of an effort to chart the play's contours. Fox and his company fondly remember how they used to seek out places where tragedies had happened. There they could satisfy a need for diversion.

PEDRO: A train crash or an explosion in a school.
FOX: Has to be children. Remember the time that
    orphanage in the Midlands burned down?
PEDRO: That sort of thing.
CRYSTAL: For three solid weeks not an empty seat.
PEDRO: Marvellous.
CRYSTAL: And a matinée every other day.

But things have changed and so have popular habits.

PEDRO: They don't flock to the tragedies the way they used
    to.
CRYSTAL: Television has them spoiled. It needs to be
    something very big.

In his final speech Fox also shows us the sad face of the
clown. That is, if we can believe his own words, how he
saw himself: 'All clowns become sages when they grow
old, and when young sages grow old they turn into
clowns. I was an infant sage – did you know that, Pedro?'
In each concept or belief is contained its own opposite.
Finally, much to Fox's amusement, he finds in the local
paper an excellent example of the grand gesture. ' "The
local Grand Opera Society held its annual meeting last
Wednesday in Sweeney's Hotel in Drung. It was agreed
to do *Faust* next April. There are four members in the
Society." ' Together these examples, in dealing with the
nature of the performing arts, inevitably also contain
expressions of human nature.

The Mundy Scheme (1969)

If the final impression of *Crystal and Fox* is one of
haunting wistfulness, Friel's next play could be seen as
an example of the opposite mood. *The Mundy Scheme*
(1969) is not a light comic interlude. Its laughter is an
expression of bitter disappointment released through
cynical satire. The play's political edge is clearly notice-
able from the very beginning, making in its subtitle, *Or,
May We Write Your Epitaph Now, Mr Emmet?*, a direct
reference to one of the golden passages of Irish political
prose.[8] In a spoken Prelude to the play Friel asks the
questions that the play goes on to answer:

VOICE: Ladies and Gentlemen: What happens when a small
    nation that has been manipulated and abused by a
    huge colonial power for hundreds of years wrests its
    freedom by blood and anguish? What happens to an
    emerging country after it has emerged? Does the

transition from dependence to independence induce
a fatigue, a mediocrity, an ennui? Or does the clean
spirit of idealism that fired the people to freedom
augment itself, grow bolder, more revolutionary,
more generous?

The Irish government, if we believe Friel's play, is a
gang of corrupted and psychologically unstable liars,
motivated by self-interest and greed, led by a prime
minister (an ex-auctioneer) who is prepared to sell the
country to the highest bidder. In the face of economic
collapse and civil unrest he first refuses the American
offer of bases for nuclear submarines in Galway and
Cork (virtuously rejected also by his Minister for
Development: 'we're going to have no dirty Yankee
sailors with nuclear warheads seducing decent Galway
girls and decent Cork girls'), only to accept the
miraculous Mundy scheme to turn the West of Ireland
into an international cemetery. After much manoeuv-
ring and double-crossing the scheme is accepted by the
government and launched with auspicious splendour.
To the play's already explosive content was added an air
of controversy with the Abbey's refusal to perform it,
thus putting Friel's name on a famous list. But despite
this pre-production excitement the play did not succeed
well when it opened in Dublin. The central idea, though
promising enough itself, is not well supported by the rest
of the play. It was thought that once the scheme is
revealed (at the end of act I) there is no sustaining
interest and the petty dealings of the government
ministers are too trivial to hold up the remaining two
acts. But there are also, I believe, more serious
weaknesses in the play. It is, first of all, untypical of Friel
in its unbalanced bias. Only rarely does he allow his
artistic stance and tone to be swayed by an undisguised
indignation. Here it is savage to the point of becoming
unsubtle and wild. Its satire is almost too strong to be
tolerated, it may even cause embarrassment; if things

are as bad as they seem to be some sort of artistic distance is necessary. This *The Mundy Scheme* lacks. There is nothing like Swift's 'modest proposal' to lift the subject out of its innate depravity. Perhaps Friel was aware of some of these problems. He submitted the play, he has said, 'with the gravest misgivings and little enthusiam' (*A Paler Shade of Green*). It was, no doubt, too personal a statement, not sufficiently honed into artistic shape. According to Sam Hanna Bell in *The Theatre in Ulster* Friel did not 'propose to write another play of what he describes as "similar here-and-now relevance"'. Soon, however, he would be working on a play of extreme contemporary relevance, *The Freedom of the City*. When he did, we shall see that he approached his subject in a very different manner.

In the light of the rest of Friel's work *The Mundy Scheme* can, in spite of the shortcomings discussed above, contribute some valuable insights. Much of his work reflects the failure of various society structures, the government, the Church, the family, to consider sufficiently the individuals who make up that structure. One important aspect of this relationship between the individual and the group is the question of communication, with Friel often stressing its linguistic features. Two examples from his previous plays will suffice to illustrate this: Private Gar's distress signal to the Canon in *Philadelphia* is a direct consequence of his failure to relate to his father:

there's an affinity between Screwballs and me that no one, literally, no one could understand – except you, Canon (*deadly serious*), because you're warm and kind and soft and sympathetic – all things to all men – because you could translate all this loneliness, this groping, this dreadful bloody buffoonery into Christian terms that will make life bearable for us all. And yet you don't say a word. Why, Canon? Why arid Canon? Isn't it your job? – to translate?

In 'Winners' the factual and detached language of the Commentators is in sharp contrast to the warm and human language of love between Mag and Joe. The politicians in *The Mundy Scheme* squabble crudely between themselves but always put on a linguistic mask of authority when addressing the public. Here language is used in order not to communicate, to hide real facts and circumstances behind officialese and empty rhetoric. The Taoiseach's private secretary, when dictating letters, achieves the intended effect through alternating between the offical style:

> ... we should certainly like to, but taking all these elements into consideration and in view of the fact that the economy of the country is currently ... less resilient than one would wish, the Taoiseach asks me to inform you that at the moment he cannot support in principle the channelling of any state monies whatever into any new industry. He wishes you to understand, however, that when the present situation ...

and the more personal (but nevertheless insincere) manner:

> Quin – he's one of the old brigade. Better make this first-person – in the vernacular. Dear Sean: How's the big heart? My God but it's bloody powerful to hear from you, even though you're complaining as usual, and aul hoor – a–u–l w–h–o–r–e. Of course I'm worried about the high emigration from your area and from the whole west. But I promise you, Sean a Vic, that I have the situation under constant survey.

At the time of writing *The Mundy Scheme* Friel seems to have been rather depressed about the role of the writer and the state of literature in Ireland. In the Taoiseach's TV speech to the nation on inaugurating the Mundy Scheme, Friel aims his satire at the businessman mentality which he saw as dominating the Irish government. His Taoiseach has not heard the name of

Ireland's foremost poet (he was, we must remember, an ex-auctioneer), and wants Ireland's 'renowned artists and writers and poets to forget the gray past and celebrate the new dawn with happy panegyric and joyful dirge and wholesome, hearty plays.' Friel was experiencing, at the end of the sixties, the accumulated effects of forty years of a generally restrictive intellectual climate in Ireland, constantly exacerbated by the existence of censorship. Friel's own view of how Ireland should be governed was idealistically different:

> One of our great misconceptions is that Ireland can be ruled only by its government and that the best government is composed of businessmen. This is a fallacy. I see no reason why Ireland should not be ruled by its poets and dramatists. Tyrone Guthrie has said that if Yeats and Lady Gregory were alive today they would be unimportant people. This is the way it is going to be, I am afraid. (*A Paler Shade of Green*)

Since then, the conditions under which the Irish writer is working have been considerably improved. The disappearance of censorship, increased public spending through the Arts Council, the spectacular growth of an Irish publishing industry, to mention but a few factors, all contributed in making Ireland in the seventies a much more promising place for the creative artist. The scathing satire of *The Mundy Scheme,* with its end-of-sixties setting, was no doubt accurate in its aim, and could perhaps be seen to signal the end of a particularly neglectful official attitude towards the arts.

The Gentle Island (1971)

The ironic title of *The Gentle Island* (1971) hides a complex web of violent and sexual tensions. As Maxwell has pointed out it was 'in a way Friel's most Irish play' so far. It contains a direct confrontation between the West and Dublin, which is, however, not fully developed but nevertheless instrumental in urging the action forward to its violent end. On the surface the play tells a straightforward story but if we examine events and their causes it becomes extremely difficult to arrive at anything but the simplest and most basic facts. On the island of Inishkeen off the west coast of Donegal a man from Dublin is shot, seriously injured and probably maimed for life. But as Manus, an old man in his sixties and head of the only family still left on the island says, 'there's ways and ways of telling every story. Every story has seven faces.' The dramatic end of the play hinges on the question whether Sarah really saw what she says she saw. Did she see her husband Philly and Shane, one of the visitors from Dublin, naked in the boathouse? Sarah's words to Manus at the end of act II, scene 1 precipitate the catastrophe:

> MANUS: What are you trying to say?
> SARAH: That he's down there in the boathouse at the far
> slip, your Philly, my husband. That he's down there
> with that Dublin tramp, Shane. That they're
> stripped naked. That he's doing for the tramp what
> he couldn't do for me. That's what I'm trying to say.
> And that if you're the great king of Inishkeen, you'll
> kill them both – that's what I'm saying.

A jury would have great difficulty in disentangling all the facts. Sarah's statement could be true. Shane's relationship with Peter, the other visitor, has definite homosexual overtones; Philly, the childlessness of whose marriage with Sarah is stressed on several occasions, seems to take a liking to Shane and becomes dangerously violent in his attitudes towards Peter. On the other hand, Sarah (and Manus) had previously had experiences of what could only be described as visions. Sarah is the key person. What would go against her version is the fact that she had offered herself to Shane and been rejected early in the play. The audience would

[125]

know that she is lying in the final confrontation with
Shane.

SARAH: (*to Manus*). Ask him is it true? Ask him! Ask him!
SHANE: *She* wanted to sleep with me.
SARAH: With that thing, Manus! Is it the truth or is it a lie?
SHANE: I wouldn't have her. That's what's eating her.
SARAH: Deny it! Deny it! Deny it! Look at the face! Look at
the slippery eyes! He can't! He can't! 'Cos I seen him!
I seen him!
MANUS: Is it the truth?
SHANE: What? Is what the truth?
SARAH: It is or it isn't? It is or it isn't?

The insistence on 'truth' is significant. Manus would
know how easy it is to manipulate reality for your own
ends. He turns the degrading incident in which he lost
his arm into something more acceptable. In the end it is
Sarah who grabs the gun and shoots Shane. Afterwards
all her aggression is gone, and she can settle down and
calmly accept or at least tolerate life on the island and
Philly's half-hearted promise that they will leave once
he has made enough money on his fishing. In this
interpretation Shane not only rejected her, he also
reminded her of her glorious summer on the Isle of Man
as a chambermaid when she wore out three pairs of
shoes going to fifty-one dances in eight weeks. The
prospect of life on the depopulated and lonely island
stands out in relief against that happy populated
summer and, when Shane refuses her, one reason for
her existence disappears. Her childless marriage, a
precise image of the end of life on the island, and her
sexual frustration are the female equivalent of Bosco
and the boys on their way to Scotland. Their coarse and
singleminded jokes hide the true complexity of their
exile. 'Get the knickers off, all you Glasgow women! The
Inishkeen stallions is coming!' is a direct flashback to
Gar's friends in *Philadelphia, Here I Come!*. The exodus
with which the play opens again introduces the subject

[126]

of emigration, but in this play the issue for or against confronts more honestly and openly the economic and social reality of the emigrants' future. The vitality of the young is countered by the tragedy that old Con feels in leaving the island. He had dulled his senses with alcohol but he still knows what is waiting for him: 'One bloody room in bloody Kilburn, son.' Manus refuses to leave and represents fully the idea of home and a different way of life.

> They belong here and they'll never belong anywhere else! Never! D'you know where they're going to? I do. I know. To back rooms in the back streets of London and Manchester and Glasgow. I've lived in them. I know. And that's where they'll die, long before their time – Eamonn and Con and Big Anthony and Nora Dan that never had a coat on her back until this day. And cocky Bosco with his mouth organ – this day week if he's lucky he'll be another Irish Paddy slaving his guts out in a tunnel all day and crawling home to a bothy at night with his hands two sizes and his head throbbing and his arms and legs trembling all night with exhaustion. That's what they voted for. And if that's what you want, it's there for the taking.

There are echoes here of Peadar O'Donnell and others, an angry protest at 'the impounding of the Gael'. But Friel first of all portrays in this and other plays events which have had an enormous influence on the Irish psyche. The historical change that has taken place since the nineteenth century is suggested in the argument between Manus and his younger son Joe.

MANUS: They'll regret it.
JOE: So they'll be back tomorrow – is that what you're
    saying? – you're saying they'll be back tomorrow,
    next week, the week after? – is that what you're
    saying?
MANUS: No.
JOE: Damn right they won't. There should never have been
    anyone here in the first place.

[127]

MANUS: Fifty years ago there were two hundred people on this island; our own school, our own church, our own doctor. No one ever wanted.

JOE: Scrabbing a mouthful of spuds from the sand – d'you call that living?

The two different generations cannot agree. Each solution, staying or leaving, contains attractions and sorrows. Manus is looking backwards and Joe forwards. There is a sense of inevitability here. Manus knows that those who left will not come back. He tries desperately to ensure the continuation of life on the island. On behalf of a reluctant Joe, he writes to Joe's girl-friend asking her to come back to marry him. Joe never sends the letter, and when he leaves at the end of the play, it is to Bosco and the boys in Glasgow he is going, not to Anna in London. Manus, Philly and Sarah are left to an impossible future.

As far as the theme of emigration and the depopulation of rural areas is concerned *The Gentle Island* repeats and extends the treatment seen in the short stories and in plays like *To This Hard House, Philadelphia, Here I Come!* and *The Loves of Cass McGuire*. But it goes further than any previous play in setting up a basic contrast between the West of Ireland and Dublin. In *The Gentle Island* we seem to have the first suggestions of an attempt by Friel to dig deeper into the Irish psyche in an effort to define its main characteristics. This is where the confrontation between the East and the West of Ireland becomes the main issue of the play. Of the two visitors from Dublin, Peter is clearly attracted by the quiet calmness of the island. He finds the epithet 'gentle' a suitable one, totally unaware of the sinister overtones of violence and death which will be heard before the play is over. In his innocent failure to understand the true nature of life on the island he bears a striking resemblance to one of Friel's later visitors to the West, the English soldier Yolland in *Translations*.

[128]

This is Peter speaking to Manus: 'It's not the weather; it's the ... the calm, the stability, the self-possession. Everything has its own good pace. No panics, no feverish gropings. A dependable routine – that's what you have.' When Yolland first arrived in Ballybeg he was immediately made aware of certain qualities governing the atmosphere: 'It wasn't an awareness of *direction* being changed but of experience being of a totally different order. I had moved into a consciousness that wasn't striving nor agitated, but at its ease and with its own conviction and assurance.' Both experiences stress the same qualities, indicating a way of life, a national psyche, different from Peter's Dublin and Yolland's England. The awareness is that of rural Gaelic Ireland, the outer characteristics of which Peter and Yolland can see and feel, but whose deeper significance evades them both. Before the plays are over they will both be exposed to forces that they, as outsiders, activate but cannot understand. In both plays the Irish language is an important factor in stressing the differences between the visitors and the native population. In *The Gentle Island* Shane's flippant few words of Irish cannot save him from the impending attack and serve only to alienate him. In *Translations* the ousting of the Irish language by English is much more central to the play's main concern and of much greater symbolic weight. It is interesting, however, and highly significant, that as early as 1971 Friel wrote a play which is in some respects close to what is probably his greatest play to date.

The irony of the title is repeated in many different contexts in *The Gentle Island*. Peter's admiration in the following quotation ironically highlights the process of depopulation that had already started: 'I envy you, Manus; the sea, the land, fishing, turf-cutting, milking, a house built by your great-grandfather, two strong sons to succeed you – everything's so damned constant. You're part of a permanence. You're a fortunate man.' Shane on the other hand, younger and more restless, sees none of the permanence. Perhaps it is also relevant that he lacks a normally stable family background. Being an orphan, he has, in a sense, no history. When Peter mentions that Manus would like them to come back to the island for Christmas, Shane's answer has much more than a grain of truth in it: 'Of course he does. Because we give support to his illusion that the place isn't a cemetery. But it is. And he knows it. The place and his way of life and everything he believes in and all he touches – dead, finished, spent.'

The basic contrast between East and West is expressed in a number of different ways. There is an affinity between Manus and his older son Philly which excludes Joe. Philly can tell the legend about the monks (in itself a symbol of frustrated escape) the way Manus wants it: 'So beautiful was she that the fish came up from the sea and the birds down from the trees to watch her walk along the roads,' whereas Joe's version is much more pedestrian and modern. 'He's ruined it,' says Manus. There is the proverbial distrust of the law which Peter obviously accepts. At the hospital on the mainland he lies about the real cause of Shane's injuries. An almost natural proclivity for violence, always reacted against by Peter, is mirrored in the language and the everyday experiences of the islanders. This may be the other side of the 'dignity and settled peace' that, according to Corkery, Synge 'not only noted but envied' on the Aran Islands, and that Peter in *The Gentle Island* and Yolland in *Translations* felt when coming to the West.

Brief mention should be made of the character of Shane. His clownish behaviour may at first militate against his credibility, but it soon becomes obvious that his jokes contain a deeper truth. He is witty and cynical but also sensitive to the deceptively calm atmosphere, always one step ahead of Peter. In one respect he stands for complete unsentimentality, a modern attitude which reflects his modern occupation of engineer; he is able to mend both the radio and the record-player. His early references to the atmosphere of the island as being sinister and too quiet, his jokes about Inishkeen being an Apache name meaning scalping island, and about the Pied Piper of Hamelin, seen only as silly nonsense by Peter, reveal the presence of a genuine threat and are eminently relevant to the themes of violence and emigration. As we have seen, he does not share Peter's ready admiration for the island, and he is perhaps the one who comes closest to summing up the difficulties experienced by all the islanders in the face of emigration. When asked by Peter if he wants to stay on the island (for a few days) he answers: 'In the circumstances, m'Lord, I'm torn between emotion and intellect, between the old heart and the old head, and the trouble is – '. Their intellects may well tell the islanders that to leave is the only solution, but their hearts keep holding them back. As a distinguishable type of character Shane would return in later plays, as Skinner in *The Freedom of the City* and as Keeney in *Volunteers*. In their unpredictability they must not be seen as spokesmen for any one ready-made view or emotion, but their presence represents a point of view that in its complicated flippancy contains sudden and far-reaching insights.

Pausing briefly at this juncture we can, if we look backwards, note again the closely knitted thematic structure of Friel's work. Certain themes appear and reappear, the focus shifts a little, a different aspect or point of view is emphasized. I have stressed the unity of the thematic development, carried on from stories to plays, most of which take as their centre the private individual and causes and factors that determine his existence. The situations presented are all genuinely Irish and strongly contemporary, dealing with the everyday reality of life in a particular region. The form of the plays has been a mixture of modernist (or experimental) techniques coupled with a strong insistence on the importance in all drama of ritual on the one hand, and perfectly straightforward realistic techniques on the other. Without wishing to enforce any rigid pattern on subsequent plays, I nevertheless believe that at this stage there are indications in Friel's work of two different directions. First, as regards form, a less pronounced urge towards 'supra-realism' in the physical sense of the word, i.e. fewer basically non-realistic techniques imposed on the framework of the play. In this sense there will be fewer commentators existing independently of the action of the play and less movement backwards in time within the plays; the presentation of the whole will tend towards a situation limited to a realistic concept of time-orientation. But these factors are all external to the main function of any play and cannot be isolated and treated on their own. As we have seen, Friel sees the question of form as inseparable from content, and it should be stressed again that no theatrical device can hide a badly conceived or written play. Secondly, as far as themes go, Friel has gradually sharpened the treatment until his role as dramatist and as 'presenter of a situation' has begun to take on the function of interpreter as well. An acute awareness of the less tactile aspects of reality has always been one of the most typical characteristics of Friel's craft. Increasingly, this has been used in an effort not only to perceive larger meanings and truths behind everyday reality but to arrange his material so that a unity of thought and feeling emerges that can express and define the Irish identity. From *Crystal and Fox* and more importantly from *The Gentle Island* Friel tackles more elusive subjects in general. He reaches for a different level of existence in an intensification of his efforts to define and interpret the Irish psyche. Alongside goes an increasing historical dimension which is lacking in most of the plays before *The Gentle Island*. The first reference in that play to this historical perspective seems insignificant enough. As most of the islanders are getting ready to leave, Con, who has not been sober for nine days, asks:

[132]

'D'you think was the Flight of the Earls anything like this?' He then bursts into drunken song: ' "My name is O'Donnell, the name of a king/And I come from Tirconnell whose beauty I sing," ' and is completely ignored by the others. But Con's words are strengthened later in the play by further unobtrusive links with the past, such as Manus's memories of what the island used to be like and the legend of the monks. This 'backward look' was to be continued in *Volunteers, Aristocrats* and *Translations*.

The Freedom of the City (1973)

The tendencies towards a less 'experimental' presenta-tion in form and an added historical dimension in content are in no way clear-cut and consistent. They are both part of the continuing development of Friel's plays and may at any time be reversed by other trends. But an awareness of them and their function will increase our understanding of the rest of the plays. Before we turn to the first play of the trio mentioned above we must examine two plays whose external characteristics are an obvious example of Friel's 'supra-realism' and whose contemporaneity is less preoccupied with an historical perspective. In a previous chapter I have sketched the events that make up the background of *The Freedom of the City* (1973). Since the renewed outbreak of violence in Ulster in 1968 there had been a growing demand that Irish writers should direct their creative attentions to 'the troubles'. Fairly soon the political situation became another typically Irish subject. Friel, however, initially refused to consider the crisis as a viable dramatic vehicle, mainly, as we have seen, a result of his own emotional involvement in it. It is not surprising then that when he came to the subject it was in a slightly roundabout way. When Derry's Bloody Sunday hap-pened on 30 January 1972, Friel was working on a play about an eighteenth- or nineteenth-century eviction in the West of Ireland, which would be 'a study of poverty'. Contemporary events changed the course of the play into an extensive analysis of the situation in Northern Ireland at the beginning of the seventies. With one important proviso, *The Freedom of the City* attempts to describe the religious, social, economic and political issues at play; it does so from a Catholic point of view. The play, quite simply, is about the minority population in Northern Ireland (but the majority of the people in Derry City) and the social, economic and political conditions that determine their lives. It is not about poverty and not about Bloody Sunday in Derry, although both help to illustrate points that the play makes. In order to relieve the play of the possibly limiting effects of too narrow an association with Bloody Sunday and in order to neutralize some of his own personal involvement in the issues, Friel used various distancing effects. The first of these was to set the play in 1970, a fact which has done nothing except cause some mild discussion about why it was set in 1970 and not 1972. Perhaps it would have been better not to give a year at all, since it hardly matters when it happened, only that it did. What happens in Friel's play cannot escape a comparison with Derry's Bloody Sunday and the ensuing Widgery Report. Although the real events of 30 January 1972 were in many respects different from those of Friel's fictitious 10 February 1970, the climate of thought and feeling in the Catholic population of Derry before Bloody Sunday must be seen as a true if not complete picture. It is typical of Friel's approach that his play does not allocate much space to the aftermath of the events described, apart from the official tribunal set up to examine these events. There is nothing in Friel's play to match the sense of outrage that swept Catholic Ireland after Bloody Sunday. It is left to the audience to evaluate what has happened. Only in the two sermons by the priest, the second of which cancels out the subdued sense of injustice suggested in the first, and in the media description of the funeral do we get anything like a reaction, and both are hypocritical and unrepresentative.

In *The Freedom of the City* two parallel events are dramatized on stage: first, there is a description of what happened in and around Derry's Guildhall on 10 February 1970; secondly, this description is constantly interrupted by the proceedings of the subsequently appointed tribunal. As always in Friel, the juxtaposition of two separate events is used to ironic effect in stressing the discrepancy between the accounts of what happened. What is shown on one part of the stage is counterpointed by what happens on another. Again, only the audience can see everything. Friel quickly establishes the play's main business. We see the three central characters dead on stage before the scene shifts to the tribunal and the judge questioning the first witness, a policeman, who gives only the names and a few basic facts about the three dead. These simple statistics are then fleshed out into detailed portraits of three individuals and how they were affected by the situation in Derry. When a civil rights meeting is broken up by the British Army, Lily, Skinner and Michael, blinded by CS gas, inadvertently make their way into the Mayor's parlour in the Guildhall. There, the three of them, in some respects at least a cross-section of the poor Catholic population of Derry, settle down to await the return of normality outside. Meanwhile their presence in the Guildhall, through rumour and exaggeration outside, is turned into a major act of insurrection against the authorities. They become, in the eyes of the British Army, fifty armed terrorists, and in the eyes of the Catholic population, heroes and freedom fighters. In reality, of course, this confrontation between three unarmed civil rights marchers and a ridiculously over-armed British Army becomes a major ironic contrast in the play. The outcome of this unfair contest predictably ends with the defeat of the former; that they should have to pay with their lives increases the tragedy. They are double victims, first of the unjust political and social system they had been marching to change, and, secondly, of its military might. The play's two parallel actions, progressing independently of each other, are mutually reflecting. Overlaid on these, and interspersed between them there are several complementary actions. Events in Guildhall Square and in the rest of Derry are reported almost documentary-style. Completely outside and separated from these actions is Professor Dodds, an American sociologist who lectures straight to the audience on 'inherited poverty or the culture of poverty or more accurately the subculture of poverty'. His appearance should disturb no one in an otherwise completely fluid presentation. His function seems to be to direct the attention of the audience to the subject of poverty, and so to counterbalance the Judge's terse statement early in the play: 'We are not conducting a social survey, Constable.' The Widgery Report, too, dealt exclusively with the events on one particular day, without any reference to underlying political or social conditions. In Friel's play, with the appearance of Professor Dodds, implicit criticism seems to be intended against the tribunal for not attempting a more thorough analysis of the background. Dodds's thesis is illustrated by Friel in the actions and behaviour of the three central characters in the Mayor's parlour. His suggestion, for instance, that the poor in general show traits of 'present-time orientation' in contrast to the 'future-orientated' middle class, that 'they often have a hell of a lot of more fun than we have', are shown in the next scene where Skinner and Lily have a bit of innocent fun with the Mayor's ceremonial robes. The third victim, Michael, does not join them; he has definite middle-class aspirations. This is only one example of a gradually emerging rift between the trio in the Guildhall, stressing the conflicting ideals that lead to suspicion and more serious division, a fate that the Northern Ireland

Civil Rights Association had to suffer. Michael's idea of responsible and dignified protest, 'people marching along in silence, rich and poor, high and low, doctors, accountants, plumbers, teachers, bricklayers – all shoulder to shoulder', is ridiculed by the less disciplined Skinner. The latter is never serious enough to state his own goals but his impulsive and intuitive understanding of the situation must not be underestimated. He knows for certain why Lily is *not* marching. *Not* for 'wan man – wan vote'; 'You got that six months ago,' says Skinner correctly. *Not* for 'no more gerrymandering'; 'I don't believe a word of it,' is Skinner's reaction. He then goes on to tell us the real reason why Lily is marching:

> Because you live with eleven kids and a sick husband in two rooms that aren't fit for animals. Because you exist on a state subsistence that's about enough to keep you alive but too small to fire your guts. Because you know your children are caught in the same morass. Because for the first time in your life you grumbled and someone else grumbled and someone else, and you heard each other, and became aware that there were hundreds, thousands, millions of us all over the world, and in a vague groping way you were outraged. That's what it's all about, Lily. It has nothing to do with doctors and accountants and teachers and dignity and boy scout honour. It's about us – the poor – the majority – stirring in our sleep. And if that's not what it's all about, then it has nothing to do with us.

This is an eloquent and moving plea on behalf of the poor. Yet, its generality only becomes valid when it is particularized in a Northern Ireland or Derry context. It is only when we see the various manifestations of poverty as experienced by Lily, Skinner and even Michael, that this speech makes sense. It must not, I believe, be seen as the play's (or Friel's) statement or point of view. Skinner, as a character, is perfectly capable of expressing such truths honestly, but as elsewhere in the play, he lacks a consistent and genuine focus for his words and actions. His 'defensive flippancy', as he realizes in his moment of death, will not achieve anything. His protective role-play may be an understandable reaction in the face of a situation that demands so much, in a life that is so desperately impossible. Skinner understands at the end 'how seriously they [the British Army] took us and how unpardonably casual we were about them; and that to match their seriousness would demand a total dedication, a solemnity as formal as theirs'. This could perhaps be taken as a tiny hint of an extension of Friel's interest in a definition of the Irish psyche. Earlier in the play Skinner had jokingly asked Michael to recite Rudyard Kipling's poem 'If', 'a poem to fit the place and the occasion'. This obvious reference to a well-known poem by a spokesman of British imperialism, extolling the virtues of a peculiarly British stiff-upper-lip mentality, was surely not included by chance. Once or twice in the short stories, there had been the odd reference to this opposition between British and Irish. In the plays it returns more frequently, seen in literary, linguistic and generally historical terms. The proper place to return to this subject will be in connection with a later play, *Translations*.

The Freedom of the City is a rich and complex play. The whole dramatic structure of the play seems to be designed as a clinical and formal analysis intent on controlling the flow of emotions. Apart from the three central individuals, and even their feelings are subdued and kept under control, the characters in the play are strangely dehumanized. This is due partly to their brief and intermittent appearance which can never establish them fully as characters. They may at first seem stereotyped, but their impact in the play is only delayed, and each of them emerges finally after having played a shameful part in the whole proceedings: the priest in his fickle and amateur dealings in politics again betrays the people; the balladeer trivializes and at the same time glorifies an event into doubtful myth; the RTE commentator (and other members of the media) peddle dangerously inaccurate information and turn the funeral of the three victims into an exercise of unctuous hypocrisy. These, we must remember, are some of the 'Irish' characters in the play, but they do not escape Friel's criticism. This is relevant when we consider the more important treatment of the British hierarchy of power, the judge of the tribunal, the British Army brigadier in charge of the operations and the soldiers who fire the shots that kill the three demonstrators. All these layers support each other, and justify each other's behaviour, they are what Skinner, in his dying speech, refers to as 'they', the opposition. But to argue that Friel is anti-British, anti-Army and anti-tribunal would be a simplification of the play. It is true, of course, that, since we know that the victims are not armed, the findings of the tribunal can be seen to have been a whitewash. But then this was the prevalent Catholic attitude to the Widgery Report. It is typical of Friel's approach that the tribunal was never explicitly criticized in the play. This realization, when it comes, is part of the ironic interplay between events as perceived from different points of view and conditioned by different values and loyalties. The individual is again confronted by an authority much removed from its opponent. Communication between them is thwarted as a simple consequence of distance, but more importantly because confrontation is the name of the game. They cannot communicate because they simply do not want to understand each other.

In many ways, *The Freedom of the City* is a most difficult play to deal with, quite simply because it contains a number of the historical indeterminacies that I mentioned in the Introduction. The play can be extolled for its virtues or condemned for its faults all depending on your political or religious persuasion. If you accept the basic thrust of the play you become a nationalist or at least anti-British. If you are English or a Northern

Irish Protestant you do not accept the play. This, of course, is not a complete picture, and several exceptions would have to be made. I believe, however, that such exceptions would only tend to confirm the general rule. Many press reactions stressed the contemporary historical context and made references to Bloody Sunday and the Widgery Report. When the play opened at the Royal Court in London (one week after the Dublin première) most English newspapers were predictably hostile to its political content, and some sort of defence had to be made: 'an entertaining piece of unconvincing propaganda' (*Daily Telegraph*); 'its bias against the English robs it of its potential power' (*Sunday Express*); the play 'suffers fatally from this overzealous determination to discredit the means and the motives of the English in the present Ulster crisis' and the writer 'is also engaged on a Celtic propaganda exercise' (*Evening Standard*); 'Friel's case is too loaded to encourage much intelligent sympathy' (*Daily Express*). These views were corroborated by the *Belfast Newsletter* which called the play 'a cheap cry' and described it as 'mawkish propaganda'. The *Daily Mail*, finally, told its readers that 'the play has angered senior Army officers in Ulster.' I do not believe that Friel for a moment thought that his insistence on the theme of poverty would make the play impervious to this kind of criticism. That is the staple response of the entrenched attitudes in Northern Ireland. The tragedy of the situation is highlighted in his honest, human and moving plea for the three central individuals, who, as human beings, are never allowed a chance to realize themselves. No single speech or statement must be taken as the play's message, but in this context, Michael's simple ideals might be worth quoting. We are not asking for very much he says to Skinner, 'a decent job, a decent place to live, a decent town to bring up our children in – that's what we want'. Here too, the basic division into two different levels of action in the play must be understood as part of Friel's intention to separate them also thematically. If we conclude that Friel is criticizing the tribunal for its findings and the Army for its role in the events, we must also accept the case that he presents in favour of Lily, Michael and Skinner in their underprivileged situation. We should be able to see that Lily, Michael and Skinner also exist, be it precariously, on a different level as typical victims of any repressive society or authority. In Northern Ireland, however, such reflections would immediately be qualified by considerations of nationality and religion.

The aspirations of the three central characters are stunted by the conditions in which they live, their lives are a human desert of unfulfilled potential. Professor Dodds in his lecture suggests that the first step out of this despair must be a realization of their condition.

> But the very moment they acquire an objective view of their condition, once they become aware that their condition has counterparts elsewhere, from that moment they have broken out of their subculture, even though they may still be desperately poor. And any movement – trade union, religious, civil rights, pacifist, revolutionary – any movement which gives them this objectivity, organizes them, gives them real hope, promotes solidarity, such a movement inevitably smashes the rigid cast that encases their minds and bodies.

But such are the complicated ironies of the play that this statement, although simple and straightforward in itself, cannot stand unchallenged. In the play's central scene we witness how fragile and difficult the unity of any organization is. But Dodds's general theory has an interesting personal parallel in Lily's dying speech. She understands, with great grief and regret, that life had somehow passed her by.

> And in the silence before my body disintegrated in a purple convulsion, I thought I glimpsed a tiny truth: that

[141]

life had eluded me because never once in my forty-three years had an experience, an event, even a small unimportant happening been isolated, and assessed, and articulated. And the fact that this, my last experience, was defined by this perception, this was the culmination of sorrow. In a way I died of grief.

A link could form itself between the two statements, making Lily's private realization a premable to Dodds's common ideal. And yet, also, they contradict each other in that the individual will always be at odds with the group. Professor Dodds and his lecture are all the time divorced from the actual events of the play, and thus from the individuals involved in them. He accurately describes only one facet of the conflict enacted in *The Freedom of the City* and does so in theoretical and generalized terms. He serves, I believe, a dual purpose. His analysis attempts to broaden the issues, but it also amplifies the fact that to see the conflict in terms of poverty alone is not enough.

Living Quarters (1977)

Before turning to the next play that Friel wrote, *Volunteers* (1975), which represents a further extension of his dramatic style, it may be suitable to consider briefly a play which, it seems to me, stands half-way between the previous works and the distinctive voice of the period since *Volunteers*. *Living Quarters* (1977) was Friel's third play to be premièred in the Abbey's new theatre. Thematically it is dominated by two subjects that we recognize from Friel's previous work: the unit of the family and the force of Fate. The play describes the events of one single day in the life of the Butler family. But the story is told in retrospect, and the format of the presentation becomes that of a rehearsal in a theatre in which the characters play themselves in a play of their own lives. Technically, Friel's play is dominated by the character of Sir, who in the rehearsal becomes the director. He alone has a copy of the script outlining the actual events that are now being re-enacted on stage. This script, which Sir carries in his 'ledger', must be seen to have been created in collaboration with Fate. One of the characters, a priest, is hurt by the description of himself as 'a cliché, a stereotype', and refuses at first to play the part. 'The assessment isn't mine,' Sir declares, suggesting a higher authority. But Sir is not just the director. At times he briefly becomes a metaphor of the writer at work, organizing the presentation of events.

> Are we all set? Good. Now – you've all been over this hundreds, thousands of times before. So on this occasion – with your co-operation, of course – what I should like to do is organize those recollections for you, impose a structure on them, just to give them a form of sorts. Agreed? Excellent! Naturally we'll only get through a tiny portion of all that was said and done that day; but I think we should attempt some kind of chronological order; and I promise you that the selection I make will be as fair and as representative as possible. So I'll call you as I require you and introduce you then.

The atmosphere of the rehearsal room, with the actors' patois and stage business is well established.

> *(Tom exits quickly – in his confusion going off left instead of right.)*
> SIR: Not that way, Tom. Over this – *(Tom has gone.)* I don't think we need those things, do we? *(He picks up empty coffee mugs, the* Enquirer; *adjusts the chairs.)*
> MIRIAM: I'm not needed, am I?
> SIR: Not for the time being, thank you. Nor Helen, nor Tina. *(Looking round the set.)* That's more like it, isn't it?

While the characters are waiting for Sir to return at the beginning of act II, Friel stipulates in the stage directions that '*throughout this sequence none of the characters obeys the conventions of the set*'. As a modern

[143]

convention Friel's technique has obvious similarities with, for instance, Pirandello's *Six Characters in Search of an Author*. The question of how to transform life into art is twice removed from the audience. They are watching Friel's description of how real events can be presented on the stage. But Friel's treatment also emphasizes how the characters perceive themselves and their roles in the play they are rehearsing. They cannot escape the events as they actually happened on this day, but they are allowed to speak their thoughts as well, opening up the possibility of regrets, analyses of lost opportunities and of decisions made or not made. Friel's play, then, adds to the physical events a psychological dimension, involving the emotions and thoughts underlying what happened. The whole rehearsal may in fact be nothing but the formalized memories of people dead or scattered all over the world who in their minds keep turning over the fateful events of this one day. That much is suggested by Sir's first speech. It is not, then, a question of a normal physical reunion of a family but an arrangement of the extra-sensory perceptions of the people involved, prompted into physical action by Sir for the benefit of the audience. This would put a different complexion on the whole exercise. There is throughout the play an insistence on non-physical elements of the action, 'inner voices', 'unease' and 'shadows' that influence the atmosphere. Father Tom's strong reaction at the end, which comes from the certain knowledge that Frank Butler is going to kill himself, would then be a retroactive expression of his own sense of guilt. From having been dead drunk one minute earlier, Father Tom suddenly stands up ('*now sober*' says the stage directions) and asks the others to stop what is about to happen. But Sir is adamant: 'You had your opportunities and you squandered them . . . We'll have none of your spurious concern now that it's all over.' Once the drama is dissolved the tension is relaxed. Sir's summing-up, 'That wasn't too bad after all now, was it?', signals the end of the rehearsal and leaves him to the factual description of what happened to the characters afterwards. Wherever they are, the events of the day, or more correctly their own perceptions of what happened, will continue to influence their lives, and there will no doubt be several more rehearsals.

As in the case of *Philadelphia, Here I Come!* and 'Winners', our understanding of *Living Quarters* as a play will be improved if we see it in a wider historical perspective. The character of Sir has been criticized for being an intrusive device that interrupts the action. Robert Hogan in his essay 'Since O'Casey' quotes from Conor Cruise O'Brien's review of the play: 'Those Brechtian and post-Brechtian devices that were supposed to be liberating from the fetters of traditional dramaturgy are beginning to look suspiciously like fetters themselves. Putting it another way, Sir is a pain in the neck.' Hogan himself adds: 'They [the devices] dissipate the dramatic energy; they are tedious,' but makes an exception for 'the one superb instance of Private Gar'. These views, and the continuing insistence on 'devices', may be understandable, but reflect, I believe, the demands of a basically realistic dramatic form. Hogan's main mistake has been to group these devices together and in doing so divorce them from the dramatic form in which they appear. Sir can be allowed to disrupt the flow of action in the play because flow of action *per se* has never been a major issue in any of Friel's plays. Dramatic energy does not depend on the question of what happens next. In none of his plays is there an increase in dramatic tension or suspense that is resolved or released in a conventional ending. Nor is there a solution to the problems or issues dealt with in the play. This is not to say that a conventionally dramatic play is inferior to the kind of play that Friel would write. But his drama must be judged according to what it is trying to achieve, not according to external standards. Within each play each 'device' attempts to intensify the process through which it works. Sometimes it may be more successful in the popular sense of the word, but I believe that in the organic unity of the play Friel's specific definition of the word 'success' can be found to be more appropriate. There is little or no doubt that *Philadelphia, Here I Come!* as a play has been and will be more successful than *Living Quarters*. But this cannot only be a result of the device of Private Gar. *Living Quarters* is less 'attractive' than the earlier play, its humour more subdued and always tinged with the grim reality of the overall atmosphere. Sir illustrates the complexity of the situation, questions motives and deepens the psychological aspects of the characters. He also explains the action to the audience, a fact which would move him closer to the role of narrator, and so, as we have seen, his presence in a play could be seen to indicate a weakness in the writer's ability to provide this element naturally in dramatic form. But one of the roles performed by the Greek chorus was to provide this information in order that the dramatized action would increase in validity and meaning. Sir also functions as a chorus in the way he controls the past and the present and predicts the future. He could be seen to express the wishes of the gods in their mastery over human affairs. 'There is no refuge from destiny and the inevitable' would describe the human condition of *Living Quarters*. The quotation is from Euripides' tragedy *Hippolytus*, and there may be in Friel's play further analogues with the classical story about Phaedra. Frank Butler's formal protest at the unfair and unjust way he has been treated in the play they have been rehearsing, and consequently by life, is, he knows, absolutely futile: 'The ledger's the ledger, isn't it?' His quiet complaint could be seen to echo those of both Hippolytus and Theseus in Euripides' drama. The former's 'Ah! Would that the human race might bring a curse on the gods!' and the latter's 'My grief! Long will I remember the evil you have done, O Cypris!' are both expressions of human frustration at the unassailability of the gods.

Friel's play relates how Commandant Frank Butler returns to Ballybeg as a hero after United Nations service in the Middle East, and how he commits suicide when he finds out that his young wife Anna during his absence had been having an affair with the son from his first marriage. In Euripides, Phaedra, when she realizes that she is in love with Hippolytus, knows that it is a sin, assumes all the guilt, takes all the blame herself and finally, to avoid the shame of having to face Theseus, commits suicide. In Friel's modern tragedy the concepts of sin and honour are treated very differently. Frank is confronted with the fact of Anna's adultery, and being a military man, does the honourable thing. He goes into his room and shoots himself. Anna and her associate in sin shake off their guilt and busy themselves with their torrid and trivial lives. So, Frank, who was innocent, dies and the guilty live on. That could be one implication of Friel's play. If this is so, then modern tragedy is but a paltry version of the real thing. George Steiner argues in *The Death of Tragedy* that tragedy is not possible in the modern world. 'But tragedy is that form of art which requires the intolerable burden of God's presence. It is now dead because His shadow no longer falls upon us as it fell on Agamemnon or Macbeth or Athalie.' In Friel's play the priest is a poor substitue for God, but he presents the Christian alternative in its simplest terms:

... but I've got to speak what I know to be true, and that is that grace is available to each and every one of us if we just ask God for it ... Which is really the Christian way of saying that our options are *always* open. Because that is the enormous gift that Christ purchased for us – the availability of choice and our freedom to choose.

It is the availability of grace that makes modern man less susceptible to the pity and terror of genuine tragedy. 'Real tragedy can occur only where the tormented soul believes that there is no time left for God's forgiveness.' But there is another aspect of tragedy that can certainly be felt also in modern life. It could be argued that the essence of dramatic tragedy resides not in unhappiness generally or in fear of the hereafter, but in an awareness of 'the solemnity of the remorseless working of things'.[9] In many of Friel's plays, and in particular in 'Winners' and *Living Quarters*, this seems to be the human condition as reflected in the writer's creative sensibility. 'The world is a comedy to those who think, a tragedy to those who feel,' wrote Horace Walpole. If such a simple distinction were possible, Friel, I suggest, would belong in the second category.

Living Quarters describes a family reunion on the occasion of the father's return as a hero. The Butler family, however, is far from a homogeneous unit, and Friel's title is an apology for the absence of the more ideal 'home'. Frank's second wife Anna is the most obvious outsider. In an extended session a family photograph is taken in the garden with Anna forlornly left inside. But in the course of events there is evidence that relationships within the family have been tainted by past failures to overcome an embarrassment between them. Frank's first wife, and the mother of all the four assembled children, returns as a ghost to trouble their consciences. Her death and her continued presence cause a rift between Frank and at least two of his children. But the general family atmosphere seems not to have been conducive to open and honest communication. Frank's own description of the family, 'measured, watching, circling one another, peeping out, shying back', is constantly echoed in Friel's stage directions. The characters are '*all isolated, all cocooned in their private thoughts*', and one of them '*remains encased and intact in his privacy*'. These qualities are amply realized in the action. Father and son again fail more miserably than the others to express a love they may after all feel

for each other. The son's impulsive urge to open his
heart is never satisfied. But, he says:

> I suppose it was just as well it wasn't said like that because
> he could never receive that kind of directness, and I
> suppose I could never have said it. But I just hope – I just
> hope he was able to sense an expression of some
> k–k–k–k– – of some kind of love for him – even if it was
> only in my perfidy –

Ben's stammer is an image of the impossibility of
gaining access to the inner emotions of the individual. It
disturbs communication generally and is caused by
some emotional inhibition, by shyness, fear or respect.
Joe in 'Winners' pretends to have a stammer when he
has to face Father Kelly after the revelation that Mag
was pregnant. He knows that, in the circumstances,
that would be an appropriate response. In *Translations*
Sarah's slow and laborious progress out of her dumbness
is checked by the insensitivity of the English officer.

Ironically, it is in the context of the family that the
failure of communication is most acutely felt. It is also
where individuals can be most seriously hurt emotionally, and where lives may be destroyed. In 'Winners'
Mag's parents reacted very badly to the news that she
was pregnant: 'My God, the things they said to me –
they seared my soul forever.' Helen in *Living Quarters*
accuses her dead mother of having ruined her marriage
with Gerry Kelly. In the face of 'her mother's bitter and
vicious opposition' he left her, and caused Helen to
emigrate to London. Ben is most relentless in his
criticism of the family. In his year at UCD he knew three
brothers from Tipperary who lived separately and who
never met once during term. One of them 'called his
father and mother by their Christian names. Spoke of
them warmly – as if they were friends of the family.'
Ben's outburst against his own family must have some
general validity: 'There must be another way of ordering
close relationships, mustn't there? (*Shouts.*) Mustn't

there?' It is only Tina, the youngest daughter who, at eighteen, is still innocent enough not to have discovered the negative influences. In the events of this one day, though, she, Sir says, was 'faced with the inevitablility of growing up'.

Another central Frielian theme is repeated in *Living Quarters*. Ballybeg itself and 'the quiet of this backwater' may have helped to drive Anna into Ben's arms. Moreover, 'this bloody wet hole' may have ruined the health of Frank's first wife. The general tendency in the play is away from Ballybeg. Frank had long been waiting for a promotion that would take him to Dublin. After his suicide, Sir informs us,

> Helen and Tina flew to London, where they now live in different flats and seldom meet. Tina works as a waitress in an all-night café and Helen has had to give up her office job because of an acute nervous breakdown. Ben went to Scotland. He came back after seven months. He has been jailed twice for drunk and disorderly behaviour.

Anna, finally, ends up in Los Angeles. Only one daughter, Miriam, can settle down to a well-adjusted life in Ballybeg. She is different from the other Butler children, married to a court clerk and with three children. She had been described by her mother as 'neither a Butler nor a Hogan. I'm afraid you're just – pure Ballybeg'. She describes herself as 'a coarse bitch', she is not present at the crucial moments of the play, and she remains emotionally uninvolved in the family antagonisms. Miriam accepts social and religious conventions, takes her role as wife and mother very seriously and must be seen as a typical Ballybeg inhabitant, not very attractive but nevertheless harmless in her simple prejudices.

Living Quarters is Friel's most consistent inquiry into the negative aspects of family life. Frank and his wife clearly fail in promoting a happy family atmosphere. Her social snobbism, 'nobless oblige! D'you hear –

nobless oblige!', may have been part of the cause, and qualities which stood him in good stead in his public role may have militated against him in private life. But just as he did in 'Winners' and other plays, Friel lifts the significance of his statement into a wider perspective. The final scattering of the family into different parts of the world is a fine image of the perilous and fragile nature of family ties and of the failure of the individual to break the rigid cast surrounding his own personality. The enormity of it all also comes out in the relentless forward movement of time. Friel's characters return in their minds to a decisive event; they interpret it and try to understand what happened and their own role in it, but, even though their own perceptions of it may vary, the event itself cannot be changed.

The single most important influence on Friel's writing career in the seventies was probably the continuing and sometimes worsening situation in Ulster. With *The Freedom of the City* he gave a voice to the politically and economically suppressed population of Derry and Northern Ireland and, in doing so, necessarily collided with the official British attitude to the conflict. There is, in that play, an air of reluctant contemporaneity about the treatment of the troubles. As we have seen, the play grew out of a more historical subject, removed from the terrible reality of actual events, and Friel, in a small way, tried to withdraw it from its immediate background by shifting the time and by superimposing the theme of poverty on its overall structure. With the exception of *The Enemy Within* all of Friel's plays had been set in contemporary Ireland. It was only in 1980 and with *Translations* that an historical perspective was explicitly introduced and the main action moved backwards to 1833. But there had been, with the plays written in the late sixties and early seventies, an increasing sense of history. Perhaps the process started as early as with *The Mundy Scheme,* when the audience were asked to compare contemporary politicians with the idealists of 1916 (and, by implication, previous centuries) and to assess the progress of Ireland since the liberation from British colonialism. *The Gentle Island* strengthened the links with the past and also made the East–West dichotomy a necessary condition of the conflict in the play. Next, but for Bloody Sunday, we might have had a play about an eighteenth-century eviction in the West of Ireland. Instead, in *Volunteers*, contemporary Ireland is excavated with pick-axe and spade in order to unearth essential qualities of Irishness and to define the nature of the Irish past. Through the seventies there was a gradual intensification of two parallel and equally important tendencies in Friel's plays. Both deal directly with the two essential dichot-omies of place in Ireland. First there is an increas-ing attention to questions of national and linguistic identity and, a concomitant of this, an unavoidable and necessary interest in the relationship between England and Ireland past and present and between the English and Irish languages.

IV

New Accents

Politics Underground: *Volunteers* (1975)

The renewed outbreak of sectarian violence at the end of
the sixties after a period of civil rights agitation, its
continuation up to the present day and the political,
social, economic and religious realities of everyday life
for people in the North have probably been the strongest
influence on Friel's career as a writer. After Bloody
Sunday in Derry, when Friel himself took part in the
march, contemporary reality forcibly entered his work;
he could no longer refuse to deal with it. In that sense,
The Freedom of the City started something new. But the
more typical phase of Friel's recent work was initiated
by *Volunteers*. It involves a treatment of history that
will assist an effort to understand today's tortured
reality.

If Field Day had existed in 1975 the company might
well have considered putting on *Volunteers*. It is a play
which introduces the main concerns of Friel's new
development. Like Seamus Heaney's *North, Volunteers*
seeks in the myth of Viking Ireland a clearer vision of
contemporary Irish politics. The Viking dig in the
middle of a modern city becomes another fitting focus for
Friel's thematic exploration of the Irish psyche. The
Wood Quay excavations in Dublin lent contempory and
local relevance to the production as did, of course, the
situation in the North. But the relevance of the play is
extended backwards into early Irish history. Friel's

'backward look' reveals no 'idyllically happy' ancestors, and it questions the values and myths that it has pleased modern Ireland to keep and cherish.

In *Volunteers* politics, like the action, exists underground. It is an obvious condition of the play, but its action and its symbols invite a number of interpretations. Internment had been introduced in the then wartorn North in 1971 and immediately condemned by the Catholic population. Friel's treatment of the subject does more than establish this political connection. Keeney and his fellow diggers are political prisoners let out on parole to provide cheap labour for the dig. Back in the prison (or internment camp) they are seen as collaborators, and a kangaroo court has sentenced them to death. When the dig is over at the end of the play they return to face certain death. In its intricate symbolic design *Volunteers* attempts to disentangle the complex web of loyalties that determines the political complications in the North. Society and language, disaffectation and alienation, as we shall see later, are all relevant considerations in such an effort. They reflect the confusion within the Irish psyche. Referring to *Translations*, Friel has suggested that confusion may be a 'fairly accurate description of how we all live, specifically at the present time. Other countries perhaps have access to more certainties than we have at the moment. I was talking specifically about Ireland' (*Magill*). Friel's interest in language as communication and in particular the connection between linguistic features and individual and national characteristics, which finds its most elaborate expression in *Translations,* has a sporadic presence in *Volunteers*. Keeney, whose well-oiled patter dominates the play's action, suggests a seemingly irrelevant cause for the death of the Viking skeleton Leif. 'Maybe he was a casualty of language. Damn it, George, which of us here isn't?' The suggestion is not pursued. Friel may intend no more than an allusion to the hazards of communication. But Keeney, like

Skinner in *The Freedom of the City*, often uses his joking cynicism in a way that undercuts the more serious stance in other characters. The true cause of Leif's death cannot be established. Keeney, however, suggests several, one being that Leif was a 'victim of his society'. In comparing himself and the other diggers with Leif, Keeney may begin to direct us toward the play's thematic centre.

In *Volunteers* the dig of self-discovery goes deeper than in any of the other plays. None of the finds can be dated or defined with scientific accuracy. The result of this was almost total confusion among critics as to the meaning of the play. And *Volunteers* is an extremely difficult play to extract meanings from. However, it may help to note that there are several parallels between the play and Seamus Heaney's *North,* a collection of poetry published in 1975. Both works incorporate images of Viking Ireland and Scandinavia into the contemporary political situation. Two key concepts evident in, for instance, Heaney's poem 'Punishment' may provide some help in understanding *Volunteers*. First there is the word 'victim', not mentioned but strongly implicit in the poem, which in Friel's play becomes of central importance; secondly there is the tough contemporary relevance of the final lines of the poem. After a detailed description of a ritualized murder of an adultress in what could be Viking Scandinavia, Heaney finds a modern parallel in Ulster:

> I who have stood dumb
> when your betraying sisters,
> cauled in tar,
> wept by the railings,
>
> who would connive
> in civilized outrage
> yet understand the exact
> and tribal, intimate revenge.

In *Volunteers* the Viking skeleton Leif and the diggers themselves are all victims of internecine strife and ferocious tribal feuding. We know, at least, that the internees will be punished by their own tribe when they return to the camp; the story of Leif's fate, on the other hand, is only a fiction, but it is executed by Pyne with such verve and authenticity that its relevance in the contemporary situation becomes inevitable. The story he makes up is about two Norwegian cousins, Leif and Ulf, who settle in Ireland; they briefly emigrate to America before Ulf becomes homesick.

PYNE: So Ulf loaded the ship with all the booty he could lay hands on; and Leif – all he took with him was the Indian girl he'd set up with out there. And on their way back they were torn to pieces by the winter gales, and Ulf and his booty were washed overboard, and the only two to make it back were Leif and his woman.

KEENEY: (*to Butt*). Ah, shure I can schmell dishaster comin'.

PYNE: And instead of welcoming them, the two families stared at Leif and his brown woman and said, 'Where's Ulf? And who is this black pagan?' And although Leif told them about the terrible Atlantic gales, they said, 'No. This black woman is evil. She killed our Ulf. Now you and she must die.'

KEENEY: Don't you know!

PYNE: And they burned the Indian woman before Leif's eyes. And then they put a rope round his neck, and strung him up, and just for good measure opened his skull. And there he is. Brother Leif. Jesus, I didn't know how that was going to end!

Keeney's increasing recognition of the story's intention betrays his familiarity with its subject. It is Keeney who expresses what may be Friel's intention. He connects the dig with history, telling a group of imaginary schoolchildren, another generation of Irish, 'that what you have around you is encapsulated history, a tangible

[156]

précis of the story of Irish man', and that 'the more we learn about our ancestors, children, the more we discover about ourselves – isn't that so? So that what we are all engaged in here is really a thrilling voyage in *self*-discovery.' These key passages occur early in the play. Later, through Keeney, the concept of the 'victim' is further developed. He becomes involved in confrontations with the other diggers and is made increasingly aware of a difference between them and himself. One such major confrontation is with Butt, described by Keeney as a consistent Gaelic-Irishman 'sustained by a cast-iron certainty'. Keeney first invites the other diggers to tell their own version of Leif's story and at that moment the play moves from Viking times into troubled contemporaneity; he then suggests four versions that he believes Butt would have told, all of them seeing Leif as a suppressed and dispossessed slave and victim of some usurping and superior authority. There are strong echoes of Irish history here, opening up the wounds of the Penal Laws, absentee landlordism and evictions. Butt himself accepts these versions and goes on to suggest a fifth of his own:

BUTT: Or he was a bank-clerk who had courage and who had brains and who was one of the best men in the movement.
KEENEY: Once upon a time.
BUTT: Yes, Keeney. And you're sure of it in your guts, too.
KEENEY: I'm sure of nothing now.
BUTT: You were once. You shouted yes louder than any of us.
KEENEY: Did I?
BUTT: Five–six months ago. Before you volunteered for this job. You knew where you stood then. Are you going soft, Keeney?

But Keeney's problem is, as he says, 'the inability to sustain a passion, even a frivolous passion'. And yet, he tells Butt, in many ways his own opposite, 'here we are,

[157]

spancelled goats complementing each other, suffering the same consequences. Is it ironic? Is it even amusing?' Keeney's new awareness seems to be that there are as many differences as similarities among the internees. His impatience with certain attitudes increases the tension between them. The key role in this context is played by Smiler, an example of an ordinary man who has been turned into a passive imbecile by the violence of authority. When one of his workmates was interned Smiler and five other stonemasons set off from their Donegal quarry on a protest march to Dublin. But they only 'got as far as the Derry border and there they whipped Smiler off to jail in Dublin and beat the tar out of him for twelve consecutive hours – you know, just as a warning'. Smiler's story, as told by Keeney, stresses the nature of his role as a victim. This is extended when, during the final day of the dig, Smiler disappears, is believed to have escaped, and then suddenly returns because he has not known what to do without Butt. Smiler's return, typically, cuts short the Keeney–Butt confrontation quoted above and everyone except Keeney starts fussing over him. Butt *'drapes a very large sack round Smiler's shoulders. It is so long that it hangs down his sides and looks like a ritualistic robe, an ecclesiastical cope'* (stage directions). While this is going on Keeney's smouldering anger finally comes out.

KEENEY: (*after a brief pause*). He's an imbecile! He's a
    stupid, pigheaded imbecile! He was an imbecile the
    moment he walked out of his quarry! And that's why
    he came back here – because he's an imbecile like
    the rest of us! Go ahead – flutter about him – fatten
    him up – imbecile acolytes fluttering about a
    pigheaded imbecile victim. For Christ's sake is there
    no end to it?

Keeney's anger, it seems to me, is here directed at a passive willingness to worship, in the guise of Smiler, the role of the victim.

In the same sense in which Owen can be seen to be the key figure in *Translations,* Butt may be the key figure in *Volunteers.* He performs his task as digger with interest and dedication. At the very end, however, it is he who destroys the green-glazed jug that George the foreman had spent much time restoring. The pieces had been found by Smiler and the jug when assembled was described by Keeney as 'Smiler restored; Smiler full, free and integrated'. In the course of the play the jug turns into a symbol that could suggest some kind of Irish heritage. Originally Butt did not want the jug damaged and his final destruction of it is not prepared for. When it happens, however, it must be seen as his decision to break with something he has lost his belief in. The jug itself can be seen as typical of the whole play. It avoids safe and clear-cut definitions and conclusions. In this sense *Volunteers* may illustrate the confusion that dominates any discussion about the political situation in both North and South. The play provides a bleak picture of a strife-torn society, confused within itself and lacking a focus for its energies. The concept of tribal warfare permeates the play. In a remarkable exchange towards the end, Keeney and Pyne progress quickly from a description of Leif as a good-natured and generous man to an awareness of his likeness to the 'Boyces of Ballybeg':

KEENEY: They all had that hard, jutting jaw.
PYNE: Now that you mention it.
KEENEY: Tight crowd, the Boyces.

                    . . .

KEENEY: Oh, he's a Boyce all right.
PYNE: One bad connection.
KEENEY: One hungry connection.
PYNE: Hungry's the word.
KEENEY: Hungry and vicious.
PYNE: Bad seed – bad breed.
    (*Keeney briskly covers the skull with the tarpaulin.*)
KEENEY: All our bad luck go with him.
PYNE: Amen to that.

The dig is over and a construction company will soon replace the diggers to build a modern multi-storey hotel on the site. This contemporary reference suggests a strong condemnation of attitudes of official and modern Ireland towards its own history and heritage. Keeney cannot understand it: 'We spend months and months making a bloody big hole and next week a different crowd of tribesmen'll come along and fill it all in. If a fella had any head on him at all, he'd be able to extract some kind of wisdom from that. Wouldn't he, Leif?' Other contemporary correspondences occur. Friel exposes the empty and ineffectual rhetoric of Des, a young Marxist student who assists in the dig. He is completely removed from the reality of the situation and promotes only his own well-being. As a character he resembles Tom Breslin in *The Blind Mice* but he is better connected to the play's action than the latter was. George the foreman sides with Wilson the warder in an effort to remove himself from the diggers. There is a wide gap between George, Wilson and Des on the one hand and the diggers on the other. The gap is filled with social, economic and political differences that make any rapprochement between them completely impossible. The social and political structure leaves the diggers at the bottom, isolated, misunderstood, confused and divided among themselves.

Volunteers, as I have suggested earlier, does not lend itself to easy interpretation. There is no mistaking, however, the disillusioned bitterness in the description of a contemporary situation. The diggers are caught in an impossible dilemma and become victims of their own society. Behind this open and confused condition lurks Friel's sense of certain Irish weaknesses, of a willingness to accept the role of victim, the inability or refusal to escape internal division to reach strength in unity and a common goal, and the reason behind this, a failure to arrive at a definition of a national identity. The play, as Seamus Heaney proposed in his review in *The Times*

Literary Supplement, 'is more about values and attitudes within the Irish psyche than it is about the rights
and wrongs of the political situation'. It is part of Friel's
effort to carry on his investigation of a national identity.
What he has uncovered in *Volunteers* may not be wholly
complimentary evidence, but he does not shy away from
a revelation of it. As for the meaning of the play, Seamus
Heaney, again, may be allowed to speak:

> Still people yearn for a *reductio*: what does he mean? He
> means, one presumes, to shock. He means that an expert,
> hurt and shocking laughter is the only adequate response
> to a calloused condition . . . and that no 'fake concern' . . .
> should be allowed to mask us from the facts of creeping
> indifference, degradation and violence. And he means to
> develop as a playwright and to create, despite resistance,
> the taste by which he is to be enjoyed.

He also means, presumably, to expose the intense
confusion within the Irish psyche, to question, with
Keeney, the wisdom of 'keeping up the protection of the
myth,' and especially the wrong kind of myth. Keeney's
antic and anarchic disposition, which he shares with
Skinner in *The Freedom of the City* and with Shane in
The Gentle Island, may be his only possible defence
against the conditions he is exposed to. His muttering,
his patter and his joking help him 'keep sane', they stop
him from going mad, which Hamlet did in the rotten
state of Denmark.

TV history: *Farewell to Ardstraw* and *The Next Parish* (1976)

Friel's urge to seek in Irish history a definition of modern
Ireland is plainly and directly manifest in two TV
programmes he wrote for the Schools Department of
BBC Belfast. Before writing *The Freedom of the City*
Friel had been interested in the idea of evictions as an
expression of Catholic disenfranchisement in the eighteenth and nineteenth centuries. *Farewell to Ardstraw*

and *The Next Parish* both deal with a different kind of eviction, emigration. In these two programmes this spectre of Irish history is approached from two different directions. In the first, Walter Glenn, a Presbyterian from the parish of Ardstraw in Ulster, is emigrating to the city of brotherly love, Philadelphia, from a religiously and politically repressive Irish climate. But the conflict is not along the familiar lines of Catholic versus Protestant, although various complaints are made by Walter Glenn about the papists in the neighbourhood, who have, we are told, been forced to leave their land to Scots-Irish settlers like himself. But the lack of civil rights that he is complaining about, and that make him risk the perilous journey to America, is exactly the same as suffered by the Catholics: lack of religious freedom and high rent imposed by absentee landlords. The point, then, that the programme is making is that Walter Glenn and his contemporary Presbyterians are in exactly the same position as the Catholics, and that their greatest enemy is the English government. The moral is obvious. Friel is trying to merge the Scots-Irish settlers and the Gaelic Irish by showing that there was more that united them than kept them apart. This is the purely historical aspect of the play. What became of Walter Glenn's descendants in America? Did they find 'the perfect society' they were looking for? The programme shuttles frequently and rather abruptly between the historical Walter Glenn, leaving Ireland and sailing to America, and his real and documentary descendant, a car salesman in modern Virginia. The historical points are convincingly made but the gap between the two parallel parts of the programme is too great. The connection between the two cannot be made to feel natural, and a good idea comes only fleetingly to life.

The Next Parish, which was the name the Irish emigrants gave to the new world, deals with the effects of the Great Famine in the 1840s and visits an Irish parish in Bronx, New York. This is more of a history lesson than the previous programme. Siobhan McKenna flies out to New York on an Aer Lingus jet and reads from various historical and fictional texts both directly to the viewer and to an audience of church-goers in Bronx. In these texts Friel has highlighted some of the most striking and haunting images of the Famine: the bare skeletons huddled together in death; the plenty of the local markets and the landlord's table; the parliamentary procrastinations before real relief was organized; the coffin ships that took the emigrants to America; and the immediate occasion of the tragedy: the failure of the potato crop, which occurred in Belgium and in Britain as well, but had a disastrous effect only in Ireland, simply because one third of the population (about three million people) depended on the potato for their livelihood. Like *Farewell to Ardstraw*, *The Next Parish* attempts to build a bridge between past and present. The latter programme succeeds better in this, even though the scenes and the interviews from the contemporary Bronx feel far removed from Ireland. But perhaps this is what Friel is trying to show. *The Next Parish* is both a tribute to the emigrants and a condemnation of the social and political order that allowed the Great Famine to happen.

The Catholic Big House: *Aristocrats* (1979)

In *Aristocrats* the range is more limited and the historical context more recent. Like an earlier short story, 'Foundry House', which the play greatly resembles, it describes the decline of a Catholic Big House. Compared with the story certain small but telling shifts have been allowed to change the emphasis. In 'Foundry House' the Hogans were 'one of the best Catholic families in the North of Ireland' whereas in *Aristocrats* the O'Donnells' large house is 'overlooking the village of Ballybeg, County Donegal, Ireland'. More important

[163]

than the change of geographical location is the new perspective of the play. *Aristocrats* examines the historical changes from within the Big House, not, as was the case in 'Foundry House', in attitudes from without.

If *Volunteers* can be said to deal mainly with politics or political attitudes and their public manifestations, *Aristocrats* attempts a more private statement on social issues. The rapid descent of the O'Donnell legal dynasty is caused by two influences. The first, the gradual weakening of several generations of O'Donnells, is curtly summed up by Eamon in a conversation with Tom.

> EAMON: And of course you'll have chapters on each of the
> O'Donnell forebears: Great Grandfather – Lord
> Chief Justice; Grandfather – Circuit Court Judge;
> Father – simple District Justice; Casimir – failed
> solicitor. A fairly rapid descent; but no matter, no
> matter; good for the book; failure's more lovable
> than success. D'you know, Professor, I've often
> wondered: if we had had children and they wanted
> to be part of the family legal tradition, the only
> option open to them would have been as criminals,
> wouldn't it?

In this sense the O'Donnells cause their own decay. But their decline is also part of the larger forces of modern history. The Ballybeg of *Aristocrats* is a village whose feudal structure is broken up with the death of the District Justice. Eamon himself personifies the levelling forces of modern democratization. He had moved from the village up to the Hall when marrying Alice and he is now witnessing the final breakdown of the class he married into. Several images from the past assemble in the background to make clear the nature of the loss. There are, on the one hand, Eamon and Willie, the boys from the village, cycling to Derry to dance in the Corinthian – 'plebeian past times. Before we were

[164]

educated out of our emotions' – and on the other, the O'Donnell children going to boarding school at the age of seven or eight and to a convent in Carcassonne to become 'young ladies'. In the present there is the well-educated Claire, an accomplished classical pianist, soon to be married to a local and successful greengrocer who drives around in a white lorry with a giant plastic banana on the roof. Claire herself is well aware of the slow slide down the scale:

> CLAIRE: Did you know that on the morning Grandmother O'Donnell got married the whole village was covered in bunting and she gave a gold sovereign to every child under twelve? And the morning mother got married she distributed roses to everyone in the chapel. I was wondering what I could do – what about a plastic bag of vegetables to every old-age pensioner?

She is forced to marry a much older man for financial reasons and in doing so she becomes part of a prevailing pattern of Irish life but one which her class had previously been exempt from. When she suddenly decides to stop playing Chopin we sense a full and pregnant moment, containing perhaps the notes of Chekhov's metaphysical string snapping.

Anna's tape-recorded message from the mission in Zambia is absurdly stuck in the past. Casimir's burrowing after the holes for the croquet hoops is his final fling at remembering what things used to be like. Casimir is probably Friel's worst mythomaniac. If he had been born down in the village, his father told him, he would have been the village idiot. His present part-time job in a sausage factory in Germany becomes an acute image of dwindled class and position. And yet, Casimir has shown admirable sense in coming to terms with his own limitations. At the age of nine he had realized that he would never succeed in life.

CASIMIR: . . . That was a very important and a very difficult
discovery for me, as you can imagine. But it brought
certain recognitions, certain compensatory
recognitions. Because once I recognized – once I
acknowledged that the larger areas were not
accessible to me, I discovered – I had to discover
smaller, much smaller areas that were. Yes, indeed.
And I discovered that if I conduct myself with some
circumspection, I find that I can live within these
smaller, perhaps very confined territories without
exposure to too much hurt. Indeed I find that I can
experience some happiness and perhaps give a
measure of happiness, too. My great discovery.

His love and concern for Helga and the boys in Hamburg
is genuinely moving. His ability to recognize and accept
failure gives him some kind of hope. Unlike Frank in
Living Quarters he does not complain about his fate. He
converts it and uses it in his life. His self-knowledge has
meant the possibility of a new departure. Hand in hand
with Friel's added historical perspective through the
seventies goes a tougher attitude to the force of Fate.
With the obvious exception of *Living Quarters* Friel's
recent plays suggest that history is made, that there are
reasons for the decline of Ballybeg Hall from which
lessons can be drawn. There is a harder edge to his
characters' perception of themselves and their reality.
Perhaps the quotation from Sartre that Friel put into his
'Sporadic Diary' during the making of *Aristocrats* is
indicative of this trend: 'You have chosen to be what you
are.' Such a dictum would demand greater responsibility
for one's actions and increase one's ability to influence
one's life.

The plastic banana and the sausage factory function
as insignia of the crass commercialism of the modern
society that the O'Donnells have already begun to get
used to. But before they are ready to leave they pay
their last respects to a way of life they once enjoyed and
which is now about to disappear forever. In a prolonged

scene of leave-taking they steel themselves for the final goodbye.

Behind the brief mention of the border between North and South in *Aristocrats* is hidden a deep and disturbing sense of the destructive influences of its existence. The difference in attitudes between the two generations of O'Donnells towards the troubles in the North accelerates the dissolution of the family. Eamon, married to one of the O'Donnell daughters, is a successful diplomat in Dublin who, when sent to Belfast as an observer, joins the civil rights movement and consequently loses his job. Judith goes to Derry to take part in the battle of the Bogside, thus causing her father the District Justice to have his first stroke. To him Judith's behaviour was an 'enormous betrayal'. In his haughty and removed position he illustrates the political and social isolation of the Catholic Big House, both from the lower-class Catholics and from its Protestant social equivalent.

TOM: What was your father's attitude?
ALICE: To Eamon?
TOM: To the civil rights campaign.
ALICE: He opposed it. No, that's not accurate. He was
     indifferent: that was across the Border – away in
     the North.
TOM: Only twenty miles away.
ALICE: Politics never interested him. Politics are vulgar.

Friel himself is no overtly political writer. Yet he is aware of the political conditions that determine much of life in Ireland. In planning and writing *Aristocrats,* as is revealed in his 'Sporadic Diary', he frequently returns to the subject and then immediately rejects its more outspoken manifestations. 'The play that is visiting me brings with it each time an odour of musk – incipient decay, an era wilted, people confused and nervous. If there are politics they are underground . . . the intrusion of active politics is foreign to the hopes and sensibilities of the people who populate this play.'

[167]

And yet, what Judith and Eamon did must be described as 'active politics'. The young generation has been prodded into action by events in Derry. The real betrayal may be found in the indifference of the District Justice. His failure to sympathize with the cause of his fellow Catholics in the North may be intended by the author to take a wider application. It certainly illustrates the confusion that was a permanent condition of *Volunteers*.

Attention is also paid to other historical and political dimensions. As in *Volunteers* certain Irish weaknesses are laid bare. There may be in the Irish Catholic countryman a willingness to accept a passive suffering that would tend to acknowledge and even thrive under strong authority. Perhaps, in *Aristocrats*, Eamon refers to a more political aspect of the same attitude. Initially, he refuses to accept Judith's decision to abandon Ballybeg Hall: 'The moment you've left the thugs from the village will move in and loot and ravage the place within a couple of hours.' Eamon, we must remember, is a simple boy from the village, but he has always admired what Ballybeg stood for. Friel is frequently content to suggest in some little detail or in a brief phrase what may in fact merit considerable attention. One such word, for instance, is 'colonizing' in the following context.

EAMON: Judith's like her American friend: the Hall can be
      assessed in terms of roofs and floors and overdrafts.
ALICE: Eamon –
EAMON: No, no; that's all it means to her. Well I know its
      real worth – in this area, in this county, in this
      country. And Alice knows. And Casimir knows.
      And Claire knows. And somehow we'll keep it
      going. Somehow we'll keep it going. Somehow
      we'll –
ALICE: Please, Eamon.
      (*Judith breaks down. Pause.*)

EAMON: Sorry . . . sorry . . . sorry again . . . Seems to be a
day of public contrition. What the hell is it but
crumbling masonry. Sorry. (*Short laugh*.) Don't
you know that all that is fawning and forelock-
touching and Paddy and shabby and greasy
peasant in the Irish character finds a house like
this irresistible? That's why we were ideal for colonizing. Something in us needs this . . . aspiration.
Don't despise us – we're only hedgehogs, Judith.
Sorry.

In this sense Eamon becomes the catalyst of *Aristocrats*. He can see first-hand the decline and downfall of
the Hall. When he told his grandmother that he was
marrying one of the O'Donnell sisters she refused to
believe it: ' "Alice? Who's Alice? Alice Devenny? Alice
Byrne? Not Alice Smith!" "Alice O'Donnell." "What
Alice O'Donnell's that?" "Alice O'Donnell of the Hall."
A long silence. Then: "May God and his holy mother
forgive you, you dirty-mouthed upstart!" (*Laughs*.)
Wasn't that an interesting response?'

The familiar format of a reunion is always a dramatic
method with possibilities, and Friel is constantly interested in differences between those who go away and
those who stay in a place. The play is meditative and
slow-moving, and the mood of Chekhovian leave-taking serves well to signal the disintegration of the
O'Donnells as a historical and social class.

Familiar themes return, but in an adjusted scale of
priority. Like *Living Quarters, Aristocrats* has the
family at its centre, but the later play differs in that it
inevitably becomes concerned with wider and more
public issues. Parental authority is seen as a negative
influence; and through the baby alarm, in which the
father's authority is artificially kept up, Casimir is
twice reminded of the old man's sternness. Willie's
implicit denunciation of the difficult father–son relationship echoes Madge's in *Philadelphia, Here I Come!*:

ALICE: . . . He didn't know me. He didn't know you either, Casimir, did he?

CASIMIR: No.

ALICE: He didn't know me either. It was so strange – your own father not knowing you. He didn't know you either, Casimir, did he?

CASIMIR: No.

ALICE: His own flesh and blood. Did he know you, Willie.

WILLIE: Well, you see like, Alice, I'm not his son.

ALICE: That's true . . .

The influence of time passing is strongly felt, and the empty Ballybeg Hall stands as a totem to the changing times. The individual, as before, struggles against various authority structures, although one of them, a strict feudal system, is now in its final stage of dissolution. O'Donnellstown has lost not only its name but all historical significance.

The general theme of linguistic communication is present in the play. A rich tapestry of voices is balanced by Uncle George's silence. He is the brother of District Justice O'Donnell and in his youth he was a very heavy drinker until, suddenly, he gave up drinking and, at the same time, stopped speaking. 'They say about here that when he wasn't going to be asking for drink, he thought it wasn't worth saying anything. But brains – d'you see Mister George? – the smartest of the whole connection, they say.' There is no mistaking the humorous intent of these lines. But, at the same time, they may contain wider meanings. Uncle George refuses to subscribe to the rich talk of the various voices in the play. He says nothing at all until near the end of the play, when he curtly accepts to go to live in London with one of his nieces and her husband.

There is also an interesting parallel discussion on the nature of private and historical myths. In 'Foundry House', where the emphasis is on the individual, Joe Brennan's private myth lingers even after the historical myth is gone. *Aristocrats,* on the other hand, considers social and political forces which expose the private myth of Eamon. Joe Brennan had to stay in the gate lodge whereas Eamon can enter the Hall and become a witness. But has Eamon freed himself of his nostalgic vision of the past? Does his dismissal of the Hall as nothing but 'crumbling masonry' sound convincing? Other characters in Friel's plays and stories have tried but failed to control the power of place and past. Friel also suggests that private myths can be turned into the larger and more reverberating myths of Irish history. An American academic, Tom Hoffnung, has come to Ballybeg Hall to chronicle the decline of the Catholic Big House. Soon, however, his conception of history meets with unforeseen problems. Casimir remembers a visit to the house by Yeats, which, Tom realizes, cannot have happened since Yeats died before Casimir was born. This simple fact suggests that at least some of the other celebrities who are supposed to have been there were equally imaginary. 'God help the poor man if he thinks he's heard one word of truth since he came here,' says one of the daughters, Alice. The sort of historical truth that Tom is after is difficult to attain. Perhaps, in *Aristocrats,* it is left to Eamon, the simple village boy who married into the Big House, to express this difficulty: 'There are certain things, certain truths, Casimir, that are beyond Tom's kind of scrutiny.' Yet Friel's latter-day 'illusionists' have found it increasingly difficult to draw sustenance from the past. In *Aristocrats* Casimir's compulsive lying is balanced by an awareness of his own limitations and his own reality, and there is a sense of historical inevitability about Eamon's slight regrets at the final phase of Ballybeg Hall.

Aristocrats was Friel's latest play to be premièred by the Abbey Theatre. As it opened in March 1979 another of his plays, *Faith Healer,* was in the middle of a pre-Broadway run in Boston.

The Artist's Strange Gift: *Faith Healer* (1979)

Friel finished *Faith Healer* in the autumn of 1977. It was obvious, however, that there would be considerable difficulty in mounting a production. Apart from the casting of three extremely demanding parts, the format created some problems. *Faith Healer* consists of four consecutive and very long monologues, spoken directly to the audience by the three actors. But Friel, who was by now used to pursuing his own idea of theatre, won through. *Faith Healer* now stands as a monument to his own dramatic kind. It is a play where form is perfectly wedded to content, held together by a strong vision of thematic unity.

The play's failure in the commercialized theatre of Broadway was completely predictable, and its indifferent reception in London was not unexpected (the Royal Court production was beset by various practical problems). The triumphant success of the Abbey Theatre production in August 1980, however, can have been no surprise. *Faith Healer* demands, to an unusual extent, the idea of a shared experience between stage and audience, of collaboration between the two. Perhaps that collaboration, in this play, comes more easily from an Irish audience.

Faith Healer could be said to be Friel's both most Irish and most remarkable dramatic presentation. In the background there is, of course, the Irish story-teller, the *seanachie,* an old tradition still practised in Ireland today. In his daring fusion of this tradition with that of the stage Friel has found as perfect a vehicle for his attempted thematic exploration as was the *alter ego* of *Philadelphia, Here I Come!.* As Manus in *The Gentle Island* told us, 'there's ways and ways of telling a story,' and in *Faith Healer* each of the three characters gives his or her own version of what is essentially the same story. Their different renderings establish the individual nature of truth and the way the emotions of the occasion exercise their influence. We must accept the agreement between Grace and Teddy that there was a stillborn baby in the village of Kinlochbervie but whether the weather was 'beautiful' as Teddy remembers it or, according to Grace, there was a 'heavy wet mist', whether Frank put up the little wooden cross (in Grace's version) or it was (according to himself) Teddy who did it, we have no certain knowledge. Both Grace and Teddy would have had reason to manipulate reality in their own favour. That Frank did we can be almost certain of; it was, in a sense, his calling or chosen profession. But that, he would say, is 'another story'. What makes *Faith Healer* so intriguing is that the three characters, in adhering to a story-telling tradition and its form, make their own lives their subject matter. Traditionally, the impression has been that in Ireland the distinction between fact and fiction has always been blurred, a circumstance which has been well used in Irish literature. From Matthew Arnold's famous phrase that the Celts are 'always ready to rebel against the despotism of fact' to the warning issued about the nature of the Irish fact in Hugh Kenner's *A Colder Eye,* both creative and critical energy has been spent to define it. An outsider, an Englishman like Leigh Kelway in Somerville and Ross's story 'Lisheen Races, Second Hand' for instance, sometimes finds it difficult to adjust to it. In *Faith Healer* Friel compassionately explores the individuals behind the versions they attempt to put across to the audience. As Friel has suggested elsewhere, each individual tells the truth as he sees it. They all, for various reasons, push aside certain aspects of reality and replace them with others. In doing this they resemble somewhat the 'illusionists' of Friel's earlier work. Teddy, in spite of his avowed intention to live in the present, is romantically and nostalgically attached to his past with Frank and Grace; for him that past may offer some solace. For the other two it clearly does not. The always available life-lie is rejected in an attempt to escape the agony of living.

In Frank's two monologues in *Faith Healer* there is a relentless and increasing emphasis on a journey towards self-destruction. The parallel between faith healer and creative artist has been well established and, although the analogy may be more general, it would seem that it is the Irish artist in particular that is intended. Not until the very end of the play, faced with the certainty of a violent death, does Frank have 'a simple and genuine sense of home-coming'. He is, of course, in Ballybeg, where his Irish welcome ends a precarious existence spent travelling the Celtic fringes of Britain with his erratic gift. From the beginning of Frank's first monologue there is an important contrast between 'the Celtic temperament' of Frank on the one hand and the Englishness of Grace and Teddy on the other. It was they who believed that 'the Celtic temperament was more receptive to us', and since Frank refused to work in Ireland that left them with Wales and Scotland. Frank, then, becomes the exiled Irish artist who, when he loses touch with his gift, returns home in search of restoration. What he finds, however, is only an occasion for self-sacrifice. But there are complications about Grace's Englishness. Frank's version of it is confident and assured and establishes certain contrasts.

And there was Grace, my mistress. A Yorkshire woman. Controlled, correct, methodical, orderly. Who fed me, washed me and ironed for me, nursed me, humoured me. Saved me, I'm sure, from drinking myself to death. Would have attempted to reform me because that was her nature, but didn't because her instincts were wiser than her impulses. Grace Dodsmith from Scarborough – or was it Knaresborough? I don't remember, they all sound so alike, it doesn't matter. She never asked for marriage and for all her tidiness I don't think she wanted marriage – her loyalty was adequate for her. And it was never a heady relationship, not even in the early days. But it lasted. A surviving relationship. And yet as we grew older together

I thought it wouldn't. Because that virtue of hers – that mulish, unquestioning, indefatigable loyalty – settled on us like a heavy dust. And nothing I did, neither my bitterness nor my deliberate neglect nor my blatant unfaithfulness, could disturb it.

But when Grace goes home she does not go to Scarborough or Knaresborough. Instead she 'got the night-crossing from Glasgow and then the bus to Omagh and walked the three miles out to Knockmoyle'. Grace, then, is from the North of Ireland; that is the conclusion we must draw. We must believe her rather than him; we know that he is a liar and she would have no reason to lie about it. And, as if to remove all doubt, Teddy's description of the night they returned to Ballybeg and Ireland clinches the argument. He has witnessed years of their uneasy union. On their return to Ballybeg things seem different.

You see that night in that pub in Ballybeg? You know how I spent that night? I spent the whole of that night just watching them. Mr and Mrs Frank Hardy. Side by side. Together in Ireland. At home in Ireland. Easy; relaxed; chatting; laughing. And it was like as if I was seeing them for the first time in years and years – no! not seeing them but *remembering them*. Funny thing that, wasn't it?

This, Teddy realizes, is what they could be all the time, united and together in Ireland. But what began as a happy night ends early the following morning with Frank's violent death at the hands of some local farmers. In the build-up to the final conflict Frank's and Grace's stories do not agree and here, unfortunately, we do not have Teddy's account to compare them with. Did Frank, as Grace suggests, issue a challenge to the young farmer with the twisted finger or was he, as Frank's version goes, threatened by him? After having successfully and miraculously straightened Donal's finger Frank over-reaches himself in trying to heal the lame McGarvey. McGarvey, as everyone knows, is an impossible case.

And in knowing that he is undertaking the impossible Frank turns himself into a victim and a sacrifice. Although he may be 'the victim of an uncomprehending society, an Irish society', he achieves in his sacrifice the certainty he had been searching for all his life.[1] For years he had carried a newspaper clipping in his pocket, a report of his feat of healing ten people in a small village in Wales that he said 'identified me – even though it got my name wrong'. Now, in Ballybeg, he throws it away because he has found his final identity.

> And as I moved across that yard towards them and offered myself to them, then for the first time I had a simple and genuine sense of home-coming. Then for the first time there was no atrophying terror; and the maddening questions were silent. At long last I was renouncing chance.

The gift that he undoubtedly possessed or that possessed him is more an enemy than a friend; in that sense he is its victim since he can never himself control it. What Friel wrote in his 'Sporadic Diary' in preparing for *Aristocrats* seems eminently applicable to *Faith Healer* and Frank Hardy in his role as faith healer/artist.

> November 11. On a day (days? weeks! months!) like this when I come upstairs at a fixed time and sit at this desk for a certain number of hours, without a hope of writing a line, without a creative thought in my head, I tell myself that what I am doing is making myself obediently available – patient, deferential, humble. A conceit? Whether or not, it's all I can do.

From an early age Frank had been impatient with the capriciousness of his gift. 'Was it all chance? – or skill? – or illusion? or delusion? Precisely what power did I possess? Could I summon it? When and how? Was I its servant?' There is no simple answer to these 'maddening questions'. Perhaps Frank's creative work was best described by Grace. In the following passage the link

between faith-healing and creative writing becomes
obvious:

> It was some compulsion he had to adjust, to refashion, to
> re-create everything around him. Even the people who
> came to him – they weren't just sick people who were
> confused and frightened and wanted to be cured; no, no; to
> him they were . . . yes, they were real enough, but not real
> as persons, real as fictions, his fictions, extensions of
> himself that came into being only because of him. And if
> he cured a man that man became for him a successful
> fiction and therefore actually real, and he'd say to me
> afterwards, 'Quite an interesting character that, wasn't
> he? I knew that would work.' But if he didn't cure him the
> man was forgotten immediately, allowed to dissolve and
> vanish as if he had never existed.

In pursuing rather ruthlessly his elusive talent he not
only burns himself out, he destroys the people around
him. There is a shift in his relationship with normal
everyday reality which he allows himself to refashion
according to his own needs and he becomes, in the eyes of
other people, a liar. As his powers continue to weaken
his return to Ireland becomes a last desperate attempt to
come to terms with them. But once again they let him
down and, genuinely exhausted with his failure, he finds
ultimate relief in a defiant act of self-destruction. In
spite of the general references to the role of the artist,
Faith Healer could only be an Irish play and Frank
Hardy could only be an Irish faith healer. Frank's
memories of his childhood may 'evoke nothing' to him,
but they suggest an atmosphere of constrained conformity. 'One of my father watching me through the bars of
the day-room window as I left for school . . . One of
playing with handcuffs, slipping my hand in and out
through the rings. One of my mother making bread and
singing a hymn to herself: "Yes, heaven, yes, heaven,
yes heaven is the prize." And one of a group of men being
shown over the barracks – I think they were inspectors

[177]

from Dublin – and my father saying, "Certainly, gentlemen, by all means, gentlemen, anything you say, gentlemen."' If, as Grace suggests later, Frank's father was *not* a guard, these images would be all the more remarkable. They are strengthened when he remembers the shame he felt because Doyle might have seen his father's rotten teeth. His own future 'career' as a faith healer would have been all the more unconventional against this strict background. In that sense the same society could be seen as having demanded a sacrifice for his efforts to liberate himself from it. There is an inevitability about his return to Ireland. He went back, he says, 'because I always knew we would end up there'. *Faith Healer*, too, though not with the same intensity as *Volunteers* for example, and in a more convoluted form, may form a part of Friel's continuing observation of the influence of an Irish habitat on his characters. Its dramatic method, certainly, is intrinsically Irish. It expresses one particular aspect of an Irish national identity that Friel is intent on pursuing. Friel's answer to the interviewer's question below makes his reasons determined and clear: 'Somebody said he was sick of the term national identity, and what the hell does it mean? "It means something very important, because it's your national ID in some way, isn't it?"' (*Irish Times*, 14 September 1982).

Questions of identity and myth, both private and national, are of a less immediately political complexion in *Faith Healer*. Yet Friel's treatment of the themes of exile, home and home-coming, suggestions of a difference in temperament between the Celtic fringes and the rest of the British Isles, even a detail like a North of Ireland judge whose obsession with ordered formality probably drove his wife (Grace's mother) mad, all become features of a political condition that stipulate certain responses. Grace, a lapsed solicitor, has to surrender to the tumult inside her; she goes mad. Life contains none of the certainties she was searching for.

She, too, becomes one of Frank's fictions, and in his refusal to name or identify her with precision (was she his wife or mistress?; was her name Dodsmith, Elliot, O'Connell, McPherson or McClure?; did she come from Yorkshire, Kerry, London, Scarborough or Belfast?), Frank, the artist, keeps remaking and refashioning his own world. At the very end of the play he and his imminent attackers lose their material existence and join his other fictions. The faith healer/creative artist has successfully plotted his own death. At that moment his gift of creative power reaches its zenith.

In spite of its Irishness, *Faith Healer* makes larger claims. The parable of the creative artist has universal applications. It is validated by Friel's sustained excellence of thematic language. The play modulates between the lyrical, the comic and the tragic. In Teddy's monologue, probably Friel's most consistently comic creation, he shifts, within a matter of minutes, from the hilarity of the description of Rob Roy's failure as a stud dog to the excruciating account of the stillborn baby in Kinlochbervie. These and other scenes contain emotions that can be recognized anywhere. Teddy knows this, and when, one night in Llanbethian in Wales, the faith healer/creative artist touches the lives of several people with his gift, the Welsh village comes to stand for the whole world.

Grace's suppressed impulse to attack her father's authority and the young Frank's apprehensions about his father's respectability contain echoes of permanent Frielian themes. The format of *Faith Healer* is in itself an expression of the theme of communication. None of the three characters communicates directly with the others. Instead we have four extended monologues following each other, presenting and revealing the relationship between the characters from three different points of view. The accounts of Frank, Grace and Teddy all differ in essential respects when dealing with private and emotional events and circumstances. Only

[179]

when some important factual event is recorded, like the trip from Scotland to Ballybeg, do their versions agree, and then, remarkably, this agreement is expressed almost verbatim. 'So on the last day of August we crossed from Stranraer to Larne and drove through the night to County Donegal. And there we got lodgings in a pub, a lounge bar, really, outside a village called Ballybeg, not far from Donegal Town.' These phrases reverberate through the play and have an almost mesmerising effect. *Faith Healer* illustrates the essentially private nature of truth. Each of the three has his or her own perception of reality. It is fashioned not out of real facts but from emotional considerations of events. For each of them, the past supplies the material for the making of a personal myth which, though partly shared by others, remains private and unique. To the characters in *Faith Healer*, and to Gar and his father in *Philadelphia, Here I Come!*, the reading of past events will yield different interpretations.

The Problem of Form: *American Welcome* (1980)

A brief playlet, *American Welcome*, which Friel wrote for the Actors' Theatre in Louisville Kentucky, may in some ways be a by-product of the three major plays, *Faith Healer, Translations* and *Three Sisters*, that he was involved with at that time. His interest in language and communication is clearly shown in *American Welcome* as is his attitude to a particular brand of American showbiz. The play exhibits another familiar Frielian contrast, that between Europe (Ireland) and America. It concerns a European playwright who arrives in America for the production of one of his plays. He is met by a young American director who, with effusive enthusiasm, shows his great admiration for the play and the playwright. Gradually, however, he reveals that, owing to certain 'problems' with the script, he has asked an American playwright to rewrite it into 'a four-character, two-act, single-set comedy that is just breathtaking'. If we examine the nature of the changes made in the European's original script their relevance for Friel becomes obvious. First problem, the American says, is language:

> Frankly we're uneasy with the language. I mean to say we're not uneasy with the language – it's just that there's a lot of it we don't understand. Simply a question of usage; or to be more accurate, simply a question of our ignorance of your usage. I've made a list here – words like 'boot', 'bumper', 'chemist' – there are maybe a dozen of them. Frankly we don't know what you mean. And since you want to communicate with American audiences and since we want them to understand you, I mean to say what we did was this. We went to our most distinguished American playwright – and you've got to meet him while you're here; he just adores your work – and what he did for us was this. He took all those little confusing words – five or six thousand approximately – and with wonderful delicacy and skill and with the utmost respect for the rhythms of the tones of your speech, he did this most beautiful job of translating the play into the language we speak and understand. I hope you'll approve. I know you'll approve.

The satirical edge becomes even clearer when we look at the second major change made by the Americans. The European's script (like Friel's *Faith Healer*) was in 'monologue form'. But according to the director, this form is not natural to Americans – 'we talk, we exchange, we communicate' – and the distinguished American playwright is put to work again. The great irony of the piece is, of course, that it is the American who speaks all the time; the European cannot get a word in edgewise. It would obviously be wrong to take this short playlet (it cannot last more than five or six minutes) too seriously. But in its concern with the concepts of communication, translation and theatrical form it is a humorous and satirical expression of ideas dealt with in a more serious manner in other plays from the same period.

Our Own Language: *Translations* (1980) and a translation of Chekhov's *Three Sisters* (1981)

In the seventies, as his stature as a dramatist grew, Friel gained a reputation for being decidedly reluctant to give media interviews. He was known as a gentle and private man who preferred to keep out of the limelight. With the advent of Field Day in 1980 and as a founder director of the company it became necessary for him to accept a more public role and to involve himself in 'theatre business'. Before and after the company's first production of his own *Translations* in Derry Friel granted several interviews to the press. One important interview appeared in *Magill* in December 1980. Here, apart from giving his own commentary on the play, Friel reveals his concern about the role of the English language in Ireland, a subject very much at the heart of *Translations*. But his interest in the subject had begun earlier and had received its first expression in the work he did on his own translation of Chekhov's *Three Sisters* which, he has said, 'somehow overlapped into the working of the text of *Translations*' (*Magill*). Friel feels that the English that is spoken in Ireland is and should be distinct from that spoken in England. I very much doubt that he would accept Micheál MacLiammóir's argument in *Theatre in Ireland*:

> For Ireland, if the older language dies, must in honesty accept a subsidiary relationship with England, from whose utterance her own will differ as vaguely in outline to the world beyond the sphere of English literature and drama as the literature and drama, say, of Bavaria differs vaguely in outline from that of Prussia, or the Andalusian from that of Castille, or the Cornish or Northumbrian from that of the rest of England. And this acceptance may not be as crushing a defeat as stubborn and insatiable

minds imagine. To me the image of Ireland without Irish is an insufferable one, but if this is to be it would be well to accept it without the futile added quibble that, by the mere fact of a different racial origin, of a few distinctive habits of expression, of a diverting dialectical form of English that becomes daily more and more akin to the English of journalism and of radio, less and less akin to the speech of Synge and O'Casey, the illusion can be kept up that England has not won the day in language and in literature, and that Irish literature in English, at its most assertively distinctive, is but the continuation of a contribution to England's literature.

Instead Friel insists on certain fundamental linguistic differences between the two languages. His urge to create an Irish version of Chekhov stems from this awareness:

I think that the versions of *Three Sisters* that we see and read in this country always seem to be redolent of either Edwardian England or the Bloomsbury set. Somehow the rhythms of these versions do not match with the rhythms of our own speech patterns, and I think that they ought to, in some way. Even the most recent English translation again carries, of necessity, very strong English cadences and rhythms. This is something about which I feel strongly – in some way we are constantly overshadowed by the sound of English language, as well as by the printed word. Maybe this does not inhibit us, but it forms us and shapes us in a way that is neither healthy nor valuable for us . . . (*Magill*)

Therefore, Friel says, 'we must make English identifiably our own language'. As an expression of a nation's identity this would be necessary for a concept of unity to develop. And the two languages are obviously different; an Irish voice is immediately recognized in England in the same way that an English voice reveals its provenance if used in Ireland.

Turning to theatre, Friel suggests that previous Irish dramatists (Synge excluded)

> have pitched their voice for English acceptance and recognition. This applied particularly to someone like Behan. However, I think that for the first time this is stopping, that there is some kind of confidence, some kind of coming together of Irish dramatists who are not concerned with this, who have no interest in the English stage. We are talking to ourselves as we must and if we are overheard in America, or England, so much the better. (*Magill*)

These considerations of language and the theory of language were directly expressed in the practical translation of *Three Sisters* into a new kind of English. This is not, in the conventional sense of the word, a 'translation' of Chekhov's play; Friel worked instead with five different standard English translations, fusing them all into a language that can live in Ireland. *Three Sisters* is also a physical manifestation of Friel's interest in linguistic communication and the nature of language as expressing a racial and cultural consciousness.

Friel has described his translation of *Three Sisters* as 'an act of love'. I have already underlined his great admiration for Chekhov's plays and his strong feelings for a need to make them more accessible to Irish audiences. He may in fact have started a tendency for new approaches to other translations of not only the classics but any play that comes to Ireland via the English language. He has, in any case, questioned the normal procedure whereby a good English translation could be seen as automatically acceptable. The nature of Friel's particular contribution can be seen if we compare any few lines with a traditional English translation. In the following passage Friel not only makes the language colloquially Irish, he also stresses a certain trait in Natasha's character. Here is Elisaveta Fen's Penguin Classics translation:

NATASHA: They've gone in to lunch already . . . I'm late . . .
(*Glances at herself in a mirror, adjusts her dress.*)
My hair seems to be all right . . . (*Catches sight of
Irena.*) My dear Irena Serghyeevna, congratu-
lations! (*Gives her a vigorous and prolonged kiss.*)
You've got such a lot of visitors . . . I feel quite
shy . . . How do you do, Baron?

This is what Friel had done with the passage:

NATASHA: Sweet mother of God, I'm late – they're at the
dinner already! (*Quick look in the mirror. She
adjusts her hair.*) It'll have to do now. (*She sees Irina
and goes to her. Her accent becomes slightly posh.*)
Irina darling, many many happy returns. (*She gives
Irina a vigorous and prolonged kiss.*) And look at the
crowd of guests! Goodness gracious I could never
face in there! Baron, how d'you do.

Friel changes, adds to and extends but cuts little of
previous translations. His wish to particularize and
localize is obvious in certain phrases. The critical
reception on the whole favoured this, except for one or
two voices which questioned the need for the whole
venture: 'Chekhov needs no special papers to take up
Irish residence. He can be at home there in a standard
translation . . .' (*The Times*, 5 October 1981) and '*Three
Sisters* is a universal and timeless play of imperishable
beauty, and it needs no colloquialised slant to enhance
its level of acceptability.' (*Irish Independent,* 10 September 1981). It is, of course, understandable that English
or anglicized city critics may have been disturbed by
Chebutykin's 'Who gives a tinker's damn?' or similar
expressions. Perhaps, however, audiences in places like
Maghera, Galway or Tralee (where, among other places,
the play toured) were made to feel more at home in the
action by the inclusion of localized detail. Similarly, it
would be for their benefit that Friel helpfully translates
Kulygin's Latin. His strong and earthy Masha, earthier
and stronger than in a standard English translation,

would inhabit more easily a town like Limerick or the old garrison town of Derry, where her small-town frustration would perhaps be real. Friel's translation of Chekhov is part of his intention of making English 'identifiably our own language'. If the Irish have not yet found their own voice, perhaps this can be done in the arts: 'Perhaps this is an artist's arrogance, but I feel than once the voice is found in literature, then it can move out and become part of the common currency' (*Magill*).

The English language is only one aspect of the complicated relationship between England and Ireland. In wider terms it has also been the vehicle through which cultural influences have penetrated Ireland. Because of the English language these cultural realities have frequently been of English provenance, reflecting the consciousness of a different race. In Friel's plays there are several references to the inheritances of an English educational system which may, for Friel with his Northern background, be particularly strong. But it is, still, the English language that carries these influences. In *Volunteers* Keats is quoted, in *The Freedom of the City* Kipling is referred to and in *Lovers* Gray's 'Elegy' has supplanted Noyes's 'Highwayman' from the story that made 'Losers'; more examples could be mentioned. In *Translations,* however, Friel got his own back. Hugh, the hedge school master, dismisses the whole English literary tradition in his supremely arrogant manner in this exchange with the young English soldier. Hugh has just declaimed a few lines from one of his own poems.

YOLLAND: Some years ago we lived fairly close to a poet – well, about three miles away.
HUGH: His name?
YOLLAND: Wordsworth – William Wordsworth.
HUGH: Did he speak of me to you?

YOLLAND: Actually I never talked to him. I just saw him out walking – in the distance.

HUGH: Wordsworth? . . . no. I'm afraid we're not familiar with your literature, Lieutenant. We feel closer to the warm Mediterranean. We tend to overlook your island.

Today we laugh at Hugh's pomposity. But we must also be prepared to go beyond this and realize the momentous historical relevance of his remarks. Such is the immense richness of *Translations* that it signals, in these few lines, the beginning of the rape of a country's linguistic and cultural heritage. Generations after Hugh would be well aware of the existence of the poet Wordsworth. In the making of the first Ordnance Survey map of Ireland and the resultant translation of Irish place-names into English Friel found a perfect metaphor for one important aspect of the historical relationship between England and Ireland.

As we have seen, the contrasts between East and West have been variously expressed in Friel's stories and in a play like *The Gentle Island*. *Translations* in a sense represents the culmination of this process. Perhaps, by applying the historical perspective, Friel was able to say more about today's Ireland than any play about the contemporary situation can do. The confusion of the language problem is only one aspect of the identity crisis we are still witnessing today. It has been Friel's particular contribution since the mid seventies to pursue with great clarity and increasing penetration some kind of definition of the Irish psyche. In order to achieve this the contemporary situation has to be filtered through the events of past history. The past must be understood and interpreted, its meaning for today made clear.

Most of the plays that he has written since the mid seventies, the application of a historical dimension, the creation of Field Day and the adoption of a more public role in his work for the company have all contributed in shaping an important development in Friel's work. There have been subtle shifts in time and point of view, achieving a balance between history and the contemporary situation, with both perspectives enlightening each other. Their expression has become less private and personal, and more public and 'national'.

Perhaps the theme of communication receives its finest and most ironic expression in the love scene between Yolland and Maire. Earlier, with Owen as translator, they had failed to reach contact. The friction between their two languages was too great. Alone, their growing love for each other becomes more eloquent than any language. As always in Friel, however, irony has a way of reviving the old differences. Yolland wants to stay with Maire in Ballybeg; she wants to leave. When she uses the word 'always', which he had just used to express his love for her, Yolland does not understand:

> YOLLAND: I've made up my mind . . .
> MAIRE: Shhhh.
> YOLLAND: I'm not going to leave here . . .
> MAIRE: Shhh – listen to me. I want you, too, soldier.
> YOLLAND: Don't stop – I know what you're saying.
> MAIRE: I want to live with you – anywhere – anywhere at all – always – always.
> YOLLAND: 'Always'? What is that word – 'always'?
> MAIRE: Take me away with you, George.

But Friel does not allow the certainty of 'always', and this scene propels *Translations* into decisive actions. The understanding generated and established by love between two individuals ironically ruptures any hope of communication in the larger context between the two nations and languages. Communication, as Tim in *The Communication Cord* would say, 'collapses' since there is no 'shared context' and no 'agreed code'. The disagreement on the national and political level was to have serious repercussions.

We have already seen several examples of Friel's increasing interest in the role of language as a medium of communication. The literary aspect of this is obvious in his translation of Chekhov's *Three Sisters*. ' "Uncertainty in meaning is incipient poetry" – who said that?' asks Owen, the translator in *Translations*, defending his inaccurate translation of His Majesty's English. The direct answer is George Steiner. When working on Chekhov's play Friel came to read Steiner's influential *After Babel,* whose subtitle *Aspects of Language and Translation* reveals the relevance for what he was doing at the time. In *Translations* he made telling use of Steiner's book in his treatment of the confrontation of English with Irish. In particular, it was in his apparent belief in the relationship between language and mind that Friel was able to magnify and transcend a simplified and dogmatic interpretation of the historical confrontation between English and Irish. In this context Friel's investigation of how mental qualities may be reflected in a language is expressed with both humorous and more serious intent. In Hugh's deliberate pomposity English possesses certain distinguishable characteristics. After his first encounter with Captain Lancey Hugh is surprised to find that the English officer does not, unlike himself and other members of the hedge school community, speak Greek or Latin. 'He speaks – on his own admission – only English.' This, however, does not stop Lancey from somehow expecting the people in Ballybeg to speak English. 'Indeed – he voiced some surprise that we did not speak his language. I explained that a few of us did, on occasion – outside the parish of course – and then usually for the purposes of commerce, a use to which his tongue seemed particularly suited . . . and I went on to propose that our own culture and the classical tongues made a happier conjugation.' English, Hugh suggests, 'couldn't really express us', and his own translation of his poem in Latin is not successful. 'English succeeds in making it sound . . . plebeian.' Any translation in *Translations*, in fact, is a complex, and difficult venture. Owen's job proves in the end impossible for him, and the confusion between Yolland and Maire over the word 'always' suggests the final failure of translation. Captain Lancey's quotation from the official white paper is only approximately rendered in Irish by Owen. The acute irony of the final sentence is lost in Owen's translation.

> LANCEY: 'Ireland is privileged. No such survey is being
> undertaken in England. So this survey cannot but
> be received as proof of the disposition of this
> government to advance the interests of Ireland.' My
> sentiments, too.
> OWEN: This survey demonstrates the government's
> interest in Ireland and the captain thanks you for
> listening so attentively to him.

Owen's brother, Manus, however, sees the more serious side of the events: 'it's a bloody military operation.' In the early stages of this operation Owen acts as an innocent do-gooder. He sees his function in translating the Irish place-names as a useful one and does not object to the English calling him Roland. There is a mild controversy between him and Yolland, who feels that what is happening is 'an eviction of sorts', that 'something is being eroded'. Moreover, Yolland wants to learn Irish but is sensitive enough to suspect that this would not be enough: 'even if I did speak Irish I'd always be an outsider here, wouldn't I? I may learn the password but the language of the tribe will always elude me, won't it? The private core will always be ... hermetic, won't it?' At this stage Owen, unaware of the deeper, more symbolic and mythic properties of language, can still suggest: 'you can learn to decode us.' Their disagreement over a possible translation of Tobair Vree illustrates the difference between them. Owen is ready to jettison generations of local connotations and accept a 'standardized' version. Yolland, on the other hand, insists that the name should remain untranslated. In the end Owen realizes his mistake. He had seen that his task was impossible. There is a suggestion that he is now prepared to take a more active part in the proceedings. From being a go-between and interpreter, mediating so to speak between two causes, he is forced to take sides to defend his own identity.

In the exchanges between Owen and Yolland can be found some of the play's key passages. But the theme of language and translation is all-pervasive. At one extreme, perhaps, is Jimmy Jack's easy familiarity with Homer and Virgil. He translates comfortably from the Greek of the *Odyssey* into his own language. But to Jimmy, Athene and Ulysses are more than literary creations or gods. He treats them, Yolland suggests, 'as if they lived down the road', always, like Jimmy Farrell's skulls in *The Playboy,* transferring them back to his own known habitat:

> JIMMY: '*Knuzosen de oi osse* – ' 'She dimmed his two eyes that were so beautiful and clothed him in a vile ragged cloak begrimed with filthy smoke . . .'! D'you see! Smoke! Smoke! D'you see! Sure look at what the same turf-smoke has done to myself! (*He rapidly removes his hat to display his bald head.*) Would you call that flaxen hair?

In the background, while Jimmy is translating his Homer, Sarah is struggling with a different kind of proficiency; Manus is teaching her to speak. The simple speech act in itself, coming as it does at the beginning of the play, is a first condition of communication and translation. Later in the play, as Sarah is beginning to learn, she is silenced by Captain Lancey. Thus, she is not even allowed to express her own identity by saying her own name. In his review of the play in *The Times Literary Supplement* Seamus Heaney invests this moment with great significance:

It is as if some symbolic figure of Ireland from an eighteenth-century vision poem, the one who confidently called herself Cathleen Ni Houlihan, has been struck dumb by the shock of modernity. Friel's work, not just here but in his fourteen preceding plays, constitutes a powerful therapy, a set of imaginative exercises that give her the chance to know and say herself properly to herself again.

In *Volunteers* Keeney's impatience with the pretence of keeping up a myth whose inadequacies make it unsuitable in a modern context may have induced Butt to let go of the green jug. Cathleen Ni Houlihan would have no place in this modern Irish context. Hugh in *Translations* again touches on what might perhaps be a particularly Irish tendency towards myth: 'it is not the literal past, the "facts" of history, that shape us, but images of the past embodied in language ... we must never cease renewing those images; because once we do, we fossilize', a quality highlighted in Owen's reply: '... one single, unalterable "fact": if Yolland is not found, we are all going to be evicted. Lancey has issued the order.'

On a less emblematic level, Sarah is not the only Friel character who struggles to express herself. There is the stutter of Joe in 'Winners' and Ben in *Living Quarters,* and the frequent grappling for the right word in other plays. But it is in *Translations* that the theme is expressed most consistently and eloquently, and perhaps within that play in the love scene between Yolland and Maire. There may even be within that scene a nice condensation of two different perceptions of reality, expressing personal and perhaps also national and linguistic characteristics. After their sudden sprint from the dance Yolland and Maire slowly become aware of their surroundings, but in different ways:

MAIRE: Manus'll wonder where I've got to.

YOLLAND: I wonder did anyone notice us leave. (*Pause.*
Slightly further apart.)
MAIRE: The grass must be wet. My feet are soaking.
YOLLAND: Your feet must be wet. The grass is soaking.

Maire's realization is impetuous and naturally innocent,
based on evidence of the senses; Yolland's suggestion is
created by reason and arrived at through deduction.

Translations makes a comprehensive statement on
the nature of linguistic communication in general and
on the conflict between Irish and English in particular.
Without going into any great detail Friel is able to
suggest certain basic differences between the two
languages in the way they perceive reality. The most
important such intimation is the well-known contrast
between linguistic and imaginary wealth and material
dearth that seems accepted as part of the Irish
consciousness. In his conversation with Yolland Hugh
elaborates on this quality of Gaelic language and
literature: 'Indeed Lieutenant. A rich language. A rich
literature. You'll find, sir, that certain cultures expend
on their vocabularies and syntax acquisitive energies
and ostentations entirely lacking in their material lives.
I suppose you could call us a spiritual people.' The
central argument of Hugh's belief is taken verbatim
from Steiner's *After Babel*. Some of the general theories
to do with language, translation and communication
show the influence of Steiner's book. But Friel's typical
use of Steiner's theory involves giving it distinct
historical and local detail and relevance. The generality
of Hugh's remark quoted above is immediately localized
and then dramatized in the action:

HUGH: Yes, it is a rich language, Lieutenant, full of the
mythologies of fantasy and hope and self-deception
– a syntax opulent with tomorrows. It is our
response to mud cabins and a diet of potatoes; our
only method of replying to . . . inevitabilities. (*To
Owen.*) Can you give me the loan of half-a-crown? I'll

> repay you out of the subscriptions I'm collecting for
> the publication of my new book. (*To Yolland.*) It is
> entitled: 'The Pentaglot Preceptor or Elementary
> Institute of the English, Greek, Hebrew, Latin and
> Irish Languages; Particularly Calculated for the
> Instruction of Such Ladies and Gentlemen as may
> Wish to Learn without the Help of a Master'.

Here, of course, Hugh is speaking English; he is
communicating with Yolland. In 1833 it was not yet
necessary for the Irish to speak English if they wanted to
'talk to themselves'. As a consequence of the events
described in *Translations* that, for a majority of the
population, would soon be inevitable.

If *The Freedom of the City,* in spite of certain
distancing effects introduced by Friel, demands political
as well as social consideration, it does so mainly as a
result of an easily recognizable contemporaneity. But
any contemporary condition or situation has in itself a
history of political events; it does not exist in a vacuum.
An understanding of the history may help in defining
and understanding the nature of today's troubled
circumstances. Furthermore, in approaching a problem
with the help of a historical dimension, it may be possible
to circumvent petrified attitudes and fixed ideas. In that
sense, *Translations* can be seen as a great education.
When we remember the generally hostile reception of
The Freedom of the City and the shouts of 'propaganda'
levelled against it, the great success of *Translations* in
London is quite remarkable. The prediction of one Irish
critic could hardly have been more amiss: 'Perhaps Mr
Friel should have taken some license in relation to
historical accuracy as a sop to the sensitivities of English
critics. As it is, his splendid and incisive work is hardly
likely to have the doors of London theatres flung open to
it' (*Eire–Ireland,* winter 1980). There may be several
reasons for its critical and popular success in London.
Translations is technically a conventional three-act

play, containing a well-balanced mixture of humorous and serious matter. Its dramatic structure emphasizes a steady growth of tension towards a point of total conflict. Certain complaints have been made about the ending, but it is difficult to see what could be justified as a possible addition. It comes soon after the dramatic climax and leaves the threat of full-scale imperial violence hanging in the air, suggesting, it could be argued, unfinished business and extending the action into contemporary relevance. *Translations* ends on a note of instability and confusion: Owen leaves to see Doalty about the Donnelly twins; Maire is left hoping for the return of Yolland; Hugh dismisses the appropriateness of the word 'always'; James ponders the dangers of marrying 'outside the tribe', and Hugh, finally, quotes falteringly from Virgil's the *Aeneid* about the downfall of an earlier civilization. All these contain powerful images of what Friel himself has described as 'the disquiet between two aesthetics' (*Guardian*, 27 September 1980). The play describes the beginning of the final linguistic and cultural take-over of Ireland by the British Empire and signals the virtual extinction of Gaelic civilization. As such it is sufficiently removed from the inflamed and entrenched politics of the contemporary situation to demand a hearing from everyone.

In many ways Yolland can be seen as the key figure for an English audience. Seeing the play through him will encourage a sense of hope, good will and understanding in the traffic between the two conflicting forces. Captain Lancey may stand as a representative of the official and military imperial machine where Yolland is instead an individual English soldier. Friel, I believe, stresses this contrast. Yolland was 'a *soldier by accident*' (stage directions), who quickly senses the impropriety of his presence in Ballybeg. He wants to learn Irish because 'I feel very foolish to – to – to be working here and not to speak your language,' and he hopes that the

English soldiers are not 'too crude an intrusion on your lives'. In this embarrassed speech to the hedge school community he reverses the existing condition and virtually invalidates the whole enterprise. Yolland in fact realizes the truth of Hugh's quotation from Ovid as translated by Jimmy: ' "I am a barbarian in this place because I am not understood by anyone." ' Lancey, in total contrast, feels no such qualms. As the voice of official colonialism his first speech reveals his unsuitability for dealing with the native population. Two strong suggestions impose themselves after his speech: the commercial and material reasons behind the Ordnance Survey make us think of Hugh's remarks about the English language; there is a certain 'take up the White Man's Burden' attitude behind the speech — the Survey is made for Ireland's sake — that recalls Matthew Arnold's Introduction to *The Study of Celtic Literature*:

> There is nothing like love and admiration for bringing people to a likeness with what they love and admire; but the Englishman seems never to dream of employing these influences upon a race he wants to fuse with himself. He employs simply material interests for his work of fusion; and, beyond these, nothing except scorn and rebuke. Accordingly there is no vital union between him and the races he has annexed; and while France can truly boast of her 'magnificent unity', a unity of spirit no less than of name between all the people who compose her, in England the Englishman proper is in union of spirit with no one except other Englishmen proper like himself. His Welsh and Irish fellow-citizens are hardly more amalgamated with him now than they were when Wales and Ireland were first conquered, and the true unity of even these small islands has yet to be achieved.

Arnold may be critical of the Englishman's methods but his point of view still seems to be that of an ideal and vague 'unity'.

The contrast between Yolland and Lancey is vital to an English understanding of the play. Yolland's sensitive realization that Ballybeg possesses a distinctive cultural climate cannot be disputed. While still being recognizably English and accepted as such he can criticize the operation. Lancey is a kind of military stage-Englishman, but his impossible position in the play will be seen by most English audiences. Neither he nor the Army in general seem equipped to deal with the situation, and here Friel may even intend a more modern correspondence.

From an Irish point of view Owen may be the key figure. Within him there is the clash between two languages and two cultures. He has been under the influence of Dublin for some time and unthinkingly accepts what he sees as the simple role of translator. In Ballybeg, however, he is opposed by, among others, his own brother. The final failure of his mission must be seen to reveal its total futility. Once the symbolic significance of the Ordnance Survey has sunk in, the disappearance of Yolland and the inevitability of Lancey's retaliation have already established a pattern for the future.

But Friel's treatment takes in more than the Ordnance Survey and the military operations involved. The state of the English language in Ireland is carefully examined. *Translations*, set in 1833, looks both backwards and forwards in time. The complexity of the situation is well illustrated within the small Ballybeg community. The hedge school itself is a vestige of the Penal Laws which forbade the education of Catholics. Having reached a certain degree of excellence its existence is now threatened by the introduction (in 1831) of a system of national education. In the new National Schools the sole language of communication will be English, a fact that in itself accounts for the rapid decline of Gaelic speakers at the end of the nineteenth century. In Ballybeg attitudes to the English language are divided. Maire wants to learn English since she plans to emigrate to America and she quotes Daniel O'Connell who, with many others in influential positions, felt that 'the old language is a barrier to modern progress'. In 1833 the Irish language had already been under pressure from the English long enough to make its position precarious. Various decisions reflecting a political and cultural imperialism can be seen to have culminated in the Ordnance Survey. It provided Friel with a powerful symbol of this process.

Other ominous notes, too, are heard in the play. The mysterious Donnelly twins are to become the perpetrators of violent actions. The chilling mention of the potato blight introduces another partly political problem. Maire's irritated and ironic dismissal of its dangers may be directed against a certain Irish propensity for poor-mouthing. The frequency with which the 'sweet smell' is mentioned as an indication of the blight reveals it as a common occurrence.

> MAIRE: Sweet smell! Sweet smell! Every year at this time somebody comes back with stories of the sweet smell. Sweet God, did the potatoes ever fail in Baile Beag? Well, did they ever – ever? Never! There was never blight here. Never. Never. But we're always sniffing about for it, aren't we? – looking for disaster. The rents are going to go up again – the harvest's going to be lost – the herring have gone away for ever – there's going to be evictions. Honest to God, some of you people aren't happy unless you're miserable and you'll not be right content until you're dead!

What Maire attacks here is perhaps also a kind of negative and unquestioning defeatism which contrasts sharply with her own optimistic and alert view of the future. It is a different aspect of the same defects in the Irish character that Eamon had castigated in *Aristocrats*. In that play these attitudes reflect mostly social

[198]

and internal Irish conditions. *Translations*, on the other hand, concerns an open political conflict between Ireland and England. But the play's great strength is that it approaches politics through history, anthropology and linguistics. It establishes various links within a racial, cultural and linguistic consciousness in order to explain events of history; it speaks for the unique individuality of that consciousness and against any interference, and it advocates attention to language as expressing that consciousness, be it in Irish or in English. So important is the role of language that one American critic thought that the play was 'obsessed with it' (*New York Daily News,* 15 April 1981). Christopher Fitz-Simon in his recent *The Irish Theatre,* after suggesting other important themes, concludes his brief discussion of *Translations*: 'but it is really about language – about the destruction of a language by that of a superior colonial power, about the basic notion of language as a means of conveying thought, and about the nature of words.' And yet the play's political content defines its action and its meaning. It must come first in any consideration of *Translations*. Friel himself, in working on the play, understood and indeed worried about its political implications. In another 'Sporadic Diary' he vacillates slightly between two points of view. On 22 May 1979 he wrote: 'The thought occurred to me that what I was circling around was a political play and that thought panicked me. But it is a political play – how can that be avoided? If it is not political, what is it? Inaccurate history? Social drama?'[2] It would of course have been possible to write a historical play about the Ordnance Survey that would have dealt mainly with the political and social aspects of the operation. But Friel's attention was elsewhere. About a week later the diary reads: 'What worries me about the play – if there is a play – are the necessary peculiarities, especially the political elements. Because the play has to do with language and only language. And if it becomes overwhelmed by that political element, it is lost.' As we know, Friel's fears were unfounded. Although the play relies to a great extent on the political confrontation between Ireland and England at a given moment of history, it is never 'overwhelmed' by it.

One important if not decisive factor in the making of *Translations* was, again, Friel's strong sense of place. He discovered that the Ordnance Survey of Ireland had started not far from Derry or Muff where he was then living. On the eastern shores of Lough Foyle an eight-mile line was measured to provide a base for a network of triangles covering the whole country. Careful surveying then took place within these triangles. Muff would have been in one of the northernmost triangles as would, for instance, Burnfoot, Ballybeg and the other place-names mentioned in the play. Friel then studied his subject carefully and made great accurate and imaginative use of several historical sources dealing with the Ordnance Survey, the hedge schools and the introduction of national education. He successfully incorporated various facts from these sources into the dramatic structure of the play. He also took some pains to acknowledge his material and in programme notes from the Irish and English productions quoted extensively from his sources. They all provide the play with a strong aura of historical accuracy and suggest the nature of Friel's use of them. Two brief examples may suffice to illustrate this. One quotation from *The Hedge Schools of Ireland* reminds us of Hugh's words about the suitability of English for 'the purposes of commerce': 'Though the use of the vernacular was rapidly falling into decay during the eighteenth century, it was owing to the greater value of English on the fair and market rather than on any shifting of ground on the part of the schools . . .'; another one from the letters of John O'Donovan, a civilian employee with the Ordnance Survey, may have provided Friel with the confusion and controversy concerning Tobair Vree in the play: 'But there are several of them such trifling places that it seems to me that it matters not which of two or three appellations we give them. For example, the name Timlin's Hole is not of thirty years' standing and will give way to another name as soon as that dangerous hole shall have swallowed a fisherman of more illustrious name than Tim Lyn.' It is rare that a dramatist so meticulously researches and records the historical background of his play. Other sources that provided Friel with facts, images and even names of some of the characters in the play were John Andrews's *A Paper Landscape* and Colonel Colby's *Memoir of the City and the North-West Liberties of Londonderry*.

As *Translations* moves towards chaos and confusion the emphasis on history gives way to the accelerating premonitions of a troubled future, and past history is extended into the present, turning, so to speak, the play into a myth of its own. The great irony, as every commentator on *Translations* must stress with Friel, is, of course, that 'it should have been written in Irish' (*Magill*). The great problem with the Irish language is that it is neither dead nor alive. In his 'Sporadic Diary' Friel said that one of the things he did not want to do in *Translations* was 'to write a threnody on the death of the Irish language . . . And yet portions of all these are relevant. Each is part of the atmosphere in which the real play lurks.' These lines seem to amount to some sort of acceptance of its demise. And yet, in the same publication that carries Friel's 'Sporadic Diary', there is talk of a 'repossession' of the Irish language. Hugh may be talking about Irish when he refers to a civilization that 'can be imprisoned in a linguistic contour which no longer matches the landscape of . . . fact', but today that language is still in existence. Its role may not be discussed with such vehemence and emotion as it used to be, but its symbolic power is still considerable. In Ireland strong contrasts and impossible opposites frequently have to exist together. The Irish language is still part of the persisting consequences of the East–West and North–South dichotomies of place. Until the concluding chapter of its history has been written it will remain one of Ireland's many indeterminacies. This makes *Translations* a more political and therefore more important piece of Irish drama. The nature of the basic relationship between Britain and Ireland is always a determining factor in Irish life. The troubles in the North are a constant reminder of one aspect of an abiding confusion. In *Translations* Friel imaginatively recreated an event that was to have a lasting and decisive influence on modern Ireland. In so doing he contributed not only a masterpiece of Irish drama but a sensitive interpretation of Irish history both in relation to Britain and within the Irish consciousness itself.

In terms of cultural and linguistic issues *Translations* may have revealed to many Irish people a vital ingredient in their own personal and national psyche. Its treatment of language approaches those areas of the subconscious where the racial and national identities are forged. With the historical dimension that has characterized Friel's work since the beginning of the seventies goes this increasing interest in questions of the Irish identity, an effort to understand and define history and especially the spiritual past and various attitudes to it. Together these two trends give to Friel's work an added urgency and edge which is of a broader appeal than the earlier plays. For all its excellence, *Philadelphia, Here I Come!* today feels a little bit dated. But then it was written in the early and more innocent sixties, well before the start of the present troubles. We are now very much aware that Friel's Northern provenance determined the direction and complexion of his later plays.

The Ancestral Pieties: *The Communication Cord* (1982)

In *Translations* the breakdown in communication has

deeply tragic consequences for the Ballybeg community, and in the historical context of the Ordnance Survey is conceived the outline of modern Ireland. From the first confused attempt at imparting information to the final collapse of the restored Irish cottage, *The Communication Cord* observes the attitudes of the contemporary Irish to their cultural and historical heritage. The decay, not of an idyll but of an experience 'of a totally different order' that Yolland has sensed in Ballybeg (or 'the calm, the stability, the self-possession' that Peter had met on the island of Inishkeen in *The Gentle Island*) is now nearly complete. The approach Friel adopts in *The Communication Cord*, therefore, is that of farce. This, to quote Friel himself, is 'a perfectly valid way of looking at people in Ireland today . . . our situation has become so absurd and so . . . crass that it seems to me it might be a valid way to talk and write about it' (*Irish Times,* 14 September 1982).

The restored cottage allows Friel a focus that is both contemporary and historical. Now Ballybeg is visited by members of the moneyed city élite who willingly part with small fortunes to return to 'the true centre' of their civilization, to borrow a phrase from Senator Donovan. They are holidaying in their own country, part-time subscribers only to the West-of-Ireland community. Now, no Irish is heard, but plenty of EEC German and French is spoken. This is, of course, the Ireland of the Common Market. Jack, who is the owner of the cottage, uses it mainly as a love nest but is nevertheless aware of its symbolic attractions to those who are susceptible to them. He has developed an impressive vocabulary in order to be able to extol on demand the virtues of the simple hearth. 'Listen, Professor. (*In parody.*) This is where we all come from. This is our first cathedral. This shaped all our souls. This determined our first pieties. Yes. Have reverence for this place. (*Laughs heartily.*)' But at least Jack is honest in his attitudes to the cottage. He has made sure that he can ride his Japanese motor bike right up to the front door. His father, on the other hand, who has to leave the car down at the main road and walk through the 'water, muck, slush, bloody cow-manure' believes that 'the penance of that introduction is somehow part of the soul and authenticity of the place'.

Senator Donovan is on the receiving end of most of the satire generated in the play, and in him Friel exposes the hypocritical and confused attitudes of official modern Ireland towards its own past. When he bends down and inadvertently chains himself to the cow-post of Irish history, his initial admiration for the meticulously restored traditional Irish cottage begins to evaporate. The homely scene he had first imagined for his scenario contains items turned by repeated use into tired clichés divorced from the reality of their origin: 'the modest but aesthetically satisfying furnishings'; 'our folk-tales and our ancient sagas'; the cow 'just chewing her cud and listening to the reassuring sound of a family preparing to go to bed'; 'a little scene that's somehow central to my psyche', he concludes before realizing that he is stuck. His pompous reverence quickly dissolves and when he rushes out of the cottage at the end of the play rural Ireland has taken on new meanings for him. Senator Donovan, on the one hand, and Nora Dan, on the other, are variant expressions of the East–West dichotomy. Nora is a Ballybeg local, or, as she is described by Jack, 'the quintessential noble peasant – obsessed with curiosity and greed and envy', and she cannot understand why anyone would want to live 'in a poor, backward place like this'. She too is satirized, especially in her poor-mouthing – 'Ah sure I'm only half-middling, Jack' – and her obsession with money – 'Oh, they'll be the bucks with the money.'

It is against the background of this muddle of insincere and unthinking attitudes to the Irish past that, in the end, the temporarily propped-up roof of the cottage inevitably has to come down. To create a stronger structure would demand sounder and more genuine attitudes.

The position *vis-à-vis* the past taken by the characters in *The Communication Cord* is in stark contrast to the one adopted by Friel himself in editing *The Last of the Name*. This book contains the folkloric and autobiographical memories of an Inishowen weaver and tailor, Charles McGlinchey, and it chronicles the final stages of a disappearing way of life. In its rich evocation of a local Donegal culture it again testifies to Friel's great sense of place and brings an authentic sense of the past into contemporary Ireland.

But the uproarious farce of *The Communication Cord* tends to push into the background serious questions about the Irish psyche and its attitudes to the past. The conventional ingredients of farce are all here: mistaken identities (some of them intended), a gusty wind blowing awkward hatches open and lamps out, a smoking fireplace that takes a definite dislike to one of the characters, people and unwanted articles of clothing which turn up at the wrong moment. Most of the action, however, depends on the collapse of communication and the loss of a common communicational structure. The authority of language is undermined and the result is utter confusion.

The worst offender, paradoxically, is Tim, a junior lecturer who has been working for seven years on a thesis on 'Discourse Analysis with Particular Reference to Response Cries'. The practical events of the play, however, may have cost Tim his academic hypothesis. 'Maybe,' he concludes at the end of the play, 'silence is the perfect discourse.'

In some respects the *The Communication Cord* can be seen as a companion piece to *Translations*. There are, as we have seen, several correspondences between the two plays. For Friel and Field Day it may have had a therapeutic influence on the historical nightmare that the earlier play records. *Translations*, in its subtle and sensitive use of Irish and English history, touched a nerve in the Irish psyche; it created its own eloquent myth and was instantly and widely heralded as 'a national classic' (*The Times*, 13 May 1981). It is possible that in choosing the modern context of *The Communication Cord*, Friel was attempting to shift some of the sediments left by *Translations*. But the play is too slight to do this – it succeeds instead in confirming the importance of the earlier play.

Friel and Field Day

It is not possible to point with any certainty to a definite year or play that can be said to have begun the present phase of Friel's growth as a dramatist. To go even further and suggest, for instance, that to point to the picture of Friel himself marching on Bloody Sunday as itself enough would be to over-simplify and to disregard other factors, other influences. But it must be stressed that an understanding of Friel's recent work is possible only against the background of the continuing troubles in Northern Ireland. It is not, however, the troubles themselves that are Friel's subject matter. From the middle of the seventies most of the plays that he has written have been notable for their increasing attention to questions of national identity. In an effort to understand and define important aspects of Irishness, Friel's plays have become involved in considerations of history, politics and language as an expression of nationality. The complex historical and political landscape in Ireland contains, first of all, the effects of the still influential dichotomies of place between East and West and North and South. Both express the fundamental split in the Irish consciousness which makes any arrival at unity so difficult. With his Northern background Friel can be said to be particularly well suited to examine the various manifestations of a divided society, and he feels, he has said, 'maybe in some kind of silly way, that the North is going to be one of the determining features of the future of this island, (*Irish Times,* 14 September 1982). Here, Field Day and Friel's strong involvement in it has been another important influence on his writing career.

But the main force behind Field Day is neither historical nor political; it is artistic. Friel agrees with the description of Field Day as part of 'an artistic fifth province', a concept revived and disseminated by Richard Kearney and others in *The Crane Bag,* rising above and covering the whole island of Ireland. Field Day does not accept a simplified and entrenched North–South division because of 'the very fact that it's located in the North and has its reservations about it, and that it works in the South and has its reservations about it' (*Irish Times,* 14 September 1982). What Friel and Field Day are looking for is 'some kind of awareness, some kind of sense of the country, what this island is about, North and South, and what are our attitudes to it'. This is very much what Friel himself has been doing in his plays since the beginning of the seventies. Perhaps the best descriptions of the original aspirations of Field Day were given by Friel in connection with the productions of the company's first three plays. They came naturally and eloquently out of his own intuitive sense of underlying historical and political complexities.

Today it may be possible to forget that Field Day was founded by Field and Rea as a theatre company to put on *Translations.* But from the first performance on Tuesday, 23 September 1980 certain stirring sentiments heightened the atmosphere in Derry's Guildhall. It is rare that the opening of a play gives rise to leading articles in the daily press, but Field Day's first production achieved that and much more. 'It was, in every sense, a unique occasion, with loyalists and nationalists, Unionists and SDLP, Northerners and Southerners laying aside their differences to join in applauding a play by a fellow Derryman and one, moreover, with a theme that is uniquely Irish' (*Irish Press*, 26 September 1980). The success of *Translations* guaranteed the success of Field Day. Derry was confirmed as its home and subsequent productions have had a period of rehearsal and preparation in Derry before opening in the Guildhall prior to a nationwide tour. In the early days Friel was involved in nearly all aspects of the running of the company, from writing the plays to helping to make the seating arrangements for the opening performance. He is still strongly committed to and enthusiastic about the various activities of the company, which are now, of course, much more diversified than earlier. The main thrust, however, remains the plays. Field Day could not live on Friel alone, and after his translation of Chekhov's *Three Sisters* in 1981 and his own *The Communication Cord* in 1982, their 1983 production was a play that was not completely alien to Field Day's Irish context: *Lena and Boesman*, by the South African playwright Athol Fugard. The most recent productions have involved some of the major contemporary Irish writers. 1984 saw Derek Mahon's *High Time* and Tom Paulin's *The Riot Act* in tandem, the latter being a version of *Antigone*. Sophocles' classical play deals with themes close to the Irish experience – as we have seen, Friel himself considered it as a subject, and in 1986 a verse translation by Brendan Kennelly was produced at the Peacock in Dublin. The concerns of these plays are all of contemporary Irish relevance, to the relationship within Ireland itself between North and South and more generally to that between Ireland and Britain; Thomas Kilroy's *Double Cross* (1986) is another excellent example of the same dramatized concern. For 1987, plays by Frank McGuinness and Stewart Parker are being planned.

From 1983 Field Day has engaged in a parallel activity, the publication of a series of pamphlets that debate aspects of Irish history, literature, culture and politics. If the plays demand a large and nationwide audience and try to adopt a 'popular' mode, the pamphlets reach only a very small audience, being increasingly specialized and ever more arcane. Since pamphlets are by their very nature aggressive and didactic there is a risk that they will be seen by some as preachy propaganda and the stance that they take as polarizing (if that is possible) the attitudes under discussion. Is more or better dialogue a likely result? Is there a danger that the artistic fifth province will find itself isolated from the other four through being mainly the playground of a comfortable and protected intellectual élite? These charges represent precisely the entrenched positions that Field Day is seeking to transform. The pamphlets have found a voice and by revitalizing stagnated concepts the company is challenging conventional inherited attitudes in an effort to articulate common sentiments that escape a limited and even mindless outlook. It is trying to shape a climate of thought and feeling that can express a united vision of Irish culture. This may sound romantic, but it is, in fact, impossible to avoid the feeling that Field Day today is trying to do what the Irish Literary Theatre (and the Ulster Literary Theatre) did nearly a hundred years ago. Those were turbulent times that required larger truths than daily ambushes and explosions, shrill arguments or booming rhetoric. Now Field Day is seeking to express these larger truths in response to a 'calloused' situation. Its idealism is intense and its most urgent belief is in the importance of culture and literature. It is this which explains their new ambitious undertaking, *The Field Day Anthology of Irish Letters*, five hundred years of Irish literature to be published in two volumes in 1988.

There is little doubt that with their plays, their pamphlets and their anthology, Field Day will have successfully created the artistic community of a fifth province. This force will address the whole island culturally, if not politically.

Politics and Failed Politics: *Fathers and Sons* (1987)

Reluctantly Friel has had to accept that his adaptation or dramatization of Turgenev's novel *Fathers and Sons* could not be produced in an Irish context. 'I would have liked Field Day to do it,' he has said, but the sheer size of the play with its fifteen characters was beyond the scope of the company. Instead the National Theatre in London accepted the play and welcomed Friel back to the Lyttelton where *Translations* was so successful in 1981. *Fathers and Sons* is not, of course, Friel's own play, but there are several areas in which the thematic content comes very close to what we have come to recognize as typically Frielian. The action of Turgenev's novel begins in May 1859, when Russia seemed to be on the verge of a major social and political revolution. Two years later the emancipation of the serfs had been proclaimed but the expected explosion had not happened. Russian society had changed dramatically but its basic fabric had withstood the strain. Soon, however, it became obvious that the reforms that had been introduced were far from adequate; revolutionary activity was followed by repression by the authorities. But in 1859 it was still possible to look both forwards and backwards. The new men and women, the nihilists, represented by Bazarov and Arkady, want to 'make a complete clearance', to plough deep into traditional Russian society in order to achieve their goals. They refuse all authority and do not accept art, love or individuality as useful concepts. To Bazarov, all people are 'like trees in the forest. Ask any botanist. Know one birch, know them all.' Bazarov is opposed by and quarrels incessantly with Arkady's anachronistic and slightly foppish uncle, Pavel. He stands for traditional values and sees himself as the perfect gentleman. There is a basic humanity about Pavel which will never find a place in Bazarov's revolutionary cynicism. On the estate of Arkady's father, Nikolai, the serfs have already been given their partial freedom in anticipation of the later proclamation. But the estate is riddled with serious problems and the new deal does not seem to work. Such, briefly, is the social and political background to the play. The confrontation between Bazarov and Pavel is in every sense the personification of the opposing forces of old aristocratic Russia and the new nihilists. The powder keg is there, waiting for the spark. But when, after the preliminaries, Pavel and Bazarov fight a duel, the reason does not seem to be political, but associated instead with love and honour. Politics, which for more than half the play was very much in the foreground, is beginning to disappear slowly from the main action. Arkady comes to acknowledge what he had always known subconsciously, that if single-minded and sacrificial nihilism will not allow him a wife and children, refuses him family life and comfort, then he is not a true nihilist. Bazarov falls deeply in love, a supremely ironic event, especially after his own dogmatic 'Principles Concerning the Proper Ordering of the Relationships between Men and Women':

One. Romantic love is a fiction.
Two. There is nothing at all mysterious between the sexes. The relationship is quite simply physical.
Three. To believe that the relationship should be dressed up in the trappings of chivalry is crazy. The troubadours were all lunatics.
Four. If you fancy a woman, always, always try to make love to her. If you want to dissipate, dissipate.

In the end Bazarov, who refused all authority, has to surrender to two forces that very much rule human life, love and death.

We do not know whether Bazarov's priorities would have changed if his love had been reciprocated – it is not, and his extreme devotion to the cause hardens him further and isolates him from the rest of the characters. When Bazarov leaves, and Arkady is getting ready to marry his sweetheart Katya and Arkady's father his former servant Fenichka (which is in itself a perfect sign of the times), Friel's stage directions stress Bazarov's isolation: *He observes the happy family from the outside.* This is the price he has to pay for his revolutionary zeal, and to quote Yeats's 'Easter 1916', 'too long a sacrifice can make a stone of the heart.' The question of loyalty and love, of blind loyalty to a cause and personal loyalty to family is, I believe, the thematic strand that Friel decides to highlight in Turgenev's novel. On the whole, Friel remains almost perfectly true to Turgenev's novel. He foreshortens time and space and concentrates the essential action. By using dramatic irony he is able to suggest ominously the illness and death of Bazarov (an event which is not prepared for in the novel), and by the use of his own Irish idiom he localizes and particularizes the play's action. He also lifts the servants more out of the background. They are allowed to act more as individuals without, however, changing the tenor of Turgenev's work.

Friel has found in Turgenev's novel moods and thematic strands that are in some kind of harmony with his own creative sensibility. We recognize in *Fathers and Sons* Friel's interest in the family, in the difference between generations, the nature of love and loyalty, in the physical manifestation of the arbitary workings of Fate, in language as expressing personality, class and nationality. But deepest and most moving of all is the expression of the human condition. Bazarov's death is deeply pathetic, even tragic, because he dies as a human being, not as a Russian or a cynical revolutionary.

Conclusion

The circumstance of place is always a highly pertinent consideration in any discussion of Irish literature. Within the small island of Ireland two important dichotomies of place express a basic pattern of opposition and division which is reflected in the national psyche. Both dichotomies have their origin in an uneasy historical relationship with Ireland's neighbour in the East. Dominated by Britain both politically and economically it has always been an unequal relationship. For centuries there was a slow and deliberate onslaught by British colonialism on Ireland which, apart from an almost total rejection of any claim for political self-determination, involved an assault on an Irish way of life, its culture, its religion and its language. Gradually, Gaelic and rural Ireland was pushed further and further west. The process was stage-managed via Dublin, and in the twentieth century the city of Dublin has continued to play its role of gateway to the West for influences from the East, now economic rather than political. The slow coming of this modern tide to the West of Ireland has meant a radical change in patterns of social and economic life. The political dimension, however, was not lost, merely given another focus with the establishment in 1920 of the Protestant statelet of Northern Ireland, loyal to Britain and hostile to its neighbour in the South. The precariousness of its existence was manifest from the very beginning, and after fifty-two years one phase of its stormy life was ended when direct rule was introduced. In 1972, therefore, Northern Ireland's *raison d'être* was formally shown never to have existed.

This study does not pretend to any great detail in the description of the historical background to modern Ireland. It is obvious, however, that a historical dimension is absolutely necessary for an understanding of the work of Ireland's best-known and most important contemporary dramatist, Brian Friel. The two dichotomies of place in Ireland, East–West and North–South, are not only reflected in various ways in Friel's stories and plays, they express his constant concern about the contemporary political situation and his efforts to arrive at some kind of understanding of history and to attempt a definition of the identity of modern Ireland. His particular habitat and background, that of a member of the Catholic minority in Northern Ireland, have contributed in making his sense of place and identity particularly acute. From his first collection of short stories to his latest play critics and commentators have noted this strong attachment to a particular area of Ireland. Friel's short stories move across the three north-westernmost counties, Tyrone, Derry and Donegal, with, it seems to me, an early base in Tyrone and Derry shifting gradually towards Donegal. Frequently this introduction into Donegal comes in the shape of a newcomer or visitor whose presence there emphasizes the basic qualities of a traditional Irish rural community slowly being penetrated by a tide of modernity. The gramophone in 'Kelly's Hall', for instance, signals the coming of modern life to a small Donegal village, and the visiting fisherman in 'The Gold in the Sea' is made keenly aware of the qualities of life that determine existence in the West. These and many other stories can be seen as expressing Friel's view of the East–West dichotomy. In various contexts he has stressed the 'peasant' quality of Ireland and set out the great contrasts between the modern city on the one hand and traditional rural Ireland on the other, confessing

[214]

himself more at home in the latter and in many respects
an enemy of mechanized and commercialized modernity, influenced not only by Dublin and Britain but also
by America.

By the very cause of its existence the North–South
dichotomy has a much more pronounced political
dimension. In Friel's short stories and early plays this
dimension is largely absent. When it does reveal itself it
is more in the form of an exploration of the social and
economic conditions that exist as a corollary of the
political situation. In 'Johnny and Mick', for instance,
there is a strong sense of a divided community, and *The
Blind Mice* expresses indirectly the schizophrenic
nature of the North in terms of religious opposites. It is
possible that Friel, in his early career, decided to keep
politics out of his literary work. His Catholic background
and his nationalist sympathies exist as a necessary
condition of his stories and plays but are only rarely set
forth explicitly. Instead they assert themselves only
obliquely in Friel's choice of subject matter and theme
and, for instance, in his refusal to even mention the
existence of the political border between Northern
Ireland and the Republic.

It must generally be stressed, however, that the two
all-pervasive dichotomies of place are not in themselves
Friel's subject matter. Instead he finds his thematic
focus in the everyday lives of Irish people exposed to
these forces. All his work shows a wide range of what
could be described as traditional Irish themes, realized
in their literary execution on the level of the individual.
These themes include: emigration and the depopulation
of the Irish countryside; the coming of the modern tide to
change a traditional, rural, land-orientated society; the
claustrophobic conditions of small-town or village life in
the West; the peculiarly Irish brand of Catholicism; the
difficult relationship between fathers and sons; the idea
of the past and a feeling of nostalgic regret about it;
the availability of mental compensations for material

poverty. These general themes could be said to be an expression of the Irish habitat, or geographical, racial and national rather than individual qualities. Friel's creative sensibility has moulded these into his own personal and private expression. They have been affected by his awareness of the essential loneliness of the individual human being, the difficulty of communicating private emotions or even the failure to communicate at all, the individual perception of life and reality and the consequent availability of an individual truth of illusion, and, finally, a frequently acute sense of the fragility and precariousness of life and love and the arbitrary and capricious workings of Fate. These qualities, I believe, suggest a basically tragic sensibility. It is expressed also in one of Friel's most typical stances, irony, which permeates much of his work. It is balanced, however, by a strong sense of humour, bitter-sweet and witty as well as broad and farcical. In his mature work, especially, he moves easily between comedy and tragedy in *Translations* and *Faith Healer*. The humour of Teddy's monologue in *Faith Healer* is created by sheer story-telling verbal magic; the farce of *The Communication Cord* is witty, satiric, situational, at once funny and serious. These three plays are in themselves ample proof of Friel's excellence in stagecraft.

With his focus settled on the individual Friel pursues another typical theme. Outside the everyday traffic between individual human beings there is the conflict between the individual and the group. There is, for instance, the village community of several of Friel's stories and plays. It has its own code of behaviour and respectability and treats newcomers with great curiosity and careful suspicion. The more formal the arrangement the more liable it is to create friction between individual and group. The family is a cornerstone in Friel's work. From the outside it suggests and indeed depends on the idea of unity and loyalty. On the inside the demands of that unity and loyalty inevitably

[216]

clash with those of the individual. The good qualities that the family can offer, such as support, comfort and love, contain in themselves their own opposites. But in spite of these hazards the family seems to be preferable to the loneliness of bachelorhood. As a form of societal organization the family, like any other group, has undergone important changes with the advent of the modern age. In Ireland especially, the idea of the family is closely linked with that of the Church. Friel's experiences at Maynooth turned him away from the priesthood and in his early work there is a strong element of anti-clericalism. Friel's criticism is directed at a strongly autocratic and institutionalized Church and its impersonal and ineffectual representatives. In his recent plays, however – his last dramatic priest appeared in *Living Quarters* – it seems that Friel has moved away from the subject of Irish Catholicism and its influence on modern Ireland. That may be another consequence of the adoption in his work of a historical and more political dimension.

It would be difficult and perhaps pointless to draw any far-reaching conclusions from this new trend. The fact, for instance, that Friel's interest in formal theatrical experimentation seems to have diminished in his most recent plays does not mean that it is gone for ever. His early striking and innovative experimentation may well return in some form. There are, however, in the new dimension of Friel's work, certain characteristic tendencies that are all, in one way or another, reflections of Friel's habitat. Many times, as a young boy in Omagh and Derry, Friel must have crossed the border between Northern Ireland and the Republic on his way to Donegal. From the end of the sixties, the sense of a fractured community and its deeply entrenched sectarian divide, was made much keener by political events. Contemporary reality forced its way into Friel's work. But the reluctant contemporaneity of *The Freedom of the City* was soon modified by the archaeological

[217]

excavation of *Volunteers*. The typical thrust of Friel's later plays approaches today's tortured reality through the historical perspective of the Irish past. *Translations* did that and much more. With Field Day and his own plays Friel is trying to explain the contemporary Irish to themselves. Such an explanation requires a definition of the Irish identity which can only be achieved through a historical perspective involving both the basic relationship with England and the concept of a divided Ireland. But the main force behind Field Day is neither historical nor political; it is artistic. It expresses in a dramatic form shaped by Friel and other writers the reality of modern Ireland, North and South.

The one and only focus of this study has been the literary work of Brian Friel. Today, Friel is very probably Ireland's most important living dramatist. His short stories provide a useful introduction to his real-life and fictional habitat. But it has been in his plays that his North-Western background has been extended to encompass the whole island. In the village of Ballybeg Friel has established a microcosm from which Ireland can be surveyed and which can express his relationship with his own world.

Notes

Introduction:

1   A. Carpenter, ed., *Place, Personality and the Irish Writer,*
    p. 11.
2   In my study I shall consistently use the terms Irish
    literature and Irish drama in preference to the equally
    common Anglo-Irish literature and Anglo-Irish drama.
    Here usage vacillates, possibly with a preference for the
    more general Anglo-Irish literature (including prose,
    poetry and drama), stressing a 'bifurcated literary herit-
    age' (Roger McHugh and Maurice Harmon in the Preface
    to *A Short History of Anglo-Irish Literature,* p. 9) and the
    more specific Irish drama, where the risk of confusion with
    drama written in the Irish language is less immediate. It
    seems to me, however, that a term, viz. Anglo-Irish, which
    in historical usage carries a distinct denotation as well as
    accompanying connotations, is a less happy one where
    literature is concerned. The term, in fact, especially if we
    are dealing with modern literature, only fulfils a necessary
    function in distinguishing between Irish literature written
    in English and Irish literature written in Irish or Gaelic.
    This, in turn, is linked to the fortunes of the Irish language.
    If the Irish language did not exist, the term Anglo-Irish
    literature would be no more relevant than, say, Anglo-
    American literature. So for as long as literature will be
    written in Irish, the term Anglo-Irish literature will
    unavoidably exist as a kind of *pis aller.* It is, one might
    perhaps suggest, another 'Irish question'.
3   From an article by Lavinia Greacen, 'Sex and the Irish' in
    the *Irish Times,* 14 June 1982, p. 10.

[219]

4 William Smith Clark, *The Early Irish Stage: The Beginnings to 1720*, p. 2.

5 Micheál ÓhAodha, *Theatre in Ireland,* p. 10.

6 From the manifesto of the Irish Literary Theatre, quoted in Lady Gregory, *Our Irish Theatre,* p. 20.

7 'Two Playwrights with a Single Theme' in Des Hickey and Gus Smith, *A Paler Shade of Green*, p. 223.

8 In Irish *Baile Beag* means 'small town'. Another common and relevant meaning of *baile* is 'home'.

Chapter I: From Killyclogher to Ballybeg

1 There are complications about the exact date of Friel's birth. It has been variously given as 5, 9, and 10 January 1929. This vacillation tells a story relevant not only for the relationship between Catholics and Protestants in Northern Ireland, but also for the historical relationship between Britain and Ireland. Friel was born on 9 January 1929; his birthday has always been celebrated on 9 January. In the parish register of the district of Knockmoyle the birth is registered as having been on 9 January and the name given is *Brian* Patrick *O'Friel*; he was baptized on the following day, 10 January. But apart from the local church register, civil registration with the local authorities is also required. It seems that when this was done the date of birth was wrongly given as 10 January. This is the date given on the birth certificate held now in the General Register Office in Belfast. But the really significant difference is that on this birth certificate the name is given as *Bernard* Patrick *Friel* (which is, of course, the English rather than the Irish form). It seems that Friel's masterpiece *Translations* was already writing itself in his mind.

2 Nicholas Grene, *Synge: A Critical Study of the Plays,* p. 120.

Chapter II: The Early Plays

1 In a letter to the present writer.

2 Jonathan Raban, 'Icon or symbol: the writer and the "medium" ', in Peter Lewis, ed., *Radio Drama*, p. 81.

3 I am using the word 'life-lie' to correspond approximately to Ibsen's *livsløgn*. In *The Wild Duck*, where the theme of the 'life-lie' is particularly strong, Dr Relling states: 'Deprive the average man of his life-lie, and you've robbed him of happiness as well.'

4 Frances Gray, 'The nature of radio drama', in Peter Lewis, ed., *Radio Drama*, p. 51.

5 John Drakakis, 'The essence that's not seen: radio adaptations of stage plays', in Lewis, p. 116.

6 Philip Hope-Wallace, 'The unities in radio drama', *BBC Quarterly* 4, 1, April 1949, pp. 21–5, quoted in Lewis, p. 126.

Chapter III: Development of Form and Content

1 Brian Friel, 'Extracts from a Sporadic Diary', in *The Writers: A Sense of Ireland*, eds. Andrew Carpenter and Peter Fallon, p. 39.

2 Carpenter and Fallon, p. 40.

3 The reaction of one Dublin critic to Friel's *Living Quarters* could be cited as an example of how some critics have chosen not to accept Friel's dramatic kind. He regretted that Friel, 'one of our ablest and most sensitive dramatists, hadn't chosen to use this particular theme for a novel instead' (*Irish Times*, 25 March 1977, p. 9).

4 In a letter to the present writer.

5 Year within brackets after the title of a play refers to year of first production.

6 The phrase is a quotation from an oft-quoted passage in Edmund Burke's *Reflections on the Revolution in France* in which Burke voices his great regret at the events in France.

7 P. Luke ed., *Enter Certain Players: Edwards–MacLiammóir and the Gate 1928–1978*, p. 21.

8 The subtitle is an ironic reference to Robert Emmet's famous speech from the dock after his abortive 1803 rising. His final words were: 'When my country takes her place among the nations of the earth, then and not till then, let my epitaph be written. I have done.'

9 Alfred North Whitehead, *Science and the Modern World*, p. 13.

Chapter IV: New Accents

1 Christopher Murray in 'Recent Irish Drama' in Heinz Kozok, *Studies in Anglo-Irish Literature*, p. 44.
2 Tim Pat Coogan (ed.), *Ireland and the Arts*, p. 58.

Bibliography

Works by Brian Friel

Fiction

The Saucer of Larks, New York, Doubleday and Company Inc., 1962; London, Victor Gollancz, 1962.

The Gold in the Sea, New York, Doubleday and Company Inc., 1966; London, Victor Gollancz, 1966.

The Saucer of Larks: Stories of Ireland, London, Arrow Books, 1969.

Selected Stories, Dublin, Gallery Press, 1979.

The Diviner, Dublin, The O'Brien Press; London, Allison and Busby, 1983.

'Nato at Night,' *New Yorker,* 1 April 1961.

'Downstairs no Upstairs', *New Yorker,* 24 August 1963.

'A Fine Day at Glenties', *Holiday,* April 1963.

'Labors of Love', *Atlantic Monthly,* April 1963.

'The Child', *The Bell,* 18, no. 4 (July 1952).

'The Visitation', *Kilkenny Magazine,* 5 (Autumn–Winter 1961–2).

Non-Fiction

'Giant of Monaghan', *Holiday,* May 1964.

'Walk to that Exit', *Holiday,* November 1963.

'For Export Only', *Commonweal,* 15 February 1957.

'The Theatre of Hope and Despair', *The Critic,* 26 (August–September 1967). Reprinted in *Everyman,* 1, 1968.

'Plays Peasant and Unpeasant', *The Times Literary Supplement,* 17 March 1972.

'Self-Portrait,' *Aquarius,* 5, 1972.

'A Visit to Spain', *Irish Monthly*, 80 (November 1952).

'Sex in Ireland (Republic of)', *The Critic*, 30, 4 (March–April 1972).

A tribute to Hilton Edwards and Micheál MacLiammóir in Luke, Peter (ed.), *Enter Certain Players: Edwards–MacLiammóir and the Gate 1928–1978,* Dublin, The Dolmen Press, 1978.

'Extracts from a Sporadic Diary', in Carpenter, Andrew and Fallon, Peter (eds.), *The Writers: A Sense of Ireland,* Dublin, The O'Brien Press, 1980.

'Extracts from a Sporadic Diary', in Coogan, Tim Pat (ed.), *Ireland and the Arts,* A Special Issue of the *Literary Review,* London, Namara Press, n.d.

'A Challenge to *Acorn*', *Acorn*, no. 14 (Autumn 1970).

'Important Places', an introduction to McGlinchey, Charles, *The Last of the Name,* Belfast and Dover, New Hampshire, The Blackstaff Press, 1986.

Drama

Unpublished Plays:

A Sort of Freedom, produced by Northern Ireland Home Service, 1958.

To This Hard House, produced by Northern Ireland Home Service, 1958.

The Founder Members, produced by BBC Light Programme, 1964.

A Doubtful Paradise, produced by Group Theatre, Belfast, 1960 and Northern Ireland Home Service, 1962.

The Blind Mice, produced by Eblana Theatre, Dublin 1963, Northern Ireland Home Service, 1963 and Lyric Theatre, Belfast, 1964.

Three Fathers, Three Sons, produced by RTE TV, 1964.

Farewell to Ardstraw, produced by BBC Northern Ireland TV, 1976.

The Next Parish, produced by BBC Northern Ireland TV, 1976.

American Welcome, produced by Actors' Theatre, Louisville, Kentucky, 1980.

Published Plays:

The Enemy Within, Journal of Irish Literature, 4, no. 2 (May 1975); Dublin, Gallery Press, 1979.
Philadelphia, Here I Come!, London, Faber and Faber, 1965.
The Loves of Cass McGuire, London, Faber and Faber, 1967.
Lovers, London, Faber and Faber, 1969.
Crystal and Fox, London, Faber and Faber, 1970.
Crystal and Fox and *The Mundy Scheme,* New York, Farrar, Straus and Giroux, 1970.
The Gentle Island, London, Davis-Poynter, 1973.
The Freedom of the City, London, Faber and Faber, 1974.
Living Quarters, London, Faber and Faber, 1978.
Volunteers, London, Faber and Faber, 1979.
Aristocrats, Dublin, Gallery Press, 1980.
Faith Healer, London, Faber and Faber, 1980.
Translations, London, Faber and Faber, 1981.
Three Sisters by Anton Chekhov, Dublin, Gallery Press, 1981.
The Communication Cord, London, Faber and Faber, 1983.
Selected Plays, London, Faber and Faber, 1984.
Fathers and Sons, London, Faber and Faber, 1987.

Works by Other Authors

Adamson, Ian, *The Identity of Ulster*, W. C. Baird Ltd, 1982.
Beckett, J. C. *The Making of Modern Ireland 1603–1923*, London, Faber and Faber, 1972.
Bell, Sam Hanna, *The Theatre in Ulster*, Dublin, Gill and Macmillan, 1972.
Brown, Terence, *Ireland: A Social and Cultural History 1922–85*, Glasgow, Fontana, 1986.
Carpenter, Andrew (ed.), *Place, Personality, and the Irish Writer,* Irish Literary Studies, I, Gerrards Cross, Colin Smythe, 1977.
Carpenter, Andrew and Fallon, Peter (eds.) *The Writers: A Sense of Ireland,* Dublin, The O'Brien Press, 1980.
Deane, Seamus, *Celtic Revivals,* London, Faber and Faber, 1985.
A Short History of Irish Literature, London, Hutchinson, 1986.

Evans, E. Estyn, *The Personality of Ireland: Habitat, Heritage and History,* Belfast, The Blackstaff Press, 1981.

Fallis, Richard, *The Irish Renaissance* Dublin, Gill and Macmillan, 1978

Farrell, Michael, *Northern Ireland: The Orange State,* London, Pluto Press, 1980.

Field Day, *Ireland's Field Day,* Field Day's first six pamphlets and an afterword by Denis Donoghue, London, Hutchinson, 1985.

Fitz-Simon, Christopher, *The Irish Theatre,* London, Thames and Hudson, 1983.

Forster, John Wilson, *Themes and Forces in Ulster Fiction,* Dublin, Gill and Macmillan, 1974.

Hogan, Robert, *After the Irish Renaissance,* London, Macmillan, 1968.
'Since O'Casey' and Other Essays on Irish Drama, Gerrards Cross, Colin Smythe; Totowa, New Jersey, Barnes and Noble Books, 1983.

Jeffares, A. Norman, *Anglo-Irish Literature,* Dublin, Gill and Macmillan, 1982.

McHugh, Roger and Harmon, Maurice, *A Short History of Anglo-Irish Literature,* Dublin, The O'Brien Press, 1980.

MacLysaght, Edward, *Irish Families,* Dublin, Irish Academic Press, 1985.

Maxwell, D. E. S., *A Critical History of Modern Irish Drama 1891–1980,* Cambridge, Cambridge University Press, 1984.

O'Brien, Conor Cruise, *States of Ireland,* London, Hutchinson, 1972.

Paulin, Tom, *Ireland and the English Crisis,* Newcastle upon Tyne, Bloodaxe Books, 1984.

Index

Abbey Theatre, 5, 7, 39, 40, 41, 107, 108, 121, 171, 172
Actors' Theatre, (Louisville, Kentucky), 180
Aeneid, 195
Aeschylus, 89
American Welcome, 27, 180–2
'Among the Ruins', 24, 48
Antigone, 88–9, 208
The Aran Islands, 44
Aristocrats, 84, 86, 133, 163–71, 176, 198
Arnold, Matthew, 173, 196

Beckett, Samuel, 14, 25, 74, 85
Behan, Brendan, 40, 184
Belfast Arts Theatre, 40
The Bell, 23, 38
Bell, Sam Hanna, 122
The Blind Mice, 49, 52, 67–70, 78, 160, 215
Brecht, Bertolt, 87, 89, 102, 145

Chekhov, Anton, 76–7, 105, 165, 169, 182–6, 189, 208
The Cherry Orchard, 105
'The Child', 23–4, 38
The Communication Cord, 188, 202–6, 208, 216
Corkery, Daniel, 9, 10, 12, 17, 37, 38, 44–5, 130
The Crane Bag, 207
Crystal and Fox, 88, 104, 108, 115–20, 132

Days Without End, 89–93
'The Dead', 5
Deane, Seamus, 15
Deirdre of the Sorrows, 3
'The Diviner', 48

A Doubtful Paradise, 36, 41, 49, 65–7, 73, 74
Double Cross, 208
Dublin Theatre Festival, 50
Durrell, Lawrence, 5

'Easter 1916', 212
Eblana Theatre, 68
Edwards, Hilton, 108
'Elegy Written in a Country Churchyard', 113, 186
The Enemy Within, 20, 31, 41, 52, 60, 68, 70, 77, 78–83, 151
Envoy, 38
Evans, E. Estyn, 5, 6, 11
Euripides, 89, 146–7
'Everything Neat and Tidy', 48

Faith Healer, 26, 27, 28, 118, 171, 172–80, 181, 216
Fallis, Richard, 6
Farewell to Ardstraw, 161–3
Fathers and Sons, 22, 210–12
'The Fawn Pup', 48
Field Day, 22, 41, 153, 182, 187, 205, 206–9, 218
'A Fine Day at Glenties', 47
Fitz-Simon, Christopher, 199
'The Flower of Kiltymore', 27
Foster, John Wilson, 15
The Founder Members, 70–1, 72
'Foundry House', 48, 163–4, 170–1
The Freedom of the City, 36, 37, 70, 86, 87, 95, 122, 131, 133–42, 151, 153, 155, 161, 186, 194, 217
Freud, Sigmund, 90
Fugard, Athol, 208

[227]

Gaiety Theatre, 50
Gate Theatre, 108
The Gentle Island, 124–33, 152,
    161, 172, 187, 203
'Going into Exile', 94–5
The Gold in the Sea, 48, 114
'The Gold in the Sea', 27, 48, 214
Gray, Thomas, 113, 186
Gregory, Lady, 9, 124
Group Theatre, 40, 41
Guthrie, Tyrone, 50–3, 87–8, 93,
    100, 124

Harmon, Maurice, 110
'He Wishes for the Cloths of
    Heaven', 102–3
Heaney, Seamus, 13, 14, 24, 26,
    31, 153, 155, 160–1, 191–2
Hewitt, John, 14, 38
Higgins, Aidan, 14
High Time, 208
'The Highwayman', 114, 186
'The Highwayman and the
    Saint', 114
Hippolytus, 146–7
Hogan, Robert, 87, 145
Homer, 191
'Homesickness', 12
Horniman, Miss, 40

'I Remember, I Remember', 13
'If', 138
In the Shadow of the Glen, 3
'In the Train', 5
Irish Writing, 38

Jeffares, A. Norman, 4, 5
'Johnny and Mick', 215
Joyce, James, 4, 5, 8, 14, 20, 25,
    82
Juno and the Paycock, 2, 3, 59

Kavanagh, Patrick, 26
Keane, John B., 14
Kearney, Richard, 207
Keats, John, 186
'Kelly's Hall', 214
Kennelly, Brendan, 208
Kenner, Hugh, 173

Kerr, Walter, 107
Kiely, Benedict, 6
Kilroy, Thomas, 208
Kipling, Rudyard, 138, 186

Larkin, Philip, 13
'The Last Mummer', 14
The Last of the Name, 205
Lena and Boesman, 208
Leonard, Hugh, 14
Linehan, Fergus, 110
'Lisheen Races, Second Hand',
    173
Living Quarters, 27, 86, 88, 89,
    115, 142–51, 166, 169, 192,
    217
Longley, Michael, 14
'Losers', 108–9, 113–15, 186
Lovers, 86, 87, 104, 108–15, 186
The Loves of Cass McGuire, 70,
    75–7, 101–8, 110, 115, 128
Lyric Players Theatre, 41
Lyttelton Theatre, 210

McCullers, Carson, 24
McGuinness, Frank, 208
McHugh, Roger, 110
MacLiammóir, Micheál, 108,
    182–3
MacMahon, Sean, 35
Mahon, Derek, 14, 208
'A Man's World', 58
Mason, Ronald, 53
Maxwell, D. E. S., 15, 51–2, 68,
    82, 124
Miller, Arthur, 65
Montague, John, 25
Moore, Brian, 14
Moore, George, 12
Mourning Becomes Electra, 89
'Mr Sing My Heart's Delight', 48
Muldoon, Paul, 14
The Mundy Scheme, 120–4, 151
Murphy, Thomas, 14
'My Father and the Sergeant', 48

National Theatre (London), 22,
    210
New Yorker, 39

[228]

The Next Parish, 161–3
North, 13, 153, 155
Noyes, Alfred, 114, 186

Odyssey, 191
Oresteia, 89
O'Beirne, Michael, 8
O'Brien, Conor Cruise, 145
O'Casey, Sean, 1–4, 14, 59, 183
O'Connell, Daniel, 198
O'Connor, Frank, 5, 12, 21
O'Donnell, Peadar, 42–3, 127
O'Faoláin, Sean, 6, 7, 8, 44
O'Flaherty, Liam, 94–5
O'Neill, Eugene, 89–93
Ovid, 196

Parker, Stewart, 36, 208
Paulin, Tom, 208
Peacock Theatre, 208
Philadelphia, Here I Come!, 16,
   20, 27, 49, 50–2, 64, 69, 73, 83,
   84, 86, 87, 89–101, 104, 105,
   106, 108, 115, 122, 126, 128,
   145, 146, 169, 172, 180, 202
Pirandello, Luigi, 89, 102, 144
*The Playboy of the Western
   World*, 2, 3, 191
The Plough and the Stars, 2, 3
'Punishment', 155

Queen's Theatre, 39, 41, 68

Rea, Stephen, 41, 207
Red Roses for Me, 3
Riders to the Sea, 3
The Riot Act, 208
Royal Court Theatre, 172

Sartre, Jean-Paul, 166
The Saucer of Larks, 48
The Seagull, 105
The Shadow of a Gunman, 3
The Silver Tassie, 3
*Six Characters in Search of an
   Author*, 144
'The Skelper', 27, 48
Somerville and Ross, 173
Sophocles, 88–9, 208
A Sort of Freedom, 48, 54, 55–9,
   62, 63, 70
The Star Turns Red, 3
Steiner, George, 147–8, 189, 193
Stuart, Francis, 14
Swift, Jonathan, 122
Synge, J. M., 1–4, 9, 44–6, 50,
   130, 183, 184

Three Fathers, Three Sons, 70,
   71–5, 100
Three Sisters, 180, 182–6, 189,
   208
Threshold, 35
The Tinker's Wedding, 3
To This Hard House, 48, 54,
   59–65, 67, 73, 74, 128
Translations, 29, 128–9, 130,
   133, 138, 149, 151, 154, 159,
   180, 182–202, 205–6, 207–8,
   210, 216, 218
Trevor, William, 14
Turgenev, Ivan, 22, 210, 212

Ulysses, 25, 40

Virgil, 191, 195
Volunteers, 115, 131, 133, 142,
   152, 153–61, 164, 168, 178,
   186, 192, 218

Walpole, Horace, 148
Warner, Alan, 13
The Well of the Saints, 3
'Winners', 88, 89, 95, 108–13,
   114, 115, 118, 123, 145, 148,
   149, 151, 192
Wordsworth, William, 187

Yeats, W. B., 9–10, 36, 37, 40,
   50, 102–3, 124, 171, 212